PAPER DOLLS

Subtitle

Unharmed

Author

Kara R. Hunt

ISBN: 978-1-965352-65-6

DEDICATION

Dedicated to the One Who paid the price for it all, so I wouldn't have to.

BOOKS BY KARA R. HUNT

FICTION:
The Habakkuk Series
Book 1 - Paper Dolls
Book 2 - Paper Dolls: Kite
Book 3 - Paper Dolls: Priscilla
Book 4 - Paper Dolls: Lydia
Book 5 - Paper Dolls: Eve
Book 6 - Paper Dolls: Mary
Click here to buy the entire series!
Audiobooks for this series are available on
audible.com

CONTRIBUTING AUTHOR TO THE
FOLLOWING NON-FICTION WORKS:
Marriage Matters
The Names of God
PODCAST
Cheer UP! Podcast

WHAT READERS ARE SAYING

Paper Dolls is filled with all the things that make women's fiction fans sit up and take notice. Family intrigue, a touch of romance, the pain of loss, the joy of reunion, and the uncertainty of life. Walk with these women as they sort out their lives, their families, and their relationships - or at least try.

- Pegg Thomas, Multiple Award-Winning Novelist

The author has an endearing style of writing. It is easy to become invested in the characters and their story. This is filled with intrigue, warfare, and relationship challenges to keep the story exciting. There are Christian and life lessons to be learned through this amazing novel. Conversations sound realistic. The adventure feels real and my emotions mimicked Kite's.

- N. Wilkerson, Amazon Review of Paper Dolls: Kite

Priscilla is Book Three in the Paper Dolls Habakkuk series by gifted wordsmith Kara R. Hunt.

This is a touching book that gave me all of the feels. I loved reconnecting with some of the past characters, my old friends. It was touching to read about the changes and growth in the characters. I love the bonds of friendship shared by this group of women.

Author Hunt has a poetic style of writing that speaks to my heart. I can picture the scenes as I read her vividly descriptive words. The Christian messages are so welcome and needed in today's world.

All fans of contemporary women's Christian books should get this series.

- Amazon Review, Paper Dolls: Priscilla

A page-turner that made my heart swell as I swiped to the last page of this book.

I enjoyed the balance of emotion and suspense in this story, all underlined by Lydia's rampant, bold, loving faith in God. There was this unfailing light at the end of the tunnel as Lydia actively worked to avoid temptations, wrath, and her struggles to forgive deceitful, deliberately murderous antagonists who plot to ruin her life. The author does a wonderful job at demonstrating the drama and reality of making mistakes and that while it isn't easy for everyone (or every Christian, rather) to flee from temptation, there is always that unwaveringly solid, golden answer: Jesus. In this case, this story contains plenty of angsty interactions between the characters and without grotesque and gritty means, Hunt writes a tasteful and humbling tale.

    – **Rosalyn Leigh, Book Review of Paper Dolls: Lydia**

Just know that you will pick this book up to read and you will not be able to put this one down!! Author Kara R. Hunt keeps you on the edge of your seat as the events play out! When you read fiction that puts Christ in the center of the story and shows the characters living for Jesus in whatever way that looks like (redemption, forgiveness, trust, new Christian, etc.), it is so refreshing! Thank you, Kara, for another chapter in the Paper Dolls series!

    – **Goodreads Review of Paper Dolls: Eve**

This book is a page turner. Mary is back home in her home town and the drama does not stop. There are fights, gun shots, a fifty year old woman.... pregnant, and prayer.

Yes, the underlying theme always comes back to faith and trust in God. I love all the twists and turns, and I don't think I'll ever whistle again!!! (read the book)

**– Duezette, Life Coach
Book Review of Paper Dolls: Mary**

Finding a woman who couldn't relate to any of the themes in Kara R Hunt's expertly crafted novel, Paper Dolls, would be difficult. Wife, mother, daughter, sibling, friend, females struggling with identity, hope, hopelessness, dreams, and dreaded decisions. The intricate plot is a layer-upon layer of deep emotional entwinement paired with strong Christian values.

Hunt's writing is superb. These characters portray the author's attention to emotion, and motivation, repressing and expressing old trauma, broken dreams, and the deepest, most horrifying fears, making them anything but paper cutouts of people. They are flesh and blood come to life in a memorable, extremely gifted, beautifully crafted story.

Dr. Deborah Maxey
The multi-award-winning author of *The Endling, A Novel*
Licensed Counselor and Marriage and Family Therapist

ACKNOWLEDGEMENTS

To everyone who has purchased, read, reviewed, and supported Books 1-6 in this series, a million thank you's wouldn't be enough to show how grateful I am for every one of you.
May this final book in the Habakkuk Series – *Paper Dolls: Unharmed* be a blessing to you as well.

A SPECIAL NOTE
TO MY READERS

The story you're about to read contains violence
associated with spiritual warfare and other Biblical themes
and elements.

While the characters and the town of Habakkuk are
works of fiction, the situations and circumstances they find
themselves in are not.

*The LORD God is my strength, and he
will make my feet like hinds' feet, and he will make me
to walk upon mine high places.*

- Habakkuk 3:19 KJV

Chapter One

Three stark figures stood on scorched concrete and stared across the pre-dawn sky to the neighborhood below. Their leader, with the onyx hair, tanned skin, and bright green eyes, stood in front. The abandoned home with the pillared porch was the perfect place for him to watch his prey. The home had been occupied by a family of five. A minor obstacle. He smiled and looked at his burned fingers. How powerful it was to set a house ablaze in a matter of moments with the snap of his fingers. It never got old.

The young woman on his left reached into her black duffle bag and handed him a pair of binoculars. He'd found the raven-haired beauty years before in Mexico, where he'd evaded the American authorities. Seven years old, cold, hungry, and clinging to a torn ragdoll, he'd found her along the violent streets of Guadalajara. He'd rescued her, fed her, and molded her. Two decades later, not a trace of that scared little girl remained. Except her voice. She talked in low, soft tones, which is why he'd named her Whisper. He laughed when he remembered the mistakes people had made when they heard such a non-threatening name. They had no idea what she was capable of. He'd trained her himself. Beauty and power were a deadly combination.

On his right was the person he'd intended to entrust his kingdom of terror to. The one he'd molded since birth. Blood of his blood. He was young, arrogant, and bore a striking resemblance. But the boy had secrets. Lots of them. Secrets the leader would expose. But not today. Today was about Jan.

He inhaled and adjusted the focus on the binoculars. He smiled and stared at the two-story brick home nestled in the middle of the quaint subdivision. He quivered. How nice it would be to catch an early morning glimpse of his elusive prey.

Instead, he saw a short, elderly woman with flaming red hair and a large leather purse. She paced in front of Jan's front door. He didn't recognize the woman and shoved the binoculars towards Whisper, who ignored them. He raised his hand to strike her when she pointed. A car drove up the street towards Jan's house. He looked through the binoculars again. Dark green Honda. Bike rack on top. Small dent near the bumper. Exactly how his spies had described it.

The door opened. A woman got out. Strands of shiny brown hair escaped from a golden clip that glistened in the morning sun. He focused the high-powered lens on her face. Defiant brown eyes stared towards him. He chuckled. His evil presence had done its work once again. She'd sensed something was wrong.

And it was.

Thirty-five years, he'd planned this revenge. She was a fiery fourteen-year-old when she'd escaped his dangerous grasp back then. But today was a new day. He handed the binoculars to the young man on his right and lifted his face towards the sky. He smiled as a gentle breeze fueled the familiar fragrance around him.

Death was in the air.

~

Not now. My grip on the car keys tightened. *Not today.*

"Jan?" Doris, the peskiest member of our congregation, ran from the porch to the walkway to meet me. "I need to talk to Pastor Eller."

"Right now, isn't a good time, Doris." I glanced over my shoulder and then up towards the older homes nestled in the cliffs above. An eerie tingle crept down my spine. The feeling that I was being watched caused me to pause. I squinted for a better look. The effort revealed nothing but a sunrise ready to peek over the horizon. I lowered my gaze and turned to Doris, who was now tapping her foot in front of me. "Doris, it's early. Ted's probably still asleep. Maybe later this eve—"

"I *need* to talk to him now."

My cell phone alarm chimes rang through the air. I pulled it from my jeans pocket. The same jeans from the night before. The screen flashed 5:00 a.m. I shook my head at Doris, slid the phone back into my pocket, and headed for the front door.

"This is an emergency, Jan. Why else would I be here before the crack of dawn?"

Why indeed?

I took a deep breath and turned my key inside the lock. "Fine. I'll see if Ted's awake." I glanced over my shoulder to make sure she wasn't planning on following me inside.

She snorted and flicked her hand at me.

I stepped in, shut the door, and ignored her annoyed sigh. I knew her well enough to know she thought not inviting her in was rude.

Doris Slater had once again shown up at the worst possible time. The argument last night with my husband Ted and the feeling I was being watched had my nerves on edge. I leaned back against the door, closed my eyes, and drew another deep breath. I hadn't slept in twenty-four hours. Maybe that was it. Perhaps I was jittery because I desperately needed sleep, not because someone was watching me. I tightened my eyes and groaned. A bristling Doris Slater was right outside my door, and I knew a change of clothes, a hot shower, and eight hours of uninterrupted sleep would have to wait until I talked to Ted. And that was the last thing I wanted to do.

Last night, he wanted to talk about Elayna. And I did what I always do when someone brings her up. I ran. I stormed out the door into the night, an emotional mess intent on ending it all.

I pushed off the door and walked towards the stairs. From the bottom step, I could see clearly into our bedroom, which meant Ted wasn't there. He never slept with an open door. I turned on the hallway light, headed to his den, and eased the door open.

He lay flat on his stomach, still asleep and fully dressed from the day before. His right arm dangled over the side of the brown leather couch he inherited from his father. I knelt beside the couch to take off his shoes. When I touched his left foot, he straightened and sat up so fast that he kicked me in the chin before I could move my face.

"Jan, I'm sorry." He reached for my arm. "I—"

"It's okay." I rubbed my chin and smiled. "It doesn't hurt. Much."

"Huh?" He winced and rubbed sleep from his eyes.

"Never mind. It wasn't important. Mrs. Slater—"

"What I meant to say ..." He took my hands and searched my eyes. "Is that I'm glad you came back. Are you okay?"

"Oh." A dull pain pulsed in my head. The lack of sleep and sudden chin kick were beginning to take their toll. "I'll be okay."

He looked me over. "Where did you go?"

"Listen, I know you have lots of questions about last night, but it'll have to wait until later."

"Why?"

"Because Mrs. Slater is outside and needs to speak with

you."

"Now?" He yawned and shook his head. "She'll have to come back later. I need to talk to *you*."

"I know. But Doris says it's an emergency."

"Emergency?"

"She didn't say what, and you never really know with Doris. But whatever it is, it's upsetting her."

He rose and reached for the blue flannel shirt he kept in the den for cool nights. "I hope everything's okay with Abner." He removed his wrinkled T-shirt and tossed it on the arm of the couch. "The old guy tends to overwork himself."

"I'll invite her in for a cup of coffee while you clean up."

Ted looked at me, his face pensive. "I'll wrap things up with Doris quickly. I don't want you to think I'm putting church members before my own family."

I waved off the comment. "You clean up, and I'll find out what's going on."

"This conversation isn't over, Jan."

"I know." I shook my head and sighed. "I'll let Doris in."

As I walked down the hall, Ted stood in the hallway behind me, his stare following me to the door. *Get ready.* I whispered to myself. *Because sooner or later, you'll have to tell him what happened last night.*

I opened the front door. "Doris, I'm sorry that took so long. Come on in." I closed the door behind her. "Ted was still asleep. He's getting dressed." Our automatic coffee maker, which was always pre-set to five-fifteen a.m., beeped, and the dark brewed aroma filtered into the hall. "Would you like a cup of coffee? Ted will be out soon."

"Hmmph." She sniffed and pushed past me towards the kitchen. "It's a good thing *I'm* not the one with the emergency. You would've found me dead on the front porch."

"Cream or sugar?" I ignored her sarcasm and made a beeline for the cabinet where I kept the aspirin and popped one into my mouth. There were members of our congregation with whom I wouldn't have minded this early morning intrusion.

Doris Slater wasn't one of them.

"I don't drink coffee, Jan." She ran a finger across the kitchen table and then put on her eyeglasses to inspect it. "Never have. Being a member of your church for as long as I have, I'd think you'd know that by now."

"Tea then?" I should've taken more aspirin.

She didn't answer.

I sighed. "Tell me what's going on, Doris. Is Abner well?"

"Abner's doing just fine, thank you very much." She pulled a napkin from her purse and wiped her hand. "Just because we're old doesn't mean we're a heartbeat away from slipping into the hereafter." She plopped onto one of the kitchen chairs and then turned to face me. "And whatever business I have to discuss, I'll discuss it with my pastor."

I placed the teakettle on the stove, poured myself a cup of coffee, and grabbed a dishtowel. "Very well. Is there anything else I can get you? A bagel, maybe?"

"You could get me, Pastor Eller."

After Ted was appointed Pastor four years ago, Abner and Doris stayed on at Cross River, our small church in Habakkuk, Missouri. Though Abner was likable, Doris was a cantankerous old woman. From day one, nothing I said or did was to her liking. I don't know why she didn't just leave.

She leaned forward in her chair. Her eyes took me in from top to bottom. "You look awful like you haven't even slept." Her brows and mouth twisted. "And where in the world would you be coming from this time of morning anyway?" She tilted her head back. "And why are you wearing the same clothes you wore at last night's meeting?"

I wondered how long it'd take for her to ask that question.

"Frankly, Doris, is it any of your business?"

She leaned back in her chair and crossed her arms. "Be careful, Jan. After all, you're the wife of our Pastor. You have an image to uphold."

"Good morning, Doris." Ted walked into the kitchen and pulled up a chair next to her. "What is this I hear about an emergency?"

Doris quickly lowered her head and clasped her hands together in her lap. After a few seconds, she looked up. Tears welled in her eyes, and her voice quivered.

This woman was something else.

"Pastor," she breathed out and swallowed hard. "It's my grandson, Cody. I … I just don't know what to do." She grabbed a napkin from the holder on the table and wiped her eyes.

Ted took her hand. "I'm sure everything's going to be all right. Why don't you start from the beginning? Is he hurt?"

"No."

"In some kind of trouble?"

"Yes."

"What kind of trouble?"

"He's, he's …. Oh, Pastor, I just don't think I can say it." Wrinkled, liver-spotted hands flew up and covered her face.

"It's okay, Doris. Take your time. Whenever you're ready."

"It's just that he's …. he's … Oh, Pastor, Cody's dating a heathen."

My coffee mug fell from my hands and onto the floor with a loud thud.

Neither of them looked my way.

"He's doing *what*?" Ted moved his chair closer to Doris.

"Cody's dating a heathen," she repeated.

"I know. I mean, I heard that part." He shook his head." On second thought, I don't know. What exactly are you saying?"

"His girlfriend doesn't know the Lord, Pastor," she spat out.

"I know what you meant by *heathen*, Doris. What I'm trying to get at is the emergency. Is the girl in some kind of trouble? Is she ill?"

"No."

"Is she pregnant?"

"Heavens *no.*" She gasped as though the mere thought of it were impossible. "I mean, I wouldn't doubt it if she is, considering her background and all, but not by *my* grandson, that's for sure."

"Okay." Ted shifted in his chair. "And the emergency is…?"

"Didn't you hear me, Pastor? She's a heathen. Troubled background and all. Comes from bad people. Not well-bred. Her mom is one of those psychos in the crazy ward. And …" She looked down at the table. "Cody told me he's in love with her."

My face burned with anger. For this, Doris showed up at our door before dawn? All because her precious grandson fell for some girl she disapproved of? This could've waited, and I should've known better. This was not the first time she'd done something like this. I have tried to work with this woman. But this was the last straw. I used the dish towel to wipe coffee off the floor. It gave my hands something else to do besides wrap them around Doris's neck.

Ted sat forward. "What would you like me to do?"

"Why, I would like you to talk with him, of course."

"Of course." He sighed and ran his hands through his hair before getting up from the table. "Let me get the youth minister's phone numbers for you. John and Norah will be more than glad to help."

"*No,* Pastor." Doris grabbed his arm. "That won't do. I mean no disrespect, but in my opinion, that young couple you hired for the youth are anything *but* ministers. No, I need *you* to talk to him. Cody leaves for work at seven, which gives us only about an hour to speak with him. Every day after work, he spends time with that girl. You need to put a stop to that, and we need to leave now. There's no time to spare."

"Doris." I threw down the towel. "You know that this is not—" But before I could finish, Ted put up his hand, stopping me mid-sentence. His eyes asked that I continue to let him handle her. Fine. I'd had enough of this ridiculous woman.

"I'm going upstairs to check on Adam." I tossed the cup and dishtowel in the sink and fought the urge to give Doris a piece of my mind.

Ted and I agreed long ago that I wouldn't interfere in his ministerial duties, but Doris had crossed the line this time. Not only that, but she'd also gotten into the habit of ordering him around as if he were her slave instead of her Pastor. After Ted dealt with Doris's "emergency," she and I were going to have a "talk." It was time I put an end to this woman's intrusive behavior, once and for all.

~

Adam, our fourteen-year-old son, lay fast asleep.

I removed my shoes so I wouldn't wake him, then walked to the foot of his bed and sat on the floor. As I leaned against the bedpost, I pulled my knees up to my chest and stared at him. Hours before, I'd contemplated plunging my car off a cliff. I now wondered if Adam would've ever known how much I loved him.

The morning sun filtered in through the curtains. I embraced its warmth and listened as he took each breath. Grateful for each one. How could I have even thought about leaving him? What kind of mother would leave one child because of grief over another?

Questions ran through my mind. Questions I knew Adam would've had if my suicide had been successful. Questions with no answers. The thought of leaving my son, my only son, and remaining child to grieve that way sent cold chills through me.

I shivered as my mind flitted back to the night before - my car feet away from the edge of Jacob's Peak, ready to plunge into its rocky depths. I'd hoped to feel every bit of the impact before death.

And that's when I knew that I'd officially lost my mind.

Or had it started earlier?

It didn't matter. All I knew was that any sanity I'd had before Elayna's death had slipped away. Slow but sure.

I stood and walked to Adam's bookshelf. Among the many books on baseball and its heroes were several framed pictures of him and Elayna. I picked up a copy of the one he'd made in his dad's workshop and placed in the casket with his little sister. The picture was taken the day before she drowned.

I wiped away tears and studied the photo. Their smiles were a mile wide as Adam had what looked to be a BBQ hot dog in his hand, and Elayna had a double-scoop of chocolate ice cream in hers. The large waffle cone bigger than her hand. Adam had painted the frame pink and white, then glued bright yellow—Elayna's favorite color—flowers all around it. The word *Laynee,* a nickname she'd had since she was little, was written in fancy green script and decorated the top right corner of the frame, an exact copy of the original wooden frame and photo that now laid on top of her heart, placed there by Adam at her funeral.

Last night, on the edge of that cliff, I grieved my precious Laynee in ways I'd never had before. Thoughts of her splashing about, in need of help, scared and alone, gutted me.

Did she call out for her brother?
Her dad?
Me?

I clutched the frame to my heart as the tears continued to fall. Last night was the first time I allowed myself to grieve as a mom. As the Pastor's wife, I'd put on a convincing charade of faith and courage after Laynee's death. I even took the time to comfort those who had a hard time understanding how bad things could happen to good people. God's people. I even quoted Scriptures to give them hope.

I placed the frame back on the shelf, walked over to Adam's bed, and sat. I pulled his robe from the post, wrapped it in a ball, and laid my face in it. Laynee had drowned in her uncle's pool while Ted and I were out of town ministering to others about the goodness of God. The message and Scriptures I'd quoted then meant nothing to me now.

Nothing.

Adam tossed and turned before nestling back into the comfort of the sheets. I glanced at the baseball clock on his nightstand and entertained the idea of joining him for a quick nap. As I moved to lay beside him, loud voices filtered into his room. Angry voices.

I wrapped his robe around my shoulders and stepped out of the room to hear more. One of the voices belonged to Libbybelle, the woman who rescued me thirty-five years ago and raised me as her own. The woman I loved to call Mom and who stopped by every morning on her way to work. The other voice was Doris's.

I rushed down to the kitchen.

"Doris Sue Slater." Mom flung her purse and keys onto the counter. "You ought to be ashamed of yourself, interrupting the Pastor's family time for something like this. Cody's nineteen years old and is more than capable of deciding on who he wants to date. If you're so concerned, why didn't you have Abner talk to him? He's the boy's grandfather. Can't he stop tinkering on those old cars long enough to talk to the boy?"

Doris stood. "They're not old cars. They're classics. And Abner thinks I'm overreacting."

"That's because you are, and you know it."

I walked into the kitchen, and Libbybelle blew out a loud breath. "Didn't mean to wake you, Janny." She tossed an annoyed look Doris's way. "But she's really put a bee in my bonnet this morning."

"It's okay, Mom, I was just checking on Adam."

"Here you go, Doris." Ted returned from the den with a piece of paper. "Call the youth ministers. I've already spoken with them, and they're aware of what's going on. Like I said, they're more than willing to help. John's planning on meeting with Cody for lunch and talking with him about your concerns."

"Pastor Eller," Doris placed her hands on her hips. "I already told you. I do *not* consider John and Norah to be ministers. Therefore, they can't do Cody any good."

"I'm sorry you feel that way, Doris," he said. "But this is exactly one of the reasons churches have youth and young adult pastors. I'm sure Cody will feel more comfortable talking to someone closer to his age. Someone he has things in common with."

"Why won't you help him?"

"Doris," he sighed and pulled out a chair. "Simply put, I cannot."

"Surely you're not refusing to help Cody?"

"I know this situation constitutes an emergency for you, but for me, it's not. If Cody was injured in any way, sick or suicidal, I would've been out of here seconds after you arrived. I would've gone myself, along *with* John and Norah. This is not an emergency situation, Doris. It's not even urgent. Don't get me wrong, I think I understand your concern, but his dating life is not reason enough for me to leave home before I've even had breakfast with my family." He sat and scooted the chair up to the table. "I'll be in the church office at nine if you want to discuss this further."

Doris snatched her jacket off the back of the chair. "What an absolute waste of time. All I wanted you to do was talk to him before things got out of hand with that girl. My apologies for interrupting your morning."

"If you'd still like me to talk to Cody *after* he talks with John, then I'll be glad to, but my first available appointment at the church isn't until three o'clock."

"He'll be there." She stormed towards the foyer and stumbled over a book bag.

"You ought to keep a better house, Jan," she fired off, then bent to pick up the bag.

Before Ted or Libbybelle could warn her, I screamed.

Alarm bells blasted off in my head at what she was about to do. "Leave it alone. Don't you *dare* touch it."

She stumbled again as she spun around to face me. "What in heaven's name is wrong with you?" Pale and trembling hands clutched her heart.

Ted and Libbybelle talked simultaneously, both trying to explain the grievous error she'd just made.

I stomped over to Doris. "That's Laynee's book bag. It's hers. Not yours. She left it here … there, that day …" My ears pounded, matching the angry beats of my heart. "She was the last one to touch it, and it hasn't been moved since. And I don't want you to move it now." I pointed straight at her, then Libbybelle and Ted. "Not you. Not them. Not me. Not ever. It will stay where it is. You hear me?"

Ted put his hands on my shoulders. "She didn't know, Janny." He turned me around and pulled me into a hug. I shook in his arms.

"She didn't know."

Chapter Two

Fall 1977

Dark waves of hair fell against her cheek as we swung back and forth. Red and gold leaves drifted in silence behind her. Their beauty enhanced by her smile. Her eyes shone and refused to be outdone by the sun's morning rays.

"Mom?" Our bare feet stirred the grass as our swings slowed. "I'm going to go into all the world and teach others about Jesus. Just like daddy did."

"You are?" She turned, and a gentle breeze blew soft black strands onto her face. The delicate whiteness of her dress highlighted the ebony undulations. "It's a big world out there, you know."

"Yep. I'm going to be a mishnanary."

"Missionary." She laughed.

"Yeah, that."

She brought my swing to a full stop. "That's a pretty big job for an eight-year-old."

"Almost nine, Mom."

"Right. Nine. How could I forget?" She leaned over and kissed my cheek. "Still, that can be a very dangerous job. Even for a nine-year-old."

I jumped off the rubber seat, climbed onto her lap, and wrapped my arms tight around her waist. "I know that,

Mommy. But God's in control, right? You always tell me that God's with me wherever I go, even the bad places. He'll be with me. Isn't that right, Mom? No reason to fear?"

She nestled close and whispered, "You're right, sweetheart."

She looked away as the swing once again began a slow, swaying rhythm.

"No reason at all."

~

Present Day

Hot, steamy water flowed over my head and onto tight shoulder muscles. The shower heads powerful jets massaged and soothed. I stood straight as an arrow and let the water work its magic. A knock on the door interrupted my trance.

"Be right out." I turned off the water and grabbed a towel from the heated rack outside the shower door.

Ted walked in, holding a pair of pajamas and my bathrobe. "Libbybelle said breakfast is ready. She told Adam to go ahead and start without us, so she could drop him off at school."

Doris's unannounced visit had turned our usual quiet morning into chaos. I slid into the pj's and robe and headed for the door. Ted grabbed my elbow. "Where are you going?"

"I want to spend time with Adam before he leaves."

"Jan, no more stalling. We need to talk. Where did you go last night?"

His words shocked me. I wasn't stalling. I wanted to hug and kiss my son before he left for school, but the look on Ted's face and the tone of his voice told me he wanted answers. He wasn't going to let this go. I shook my head. The calming effect of the hot shower began to fade. I walked to the bathroom vanity and reached for my hairbrush. "I went for a drive."

He took the brush out of my hand. "Where did you go?"

I stared into the sink. *Should I tell him or not?* When the sink didn't answer, I looked at the floor and counted the tiny beige tiles. Telling him the truth was risky. Attempted suicide, coupled with my unpredictable behavior the past several months and the verbal attack on Doris this morning, showed a field of red flags. Ted might have me committed.

"Fine. If you're not going to talk, then listen." He walked over to the counter and leaned against it. "I've made you an appointment with Dr. Schultz."

I knew it. "Dr. Schultz from church? She's a mental health counselor."

"You need to talk to someone."

"About my mental health?"

Dark brown eyes stared into mine.

I walked towards him. "Please tell me you're joking."

"No. I'm not. It's been over a year since Laynee died. If anyone brings her up, you bolt or go into hysterics. Our son walks on eggshells, and you've been pushing me away for months. And you haven't talked to your friends in who knows how long." He slid his hands into his jean pockets and stood. "We leave at one o'clock."

I stepped closer. "If you think I'm going to see a psychotherapist, especially one that's a member of our congregation, then you're the one who's lost his mind, not me." I turned and headed for our bedroom.

He followed. "Not a problem. There are others. I printed out a list." He reached into the pocket of his dark green hoodie and pulled out a piece of paper. "Choose one."

I balled the paper up and threw it at him. "You're a professional counselor. Counsel me."

He grabbed my wrists and pulled me close. "I'm not your counselor. I'm your husband." He sucked in a deep breath and loosened his grip. "Besides, I've done everything I've been taught to do. I've listened. I've been patient. I gave you space, and you're still on the verge of an emotional breakdown. With all my counseling and ministry training, I've been unable to help my wife. And would you like to know why? Because Laynee was my daughter, too. Somehow, you've forgotten that."

Last night, I thought it would be impossible for my heart to hurt any worse, but a heart-wrenching ache assured me it could. The quiver in his voice reminded me that this was still raw for him, too.

I sat on the bed. "I don't know what to do. I feel stuck. I can't seem to move on, and I'm not sure I want to without Laynee." Fresh tears slid down my cheeks. "Every morning, I wake up angry that she's not here. And every night I go to sleep angry that I am. I can't go on like this."

"What are you saying?"

I blew out a breath and looked up at him. "Last night, I drove up to Jacob's Peak. I planned to drive off of it."

He jerked backward and stared at me. His naturally tanned complexion now lacked color. He rubbed the back of his neck and then began pacing the floor. "Now it all makes sense." He stopped in front of the window and looked out towards the wooded tree line. "Maybe that's what it was all about."

"I don't understand."

"Last night after you left …" He shook his head. "I knew something wasn't right. We'd had fights before, but last night you seemed … I don't know, more on the edge. Anyway, at first, I thought you'd go outside and cool off, but when I heard tires screech out of the driveway, I knew you planned to do something awful, so I got my keys ready to go after you, but then I had to stop."

"Why?"

He sat next to me on the bed. "This is going to sound strange," he sighed, placing my hand in his. "But I knew not to go after you."

I yanked away from him. "You knew I planned to do

something stupid, and you changed your mind?"

"I didn't change my mind; I changed tactics because I knew I was supposed to do something else."

"Like what?"

"Pray."

Here we go. Ted, of all people, knew I did not want to hear this.

"And pray hard," he continued. "God had me on my knees before you reached the end of the road. Keys in hand, praying. I stayed that way for hours until the phone rang. I thought it might be you, but it was Libbybelle. I told her about the fight, the unshakeable feeling that something was terribly wrong, and the strong impulse to pray. She said she would do the same until she heard from me again." He paused. "This morning, when you were letting Doris in, I called and told her our prayers had been answered and that you were home safe."

"Whatever." I waved my hand and fell backward onto the bed. The night's events and no sleep continued to weigh in on me. "I doubt it was God who stopped me from driving off that cliff. Besides, you make it sound like He cares enough about me to *want* to intervene."

"Don't be childish, Jan. He cares. You've been a Christian long enough to know how God works."

I sprang up to face him. "Really? Let's talk about how God *works*. My dad was murdered days before I was born. Then, my mom died in her sleep ten years later. No warning. No time to say goodbye. You want to know what they both had in common? A love for God. And they got nothing in return for that love but heartache. If He cared, He could've intervened. For crying out loud, He *should've* intervened. But He didn't. That's how God works."

Ted stood. "Jan—"

"Oh, and let's not forget about the horrors I endured under the care of Aunt Ginger and her cult. But did I let that get in the way of my relationship with God? No. My mother taught me well. She said keep the faith no matter how bad things appear. So, I did. Until I got the phone call that my eight-year-old daughter was dead at the bottom of her cousin's pool."

"Jan, please come down and eat something." Libbybelle's voice came from outside the bedroom door. "I've already dropped Adam off at school and made a fresh batch of blueberry pancakes for you guys. Come eat while it's still hot."

Ted walked over to the door and opened it. "Thanks, Libby, we'll be right down." When she stepped away, he walked into the bathroom and returned with a damp washcloth. He sat next to me and gently wiped my face. "It was a long night for both of us, and we're both tired and saying things we don't mean. A hot breakfast and a few hours of sleep will do us both good." He pulled back the sheets. "I'll bring breakfast up, and then you can rest. I'll wake you around noon, so we won't be late for your appointment with Dr. Schultz."

I crawled under the covers and turned my back to him.

"You know I was thinking," he made his way around the bed to face me. "I'll make my appointment with Cody, the last one for the day. Afterward, let's pick Adam up from school and take him to that movie he's been begging to see. We could then stop for pizza and ice cream before heading to the butterfly exhibit in Midtown that everyone's talking about. I know how you love butterflies."

I said yes to the movies, pizza, and ice cream but no to the exhibit. The drive there and back would take up most of the evening, and though he hadn't mentioned it yet, I knew there was someone else from our congregation besides Dr. Schultz that he wanted me to talk to.

Someone who wouldn't be glad to see me.

Chapter Three

Winter 1982

"But I don't wanna go!" I threw my young teen body into Mrs. Gibbons's soft, elderly one and held on for dear life. "Please don't make me go. I'll be good. I won't cause any trouble, I promise."

"My darling angel." Mrs. Gibbons of New Life Church cupped my face in her hands. "I know you won't cause any trouble, and we don't want you to go anywhere either, but this was your mother's last request of us, dear. She asked that we try to locate her sister, April, to care for you if she died. And if we were unsuccessful in finding her, to take you in ourselves."

"So why do I have to go?"

Mrs. Gibbons took a step back, and I watched her trembling fingers rub across the balled-up Kleenex in her hand. "Because this is good news, sweetheart. It took us a while, but we've located your Aunt April. She was devastated when she heard your mom had passed away. We also shared with her June's request for her to be your legal guardian, and of course, she said yes."

"But I don't even know her." I continued to cling to Mrs. Gibbons, the first lady of the only church I'd ever known and the only grandmotherly figure in my life. The Gibbons's tiny

three-bedroom ranch house had been home to me for five years. "I haven't seen Aunt April since I was little."

Tears spilled down her cheeks. "Janny, Mr. Gibbons, and I have talked and prayed about this over and over. As much as it pains us to let you go, we know in our hearts that being with your mom's family is what's best for you right now." She looked me in the eyes. "But listen. Here's some more good news. Your Aunt doesn't live that far away, and she promised that you'll be able to come back and visit us." She gave the tissue in her hand another squeeze. "And if things don't work out, we'll bring you back here and continue caring for you ourselves. So, see, angel, it's not all bad. We'll still be here when you need us." She pulled me in tight and rocked me with arms that were warm and soft and fed my soul. "And remember, we're only a phone call away, Janny," she whispered.

"Just a phone call away."

~

Present Day

My cell phone rang.

I shifted the pie I was carrying and stared at the name and number that flashed across it. Mary Rabin.

Mary was a dear friend who was originally from Habakkuk but grew up elsewhere. She and her family moved back around two years ago, a few short months before Laynee died.

We met through mutual friends, but the two of us had become close. Her daughter and my son, Adam, were about the same age, went to the same school, and were also good friends.

But when Laynee died, I stopped being friends with everyone. I wasn't angry at them; I just didn't have the energy to talk, text, chat, fellowship, or hang out.

I just wanted to be left alone.

The phone vibrated in my hand. She'd sent a text, just like she always did when I didn't answer, which was ninety-nine percent of the time.

She asked if we could meet for brunch soon. I thanked her for asking and explained that "soon" wasn't a good time for me. I expressed my love, thanked her for being patient, and sent the text.

My phone vibrated with her reply. She said she understood and told me to call her if I needed to scream at someone.

I replied with a laughing emoji and slid the phone into my purse.

Normally, Mary asked me to call if I wanted to talk. It had been almost a year since I'd done that, so I guess she decided to stop asking.

She'd never mentioned the screaming part before. That was new. And one day, I just might take her up on that.

But right now, there was someone else I needed to talk to. And I wanted to get it over with as soon as possible.

No matter how many times I visited Doris's home, the beauty of her home's surroundings always managed to take my breath away.

The Slaters were nestled in the rural wooded areas of Douglas Springs, miles from the suburbs where Ted and I lived. Rose bushes lined each side of her driveway. Their fragrance lingered and continued to greet me long after I climbed the wooden steps of the wrap-around porch. A large white oak graced the side yard. Its impressive spread provided much-needed relief from the piercing rays of the August sun.

The sound of metal clanking against metal came from the back of the house. Abner was obviously tending to his hobby. I rang the doorbell and waited for Doris to answer. After several rings, the door yanked open.

"Well, don't just stand there," she snapped. "Come in."

Taken aback by her *invitation*, I hesitated. This was a bad idea.

"Fine." She moved to close the door.

"Wait." I thrust my foot out to keep it open. "You startled me, that's all. Perhaps I should've called first."

"Call for what? I knew you'd show up at my door sooner or later."

I removed my foot from the door. "You did?"

"They always do."

"Who?"

"You intend to carry on this conversation outside my front door?"

I looked down at the pie and forced myself to remember why I was there. "I want to apologize for this morning. You had no way of knowing about the book bag. I'm sorry, and I hope you'll accept this pie as a peace offering."

"Apology not accepted." She stepped aside and waved at me to come in. When I did, she slammed the door loudly behind me. "If you want my forgiveness, you'll have to admit how mentally ill you are."

I stared at her in disbelief. What was it with people and my mental state?

"Don't act surprised. You know what I mean."

I gripped the pie plate. If Doris never forgave me, I wouldn't lose any sleep over it. This was something Ted had asked me to do. We can't *ostracize members of the congregation*, he cautioned. But once again, Doris's behavior reminded me why my heart wasn't in this. It would be a cold day in Hades before I admitted anything to her.

She led me down the hallway to a small sitting area with a spectacular view of a large field of wildflowers. "Since you're here, there are some things I want to talk about."

I sucked in a breath and sat across from her. The Cottage-style chairs added charm and warmth to the room. "What do you want to talk about, Doris?" I put my purse on the floor and slid the pie onto the coffee table between us.

"Not what. Who."

"I'm not going to take part in any gossip."

"The *who*," she furrowed her brow and leaned towards me, "*is you*."

I crossed my arms and sat back further in the chair. "Get to the point."

"Who are you? I mean, before you were Pastor Eller's wife?"

"What business is that of yours?"

"Your husband has led our church for four years. I know him, but I don't know you. And you haven't taken the time to get to know me either. If you knew anything about me, you wouldn't have gotten so upset this morning."

I'm the one at fault? "Doris, you showed up at my home, unannounced, before daybreak, for a fake emergency. As far as Laynee's book bag goes, I've already apologized for that." I blew out a breath and softened my tone. "And I've tried to get to know you. We serve on the same committees, deliver meals, and even visit the sick and shut-ins together. You even take part in my ladies' meetings. But whenever I try to strike up a conversation with you, I get rude remarks and haughtiness for my trouble."

She shook her head and stood. "You're all alike."

"*Who* are all alike?"

"You pastors' wives. Always pretending."

I resisted the urge to reach up and rub my temples. The slow, painful crawl of a migraine began to surface. I pushed myself up from the chair, refusing to let her stance intimidate me. "Doris, get to what's really on your mind. If you have something to say, say it."

She stepped closer. "You don't think I see through the 'everything's-gonna-be-all right' attitude? You can't fool me, sweetie. I've been there."

I tilted my head. Ted never said anything about Abner being a former pastor.

"You were a pastor's wife?"

She tsked. "Not on your life, honey." She walked over to an antique mahogany China cabinet and pulled down two cups with saucers. "Abner can't teach a fish to swim, let alone help someone understand God's Word. And I wouldn't have any part of it if he could."

"But you said—"

"What I'm saying is that my father pastored a church for forty years, and my mother was the biggest pretender of them all."

Doris looked to be in her mid-seventies. Was she seriously still having mommy issues?

"My mother smiled and laughed and patted people on the back and told them *everything would be just fine*. She said that a lot. But they weren't there when she cried herself to sleep at night. Or stuffed her mouth full of pills. And they weren't there when she sliced her wrists. It didn't take long for me to figure out that everything was *not* fine."

The look in her eyes confirmed my suspicions. The conversation was no longer referring to her mother.

It was time to leave.

I grabbed my purse and searched for my car keys. "As a pastor's wife, sometimes, when it comes to our problems, you have to let go and let God handle it. I'm sure your mother did her best."

"My mother didn't believe in God."

This time, I did reach up and rub my temples. "Doris."

"My father was a pastor. A true follower of God's truths. My mother played a role."

I found the keys and gripped them tight in my hand. "Why are you telling me all this?"

"Because you don't believe in God either. Whether or not you ever have is not for me to say. At church, I've watched you teach, pray, worship, and sing. It's all baloney. You don't believe any of it."

I placed my hand on my stomach to stop the pizza and ice cream I'd eaten earlier from spilling onto Doris's plush light blue carpeting. The fact that Doris saw through my carefully crafted façade unnerved me. But did I really care? I didn't. And who was she to judge me anyway? Indignation replaced my urge to leave.

I let my purse slide back to the floor. "Okay. You think I'm a phony. Now what? Is this the part where you tell me that you're the one who's going to show me the way?"

She turned her back to me and walked into the kitchen. Seconds later, she returned with a silver carafe. "Hardly." She poured coffee into one of the cups. My mind flashed back to her chide earlier about me not knowing that she didn't like coffee. She placed two cubes of sugar into the cup and stirred. No cream. I gritted my teeth at her unspoken message. She knew I liked coffee and knew exactly how I took it.

She placed the coffee pot on a warmer and walked to the huge picture window. She stood there quietly. I knew she wanted to say more, so I waited and watched a beautiful array of birds dallying at the feeders outside her window and listened as dogs barked in the distance.

"I have four children, Jan. Did you know that?"

I plopped back down in the chair. This was going to take a while.

"I only know about Lauren, Cody's mom."

"Abner Jr., David, Lauren, and Abigail. Four of my own flesh and blood, and I have no idea where any of them are." She sighed softly and continued staring out the window. "I was too overbearing, they said. And one by one, they left, even my darling Abby, when she turned eighteen. None of them left a forwarding address." She lowered her head before looking at me. "Nine years ago, Lauren dropped by. Two days after that, she left a dirty and disheveled Cody on our doorstep."

I looked at my hands. After a brief pause, I asked, "So, Cody has no idea where his mother is?"

"In the beginning, she wrote him letters. Always from a

different state as she traveled with different men. After that, she called him a few times, most recently two years ago. Today, I couldn't tell you if she's dead or alive."

Why hadn't Ted told me any of this?

Doris went back into the kitchen. This time, she came out with a copper tea kettle and a small container of loose tea. "That's one of the reasons I'm so hard on Cody. After his mom left, it took forever before he stopped crying himself to sleep. The girl he's with now will bring him nothing but heartache, just like his mother did." She shook the tea into a strainer she'd placed over one of the cups and then added hot water from the kettle. She lifted the cup and saucer, then sat in the chair across from me. "He's all I have left. His mother left him in shambles, and I'm going to make sure he isn't heartbroken like that ever again."

"Doris," I paused to gather my thoughts. I was still angry with her but didn't want my words to come out that way. She was hurting, and I wanted to help. "Ted spoke with Cody and his girlfriend, Stephanie, this afternoon. Ted described her as delightful. Cody told him that he'd been witnessing to Stephanie for a while. Ted talked with her, and she decided to accept Christ." I swallowed. The next part would be hard for her to hear, but I hoped she'd see it as a blessing. "They want to get married, Doris. They asked Ted about it, and he suggested they go through pre-marital counseling first. They agreed. After that, he'll talk with them about the next steps. He believes they're making the right decision."

"She is *not* going to marry my Cody. I don't know what kind of tricks she's playing or what kind of spell she's put my grandson under, but he is not going to marry her. I'll personally see to that."

"Ted has great discernment when it comes to people, Doris. And you know it, too. I've heard you tell others in the congregation the same thing."

"He *used* to have great discernment is what I'll tell them

now."

She was bluffing. The one thing I *did* know about Doris was that she respected Ted.

"Well, they're planning a long engagement. If their commitment stands up to the test of time, that'll be your answer."

"She's not good for him."

"Not good for him or for you?"

"What?"

"Could it be that you're afraid of letting Cody go? It's obvious how much he means to you. Maybe it isn't so much that you don't like Stephanie. You're just finding stuff *not* to like about her. Not because she's a bad person, but because she's a threat."

She placed the teacup on the table between us. "A threat to who?"

"A threat to you. A threat to your relationship with Cody."

Her eyes narrowed. "Time for you to leave." She stood and stormed towards the front entrance. I heard the doorknob turning in her hand before I was even able to get out of my chair.

I grabbed the pie off the coffee table and walked quickly towards the door. "I'd still like for you to have this." I offered the pie. "My intention wasn't to come here and fight, Doris, but to make amends." I left out that the whole thing was Ted's idea, not mine. "Besides, it's my most requested recipe."

"I don't like blueberry pie."

"You don't?" I had gone through a lot of people and a lot of phone calls to find someone who knew Doris well enough to know her favorite dessert. It seemed I wasn't the only one who didn't know Doris Slater all that well.

"But … I spoke with Ethel. Your best friend. She told me you loved blueberry pie."

"Ethel is deaf in one ear and can't hear out the other. I

never told that crazy old bird I loved blueberry pie. Blackberry is what I said."

I didn't move.

Doris yanked the pie from me with one hand and held the door open with the other. "The Maestro will enjoy this."

I stepped onto the porch. "Maestro? I didn't know Abner was a master musician."

"He's not."

"Oh. Then who's Maestro?"

"The dog," she answered and slammed the door. The sharp needles of the evergreen wreath that decorated it scraped across my nose.

The tiny cuts felt like fire.

And I was livid.

Chapter Four

Spring 1982

"I wish I could invite you in, Mrs. Gibbons." Aunt Ginger leaned against the doorframe of her home. "But I have a meeting to attend, so I'd like to get Jan settled as soon as possible. I hope you understand."

"Oh, yes." Mrs. Gibbons's shoulders slumped before she peeked around Aunt Ginger to glance inside. "I must get going. The drive was a lot longer than I realized."

"It's also getting late. Trust me, you don't want to be on these roads alone after dark."

I moved from behind Mrs. Gibbons to get a better look at Aunt Ginger. My heart raced. The resemblance to my mother was uncanny. If it wasn't for the fiery red hair pulled into a tidy bun at the nape of her neck, I would've thought my mother had come back to rescue me.

When Mrs. Gibbons didn't leave, Aunt Ginger groaned and dropped her arm from the doorframe. I followed Mrs. Gibbons inside.

What appeared to be a nice home on the outside now looked more like a prison. No photos, artwork, or mirrors decorated the walls. The windows were closed, the curtains were drawn, and doors to the inner rooms were shut. The living room was dark and dingy and had six wooden chairs scattered around it. It didn't look like anyone lived here.

"Mrs. Gibbons, I really need to get to my meeting."

Mrs. Gibbons glanced my way before turning to leave. "Ginger, I don't think Jan should be left alone right now. She hasn't seen you in a while, and living in a new place can be scary. How about I take her back with me? I could bring her back in the morning so you wouldn't have to rush home from your meeting. Or you could pick her up Sunday after church." Mrs. Gibbons sucked in a breath. "Unless you'd rather join us for Sunday services?"

The more I looked at "Aunt Ginger', the more I realized some of her features didn't resemble my mother at all. They both had brown eyes, but my mother's eyes were soft and compassionate. Aunt Ginger's eyes were hard and stayed oddly still when she talked. My mother had a wonderful smile, and I often got lost in its warmth.

Aunt Ginger's smile was fake and cold as ice.

And that smile now turned sinister.

~

Present Day

"Ted!" I slammed the car door, and he appeared at the entrance that separated the garage from the house.

"What?"

"You won't believe what happened."

He looked me over, then the car. "Did you run over Olivia Jenson's mailbox again?" A sly smile enhanced the one dimple that teased his face.

"Olivia!" My fingers paused over the close button on the garage door remote. Months had passed since I last talked to her. Olivia and Brad Jenson were neighbors as well as members of our congregation. Brad died six months ago from a work-related injury. However, Olivia and their

seventeen-year-old daughter, Anna, still lived in the house across the road from us. Unfortunately, I managed to hit their mailbox regularly. Fortunately, Olivia was a very forgiving friend and neighbor.

"Have you seen them lately?" I asked. "Olivia and Anna, I mean?"

"No. Not even at church. I figured they'd gone to Montana to visit Olivia's mom," he rubbed the back of his neck. "Now that I think about it, the last time I talked to Olivia, she was concerned about Anna. I asked for details, but she didn't share them." He stepped down into the garage. "I'll go check and see if they're home."

"No, let me." I pulled my purse and jacket from the car. "Olivia's my friend. It's been a while since I've spent time with her, but I still don't think she'd leave town without telling me."

Ted spread his arms wide. "Wait. You forgot to tell me what happened."

"You won't believe it. Doris gave my pie to the dog."

His jaw dropped. "She did what?"

"The pie I skipped the exhibit for, made from scratch, and spent most of the afternoon baking? Yeah. She gave it to the dog."

He chuckled. "Wow."

"Exactly."

"But why did she do that?"

"Because Ethel's hard of hearing, and Doris doesn't like blueberries." Memories of the visit triggered the dull, familiar ache of a migraine. "Before that, I said some things she didn't like. She got angry, told me to leave, then gave my pie to the dog."

"She kicked you out of her house?" He laughed. The roaring sound echoed off the cement walls.

"Ted, this is not funny!"

"I'm sorry," he said, still laughing. "But come on, an old woman throws you out of her house and feeds your pie to the dog? You don't think that's funny?"

"Stop it." I stifled a laugh. I didn't want to make the headache worse, but the more I tried to hold the laughter in, the more I realized how absurd the whole thing was. Finally, I let go and laughed with him, making Ted laugh even harder. I sucked in a breath, hoping to halt the madness. Instead, I slid down the side of the car to the garage floor, laughing just as loud and hearty as Ted.

When we were both out of breath, I tossed my purse and jacket on the ground next to me and wiped tears from my eyes before looking up at him. I let out another chuckle. "See what you've started?" I pointed a finger in his direction. He paused to look down at me, and his laughter slowed. The lines in his face that had been creased with laughter only a few seconds ago now appeared thoughtful and pensive.

I scrambled off the floor. "Ted, what's wrong?"

He placed his hands in his pockets and shrugged before grabbing my hand and pulling me closer. "It's just that … it's been a long time since I've heard your laugh."

"That makes you sad?"

"No. It just makes me realize how much I've missed it." He tilted his head to the side. "And who would've thought that of all people, Doris Slater would be the one to make it happen?"

"Yeah." My mind whirled with the events of the past eighteen months. Not one memory of joy surfaced. I remembered others having moments of lightheartedness, but not me. "Who would've thought?"

"You, okay?" Ted asked.

I looked away from him. "I don't know."

"Wanna talk about it?"

I shook my head.

He dropped my hand, and a sudden chill followed.

I looked back into his eyes. "Ted—"

He tightened his lips and then walked back through the door that led to the kitchen. I followed and closed the door quietly behind me.

He leaned against the kitchen table. "Let me re-phrase that question. *Where* do you want to talk about it? At the table, on the sofa, upstairs?"

"What are you talking about?"

"I'm talking about how you're not *talking*. Not about Laynee anyway, and I know you were thinking about her out there in the garage."

I crossed my arms. "What do you want from me?"

"I want you to talk to me."

I stared at the car keys still in my hand, then glanced at the door behind me.

He grasped my wrist. "Don't." He turned my face towards his. "No more running. We can do this. We'll take baby steps like Dr. Schultz suggested."

Dr. Schultz apparently didn't tell Ted what I suggested she do with her suggestions.

I turned my face back towards the door. "You have no idea what you're asking."

"I do, Jan." He took the keys and placed them on the table. "Five minutes. For five minutes, we'll talk about Laynee, okay?"

I pulled away from him to walk towards the door, but he wrapped an arm around my waist and led me to the living room sofa. "Adam's spending the night with Libbybelle. No one's here but us. It's a cool evening. How about I start a fire?" He poked at the wood in the fireplace.

I forced my feet to point away from the door. I pinched the bridge of my nose and tried to ignore the tightness in my chest.

None of that worked. I still wanted to run screaming into the streets, and it hurt to breathe.

"I'll never forgive her, Ted." The words were out before I knew it. I didn't even remember thinking them. Yet, there they were.

He sat on the hearth. The look on his face told me he

knew exactly who I was talking about. "You keep looking for someone to blame, Jan. First it was God. Now you want to blame Sarah?"

I bit my lip and focused on the pain and not the desire to bolt. "You promised to never mention her name."

"Jan, Sarah's my brother's wife and your sister-in-law. You're talking about someone who loved and babysat Laynee since the day she was born. She did everything she could. It was an accident."

I rolled my eyes. "An accident that didn't have to happen. Laynee was a good swimmer. And she knew the rules. No way would she have continued playing in the water if she'd known everyone else had gone inside. Your brother's *wife should've* made sure Laynee was in the house with the rest of the family, but a phone call took precedence over my daughter."

"*Our* daughter."

I looked away from him.

He continued, "Our daughter followed Sarah into the house then went back out to retrieve her bracelet. You know this, and you also know how much she loved that bracelet. Sarah answered the phone because she didn't know Laynee had gone back outside. Laynee slipped and fell into the water, hitting her head on the stones in the process." Ted stood and then sat next to me. "It was an accident."

I looked down at my hands. Three adults and nine kids, and no one heard my daughter leave the house. Everyone suspected she'd gone out to retrieve her bracelet because she'd had it on when they found her, but not when Sarah had corralled everyone inside.

If Adam hadn't been out with his uncle Gabe, he would've noticed his sister was missing. Why didn't the rest of them? My eyes stung. I leaned forward and laid my head on my arms.

"You know what?" Ted scooted closer. "That's enough talking for tonight." He gently lifted my head from my arms and laid it in his lap. He then ran his fingers through my hair and kissed my forehead softly. The warmth of his touch reminded me of when I was a little girl, snuggled up to Mom. She played with my hair the same way he did now. Then she'd pray over me until I fell asleep. Her final prayer forever etched in my memory.

If Mom were alive, she'd be embarrassed by my behavior. I'd alienated everyone who tried to help me, including my husband. The fact that Ted had to remind me twice today that Laynee was *our* daughter weighed heavily on my heart. I wiped away more tears and shifted to look up at him. "I'm sorry I haven't been able to be there for you."

He continued stroking my hair. "I know."

"I'm going to try to fix that, but I can't make any promises."

"I know."

I grabbed his hand and kissed it. "But I can tell you that this helps. Thank you."

"I miss doing this." He resumed stroking my hair, and his one-dimpled smirk made another appearance. A playful glint also danced in his eyes.

I straightened to stretch and gave an exaggerated yawn. My hair bounced onto my shoulders. I tossed it to the side and batted my eyes at him. "It's been an awfully long day, and that nap earlier didn't quite do it for me. Will I see you upstairs?"

His eyes widened. "Are you … asking me to join you?"

I smiled. Several months ago, I'd decided to sleep in a separate bedroom for a reason that escaped me now. And every night since then, Ted had let me know just how much he hated that decision.

I reached out my hand to him. "I don't want to be alone anymore."

He stood and clasped my hand. "Neither do I."

Chapter Five

Spring 1982

Mrs. Gibbons headed back to her car, and I ran after her. She couldn't leave me here. She just couldn't. I grabbed her elbow. "Take me back with you, Mrs. Gibbons." I cried. "Please."

Her eyes watered and she clasped my hands in hers. "I wish I could, Janny, I really do, but your aunt is your legal guardian now. She said I can't take you with me, and I have to honor that." She sniffed, then pulled me close and whispered in my ear. "Never forget all that your mother taught you, Janny, you understand me? Never forget who she was, what she stood for, and Who she believed in." She dropped my hands and then rummaged through her purse. "Found it," she said before pulling out a small black notebook and slipping it into the back pocket of my jeans. "If you need anything, anything at all, call me or one of the church members in that book. I mean it, Jan. We'll take care of you." She hugged me again and said softly, "And always remember how much you're loved. By God, me, and the rest of your church family."

The click of high heels on the pavement startled us. Aunt Ginger stopped and stared at Mrs. Gibbons. A cold breeze rippled through Aunt Ginger's tan slacks and white silk blouse before she continued walking toward us. Mrs. Gibbons wrapped her arms around me one more time, then she got in her car and left.

When her car faded into the distance, I glanced at Aunt Ginger. The look on her face told me that the world, as I'd previously known it, had just ended.

~

Present Day

Normally, Saturday mornings were set aside for housecleaning. I'd managed to vacuum a room or two over the past couple of weeks, but anything more than that was ignored. I simply didn't have the emotional strength to do anything more. Ted and Libbybelle, of course, offered to help, but the uncleanliness of the house comforted me. It brought me an odd sort of peace. I felt a connection with the chaos and uncleanness. Though, I often wondered if that connection had more to do with the condition of my soul rather than the house.

Nevertheless, a deep cleaning of the home was definitely needed.

My soul would have to wait for another day.

I grabbed the basket of cleaners and dust cloths from the bathroom closet and headed to Ted's den. He loved the look and feel of real wood, and so did the dust.

I pushed open the heavy oak door, ready to wrestle with the bunnies, but the office was spotless. A finger along the wooden window sill confirmed it. The window panes were so clear I tapped my fingernails against them to make sure they were still there. The hardwood floors reflected sunlight from the windows, and the tingling aroma of lemons followed me throughout the room. *Libbybelle.* When it came to housekeeping, she was the best, and apparently, she'd had enough of watching my home turn into a disgusting pit. Part of me was angry that she'd ignored my request to leave the cleaning alone, but I was also relieved. Now, I didn't have to force myself to do something I didn't want to do in the first place. But when your fourteen-year-old son tells you that he's run out of clean clothes to wear to school and that his shower enclosure was too grimy to shower in, then you do what's necessary to keep everyone else's world from falling apart.

My husband and son deserved better, and I'm glad Libbybelle had stepped up to the plate.

I needed to call and thank her, but that would have to wait. I needed a couple of hours to prepare myself for the stern lecture that would follow. Self-pity did not happen in my mother-figure's world.

I owed my life to her and Papa George. Thirty-five years ago, Billie Sue, Libbybelle's sister, an over-the-road truck driver, found me on a dirt road in the middle of the night. She then took me to the small diner her brother-in-law owned and left me in the care of Papa George and Libbybelle.

Together, they breathed new life into me.

It took days for the police and investigators to confirm everything I told them that had happened. Still, even after being made aware of the details, Libbybelle refused to pity me.

On the days I wouldn't get out of bed and hoped only to curl up and die, she dragged me out of it. Literally. After a cold shower and a hot meal, she'd put me to work in the diner. Over warm milk and graham crackers by my bed at night, she and Papa George would explain why it was important for me to keep putting one foot in front of the other. They also told me that God wouldn't want me to wither away and die but to live and thrive and that my mother would want that, too. I believed my mother did. But God? I wasn't so sure.

I set the cleaning basket on Ted's desk and looked out

the window. I often teased Ted about choosing this room for his office instead of the more spacious one across the hall. This room gave him a sweeping view of our small semi-rural neighborhood. There are ten homes, and the curved panoramic window let him see the comings and goings of everyone who lives there. Over half of the people in those homes attended our church. Ted would laugh at my teasing and respond that he just wanted to make sure the members of our congregation were behaving themselves.

I pressed my thumb against the window latch to unlock it and let in fresh air when Olivia Jensen's van pulled into her driveway. I grabbed a jacket from the hall closet and jogged over to her place. Ted mentioned he thought she'd been in Montana visiting her mother, but I still wasn't convinced Olivia would take a trip like that without letting one of us know.

The late August sun had risen an hour ago, but an early autumn chill filled the air. I walked up the steep incline of Olivia's driveway and tightened my jacket around me. Gravel crunched under my tennis shoes and echoed throughout the quiet morning air. Olivia got out of her car and frowned.

"I'm sorry I haven't been over to visit." I moved to hug her, but she took a step backward.

"Olivia, is everything okay?"

She looked towards her house then back at me again.

Silence.

"Olivia, what's going on? Is someone inside your house?" I looked in the passenger door window. "And where's Anna?"

"Nothing's going on, okay? I'll come by your place later, but right now, I gotta go." She reached inside the car and pulled out a pile of books. She then hurried towards her house.

"Wait!" Something was wrong. I could feel it. I caught up with her and looked closely at her face. Olivia was a natural beauty and had always been meticulous about her appearance. She was the only person I knew who could make an up-do hairstyle look casual by sporting one with faded jeans and a T-shirt.

Now, puffy red circles shadowed her dark brown eyes, and her olive complexion had paled. Her hair, which was the same color as her eyes, flowed wildly towards her waist and looked as though it hadn't seen a brush in weeks. She was also a former swimming champion and coach and was zealous about healthy eating and exercise. But as I glanced over the rest of her body, I gasped. Olivia's athletic build had withered away to skin and bones.

I placed a hand on her shoulder. "Please tell me what's going on."

She dropped the pile of books at our feet and grabbed my hands. "I *want* to talk to you, and I've been wanting to talk to you for a while now, but I can't. They won't let me."

"Who won't let you?"

"Anna."

Anna was Olivia's seventeen-year-old daughter. Anna had also spent quite a bit of time at our house. Laynee had often invited her to tea parties, and she'd graciously accept— even though stuffed animals and a rag doll were the only other guests. "I don't understand. Why wouldn't Anna want you to talk to me? And you said they— who's they?"

"I don't know what to do, Jan. I've tried everything. I've talked to her teachers, her doctor, a psychiatrist, and a psychologist. They all think I'm blowing everything out of proportion or making it up." She squeezed my hands. "But they haven't seen the things she's done. I'm scared and don't know what she'll do next. Something's happened to my daughter. She's not the same Anna." She stepped away from me. "I'm rambling, and you probably think I'm nuts."

I looked down and read through the titles of the books she'd dropped. They were about abnormal behavior patterns in teens.

"Olivia, I don't know what's going on with you or Anna, but I know you're not nuts." I reached for her hand again. "But we should finish this conversation inside, maybe over tea?"

She blew out a breath and smiled. "A cup of tea sounds nice." She bent to pick up the books, then stopped. "There's something I need to tell you before we go inside. I don't want you to be alarmed, but—"

"Jan!"

We turned to see who'd called my name. Doris ran across the street to us from my house. Seriously? What in the world did this woman want now?

We cut across the lawn to meet her halfway.

"I need to see Pastor Eller right now. Where is he?"

"Hi, Doris," Olivia said.

Doris flicked a hand at her, then snapped her gaze back at me. "Well, where is he?"

Dr. Schultz and Ted warned me about letting my true feelings bubble up inside and fester, and they encouraged me to share them instead. The good, bad, and the ugly.

I wondered what they'd think when they learned I'd unleashed them all on Doris Slater.

"Go away, Doris."

"What?"

"You heard me. Get lost. I don't want to talk to you." I folded my arms across my chest. "As a matter of fact, I don't want to see you, either." I looked across the road and stared at the 1969 Oldsmobile in my driveway. "Remove that vehicle from my home and leave. Otherwise, I'm calling Abner to let him know that one of his beloved vehicles is about to be towed."

"I'll bust your nose if you do anything like that."

"Then leave, Doris. Now. Before I preemptively bust yours instead."

Her cheeks reddened. "How dare you."

"No," I rushed towards her until my face was inches

away from hers. "How dare you show up and demand anything from me or my husband. Who do you think you are?"

"I'm a member of your congregation."

"Then act like it and show some respect."

Her eyes tightened. "I don't have time for this. Just tell me where Pastor Eller is."

"You have a church calendar just like everyone else. You should've consulted it before driving over here. But oh, wait. Why would you do that when you can come here, scream in my face, and try to manipulate my husband into doing your bidding?"

"Jan," her hands balled into fists. "I'm telling you right now that if you don't tell—"

"It's the last Saturday of the month, Doris." Olivia moved between us. "He's at the Men's Breakfast."

"Where are they meeting?"

"Barney's Pancake Barn off Elm Street."

She headed to her car. "Fine, I'll talk with him there."

"Don't do it, Doris," I said. "Let my husband eat and minister in peace." I glanced at my watch. "They'll be done in an hour."

"An hour?" She stomped back to me and Olivia. "In *an hour*, Cody and that heathen girlfriend of his will be across state lines. They went off to get married!"

I narrowed my eyes. Doris always over-dramatized anything that had to do with her grandson. "Cody told you this?"

"Of course not." She stepped closer to me. "But I haven't been able to contact him for two days. *Two* days." She shoved two long, wrinkly fingers toward my face. "He hasn't been home, and he hasn't called. I just came from that crazy, loony house that girlfriend of his lives in, and her family hasn't seen her either in two days. *Two* days."

I threw my hand up and blocked her fingers from being thrust back into my face.

Her nostrils flared. "I knew something like this would happen. I told you and the Pastor that those youth ministers weren't any good, and now look at what's happened. Cody and his girlfriend have run off to get married, and those incompetent youth leaders are probably driving the getaway car!"

I made my way back to the books Olivia had left in the driveway. "Doris, Ted will be done in an hour. Call on him then, and only then."

"I'm going to that restaurant."

"No, you're not." I picked up the books and turned to her. "Cody and Stephanie are adults, and they've only been gone two days." I resisted the urge to point two fingers in her direction. "Obviously, no one suspects foul play or the police would be here instead of you. Let my husband finish his meeting."

"You can't stop me from going."

"No, she can't," Olivia said. "And neither can I. But I can *ask* you not to go. Will you please wait until Pastor Eller is done? Jan was in the middle of helping me with something, and I'd appreciate it if you'd let her focus on that."

"Fine, but if those two get married while the pastor's stuffing his face with biscuits and gravy, I swear, I'll never let you hear the end of it."

Olivia nodded. "I'll take full responsibility."

"Oh, *O-livia,* you will. I'll see to that."

Chapter Six

Spring 1982

Aunt Ginger gripped my arm. I winced at the pain, but it still didn't hurt as much as watching Mrs. Gibbons leave without me.

Back inside the house, Aunt Ginger laid out her rules. "First," she said, "Don't call me Aunt Ginger, or someone could get hurt. It's Gingie, got it? Gin-G. Second, there are six rooms in this house. The one we're in, the kitchen, two bathrooms, and two bedrooms. Your room has a bathroom, and it's down the hall to the right. My bedroom is on the left. Under no circumstances are you to go in there. If it's on fire, let it burn. As for this room ..." she extended her arms and walked in a circle. "There's not much in this area, and it's that way for a reason. You have free reign here except on Friday nights. Grab everything you need on those nights— food, water, or whatever, then go to your room and stay there. Don't come out until noon the next day. Any questions?"

"Whatever, Gingie." I flopped down on the suitcase Mrs. Gibbons had packed for me and fought back tears.

Gingie ran towards me and grabbed my shoulders. Her face was so red it frightened me to my core. "June and Mrs. Holier-than-Thou may have let you get away with that sass," she hissed. "But it won't work here." Her breath smelled of peppermint and smoke. "Another remark like that, and you're toast. Understand me?"

I trembled.

She blew out a breath and slowly walked to the other side of the room. "Listen," she pulled at the pins that held her tight bun together. "There'll never be another person on earth like your mother. June and I hadn't spoken in years. I'm a bad influence, and your mother knew that. That's why I haven't been around much since you were little. But I'll never forget how she took care of me and our brothers when we were kids. Our parents were losers, but June watched out for us. That is, until the state intervened. Still, she never abandoned us, and that's why you're here now." Hair fell away from the bun and landed on her shoulders. "I promise to take care of you the way she took care of me." She locked her eyes on mine. "But you will follow the rules and rein in that sharp tongue of yours. Got it?"

I picked up the suitcase containing only remnants and memories of the life I'd held dear. "I'm going to my room." I paused, embarrassed at how easily the manners my mother taught me had evaporated. "If that's okay with you, ma'am."

She nodded and smiled.

"One more thing." The momentary softness in her features returned to their familiar edge. "Do you have a Bible?"

"Yes."

"Then get rid of it." She grabbed a set of keys off a hook near the door and then turned on her heel to leave. "Because if I come across one of those around here ..." She looked me straight in the eyes. "Let's just say it won't end well. Not for you or the Bible."

~

Present Day

Olivia tried to warn me about what awaited us inside her home, but her description didn't come close.

The massive crystal chandelier that had decorated her entryway for as long as I could remember dangled dangerously low over our heads. Only a few thin wires secured it to the ceiling. Broken glass crunched underneath Olivia's pink New Balance tennis shoes as she closed the door behind us.

I tiptoed around the shards. Family photographs had been ripped into pieces and thrown onto the marble floor. Coats, jackets, hats, scarves, and rain gear from the foyer closet lay slashed and scattered throughout the large entrance, and the white six-panel closet door had a gaping hole. It looked like someone had taken a large, heavy object and caved it in.

"What happened?" I asked, pointing at the door.

"Anna happened. She did that with her bare hands."

A baseball bat lay against the wall near the door. I picked it up. "Are you sure she didn't use this?"

"No. She used that to shatter the chandelier."

I stood the bat in a corner, and Olivia continued explaining the damage done to her home as we went from room to room. My memory of the adorable teen with bouncy black ponytails and freckled cheeks didn't fit with the destruction around me. "Anna did all of this by herself?"

Olivia nodded. "I watched it happen. Last night was her most recent episode." She motioned for me to follow her into the kitchen. "There's more."

The kitchen air smelled of burnt flesh and smoke. I coughed and covered my nose. Scorch marks and smoke damage surrounded the cabinets and stove.

"Anna tried to set herself on fire," she said.

"What? Olivia, I had no idea how much you were struggling with her. We've got to get her some help."

She pushed several large crates with dishes from the cabinet around the kitchen counter until she found the tea kettle. "I've tried getting her help, but they think I'm the problem. The general consensus is that I'm 'a recently widowed and overwhelmed single mom with an out-of-control teenager who's looking for attention. It's a phase. She'll grow out of it.' I'm telling you, Jan, I've heard it all."

I lifted two chairs from the kitchen floor and sat at the table that, fortunately, was still standing. "Where is she now?" I asked.

"My brother-in-law, Luke, and his wife, Diane, flew in this morning. They picked up a rental and then drove her back to their ranch in Montana. It's so far away, but I didn't know what else to do. The only person she listens to since her dad died is her Uncle Luke. Diane's a trauma nurse, so she was able to take care of Anna's burns." Olivia turned to me. Tears welled in her eyes. "I love Anna and wanted nothing more than for her to stay here with me, but I couldn't because all we do is fight." She wiped at her eyes and then rolled up her sleeve. Her arm was covered in bruises. A nasty wound was also bleeding through a bandage.

I gasped and pushed away from the table. "We need to get you to a doctor,"

"And involve the authorities? I can't risk Anna getting arrested." She rolled down her sleeve. "Besides, this happened when I wrestled with Anna to get her away from the fire. It looks worse than it is. But there've been times when she's intentionally tried to hurt me."

I pulled out the other chair. "Olivia, sit down and start from the beginning."

She wiped her cheeks with her hands and sat.

"Tell me everything," I said.

"Okay." She shuddered and blew out a breath before continuing, "It started this past year. Anna and I had our disagreements from time to time— you know that— but never anything like this," she waved her hand around the room. "You know how she is. Stubborn and opinionated but also an honor student and an athlete, everyone loves her.

But earlier this year, she started hanging out with a new group of friends. I didn't like them. They were strange. They laughed at stuff that wasn't funny and groaned and complained about stuff that was good. And they were all much older than her. One night, when they were all over here watching a movie, I got the weirdest vibe from them. It was strong, and it was creepy. I asked them to leave, but they wouldn't, so I threatened to call the police. When they finally left, I told Anna to stay away from them. After that was when all the trouble began."

"Do you know anything about them? Who they are, where they live?"

"That's just it. I'd never seen them anywhere around here before. And no one else knows them either. I know because I've asked around. And now they seem to have disappeared."

"Well, the good news is that we're in a small town. I'll have Ted look into it. Somebody has to know something. He's also good friends with the sheriff. Together, they should be able to find something out."

"Thanks, but I suspect they were drifters and are long gone."

"Maybe. But it wouldn't hurt to know for sure. Do you think they gave Anna drugs?"

"Yes, and I had her pediatrician test for it, but the results were negative."

"That's good."

"It is, but I know those kids did something to my daughter. It may not have been drugs, but she was never the same girl after she met those people. She'd become frustrated at the slightest thing, then explode and start destroying stuff." Olivia sniffed. "She also began hearing voices." Olivia wrung her hands and continued. "One night, before bed, I went to check on her. She was sitting in the dark, on the floor in the corner of her room. When I asked what she was doing, she yelled at me to get out. She was conversing with someone, and apparently, I'd interrupted it."

"A conversation? But she was the only one in the room, right?"

"Yeah, but I definitely heard her talking to someone, and she wasn't on the phone either. I had taken away all of her devices because I was afraid she'd find a way to reach out to someone in that group. I then asked if she was talking to herself, and she said no."

"Did she say who she was talking to?"

"Yeah, somebody named Ruin."

The blood in my veins ran cold. "Did you say *Ruin*?"

Olivia nodded. "But like I said, nobody was in the room. And the strange thing is, before I had opened her door, I could've sworn I heard two voices. Which means they both had to come from her … right?" She wiped her eyes with her sleeve. "My daughter is losing her mind, Jan, and I have no idea what to do about it."

I sat frozen in my chair. *It couldn't be.*

"Olivia, listen to me carefully. Are you sure you heard two distinct voices?"

"Yes. Anna's voice and a male one." Her brows furrowed. "Why? What are you thinking?"

I scooted away from the table and forced a smile. "I'm thinking some fresh air will do us good. How about we go for a walk? Then we'll call some ladies from the church to help us clean up this place. Okay?"

"A walk sounds good. Give me a minute to put a new bandage on this wound, then shower and change. I won't be long."

She disappeared down the hall, and I fell against the table and held on tight.

My skin tingled.

Invisible eyes stared at me.

And a familiar presence made sure that I knew it.

I swallowed. It couldn't have followed me here. Not after what happened. Not after all this time.

I tightened my grip on the table.

Could it?

Chapter Seven

Spring 1982

Plush wall-to-wall carpeting lined my bedroom, and a white, four-poster, full-sized bed sat in the middle. A thick, pastel pink comforter covered it, and the curtains on the windows matched. Three tall, white bookshelves were spread along one wall, and the other displayed an entertainment center, a TV, a VCR, and an expensive-looking stereo system. A nightstand was on each side of the bed, and a nostalgic pewter frame sat on top of the one on the right side. Inside the frame was a picture of my mother.

Had Aunt Gingie done all of this for me?

I had no idea, but I did know I wanted to find out where the phones were.

I loved my room, especially the bright pink walls and photo of my mother, but on the wall next to the nightstand was a place to plug a phone in to, but there was no phone.

I placed my suitcase on the bed and headed into the kitchen.

A white Kenmore refrigerator and other appliances filled the tiny kitchen. The fridge still bore the purchase sticker, but the inside was piled high with food. I grabbed an orange soda and looked around the kitchen again.

No phone.

A quick glance down the hallway and into the living area confirmed my fear.

There was no phone inside the house.

~

Present Day

"Pastor, Cody doesn't understand now, but he will," Doris said. "I only have his best interests in mind. Once that girl is out of his life, he'll be able to see that."

I tossed my keys on the foyer table and headed to Ted's office, where Doris's voice came from. Ted was at his desk, and Doris sat across from him. John and Norah Baxter, our youth leaders, were on matching stools near the window. Ted motioned for me to sit on the couch.

John leaned forward. "Doris, Cody, and Stephanie did not run off and get married. They've been staying with us the past couple of days."

"Why didn't you say that in the first place?"

"Because—"

"I hope you weren't dumb enough to let them sleep in the same room."

John's face flushed red. "Of course not. Norah and Stephanie shared a room, and Cody and I bunked in the other."

"Then why are they at your place?"

"Stephanie and her sisters got into an argument. It was bad enough that her sisters vowed never to speak to her again, and she took it pretty hard. Cody brought her to our place so that she could talk to Norah. He also didn't want to leave her side. Norah and I are bringing the sisters together to make amends, but it's complicated. Stephanie's staying with us in the meantime, and Cody said he would, too."

"If you want to help that girl out with her crazy family,

so be it. But send Cody home."

John and Norah shared a glance. He continued, "Mrs. Slater, Cody promised Steph that he'd stay with her until the situation with her family works itself out." John placed his elbows on his knees. "He also knows that you're worried about him. He asked us to let you know he's okay, but he won't be home anytime soon because you'll try to keep him from Stephanie. He plans to stay with us for a while."

Doris shifted in her seat and looked at Ted. "Pastor, tell this man to send my grandson home."

"He's nineteen years old, Doris," Ted said. "According to the laws of our state, that makes him an adult. If he wants to stay with the Baxters', and they're not opposed to it, there's nothing I can do to change that. If you want him home with you, you're the one who's going to have to talk him into it."

"I'll talk him into it, all right." She spun in her chair toward John. "Where do you live?"

"Near Crater Lake. Why?"

'I'm going to get my grandson, that's why."

"Ma'am," John stood. "That's a bad idea."

She rose from her chair. "What is your address."

"What's more important to you, Doris?" Ted said. "Making a scene and forcing Cody to go home with you? Or repairing your relationship with him?"

She threw her hands up in the air. "I thought I made this clear. The most important thing to me is that *he doesn't marry that heathen*."

John shook his head. "Mrs. Slater, Cody loves and respects you a great deal. But right now, you're the last person he wants to see. Those are his words, not mine."

Blast it. I was starting to feel sorry for her. Doris was gruff, but she truly cared for Cody and didn't want him to suffer any more heartache. But Ted and John were right. Her showing up unannounced and talking to Cody like a child in front of his fiancé was a very bad idea. What if he responded the same way her children did and refused to communicate with her at all? I cleared my throat. "Doris, how about the three of us—me, you, and Norah, go to your place and pick up some things for Cody. He showed up at the Baxters' house with the clothes on his back and would probably appreciate some clean clothes. I know it's not what you had in mind, but when Norah tells him you packed a few of his favorite things for him, maybe he'll consider reaching out to you."

Her cheek twitched. "Spicy taco casserole."

"What?"

"My spicy taco casserole. Cody loves it. I'll make it and send it with his things. He'll reach out to me after that. I know it. Let's go."

Ted walked to the door and opened it for us. I felt sorry for Doris but was also eager to get her out of our house. Apparently, Ted was too. "Everything will turn out okay, Doris," he said. "The most important thing is that Cody's safe."

"And single." She added and slammed the door behind us.

~

After my walk with Olivia earlier, I'd invited her over for dinner.

I hated thinking of her in that house all alone.

Libbybelle had also decided to join us, so I prepared a roast, potatoes, steamed vegetables, and salad. However, despite Doris's invasion of my home earlier, I couldn't stop obsessing over what I experienced at Olivia's—an all too familiar and tangible presence that taunted me.

If Ruin was here, did the others follow?

I shivered, and my heart sank. God had allowed this to happen again. But why was I surprised? He'd stopped caring about what happened to me a long time ago.

I popped a cherry tomato in my mouth and let the lively tone at the dinner table distract me from my thoughts. Everyone laughed as Libbybelle described the hilarious chain of events that had happened to her and Adam while they were out on "Grandma Saturday." A name the kids had come up with years ago.

One Saturday a month, she'd take Adam and Laynee out on one of her adventures. They never knew beforehand where they were going or what they would do, and they didn't care. Back then, they'd leave before sunrise and return late in the evening. They were so worn out when they got home that Ted would have to carry them to their beds. Excited chatter about their adventures with Grandma would wake us the next morning, and it took all our energy to get them focused and dressed for church.

I blinked away tears. Libbybelle and Adam never said anything, but I knew it was hard for them to continue with Grandma Saturdays now that Laynee was no longer with us.

After dessert, Libbybelle waved goodnight to everyone, and Adam helped me with the dishes. Ted and Olivia went to his office to discuss Anna, but Olivia was in over her head.

Earlier, during our walk, she'd described another strange encounter with Anna that chilled me to the bone.

One morning, after she dropped Anna off at school, she met with a group of physicians at the New Hope Mental Health Care Facility to discuss Anna's symptoms. She never mentioned that appointment to Anna.

That afternoon, Anna left school early and returned home furious. She confronted Olivia about the appointment and destroyed the house in the process. Ruin had told her everything, she said. She also let Olivia know that every step she took was being watched.

Which was why Olivia had been so skittish earlier when we were in her driveway. That encounter with Anna had scared her into silence. From that point on, she didn't talk to anyone about her struggles with Anna. The only people she'd confided in were her in-laws, who were already aware of Anna's issues. And now she was talking to Ted.

"You okay, Mom?" Adam asked.

I nodded and filled the sink with hot water and dish soap.

He held out a dish. "I can take care of these for you if you'd like to go lay down."

I tousled his hair and dropped the dish in the water. "Thanks, but I'm okay. Just have a lot on my mind."

"Were you thinking about Laynee?"

My heart stopped.

One day soon, I was going to stop having that reaction to her name. Instead of heartache, her name will bring a smile to my face and fill my heart with tender memories. At least, that's what Dr. Schultz said.

I wish that day was now. My son needed me. Obviously, he wanted to talk about his sister.

"It's okay if you were," he continued. "Grandma and I think about her a lot. We talked to her today, you know."

I turned to him. "You did what?"

"Yeah. Every time we go out for Grandma Saturday, we gather all the yellow flowers we can find … remember how much she loved yellow? Anyway, we take them to the cemetery and place them on her grave. We talk to her while we're there."

I blinked away tears. Dr. Schultz said one day, they were going to end, too. "How long have you and Grandma been doing that?"

"We've been going to the cemetery to talk to her for over a year now, but Grandma and I have been sharing our feelings about Laynee since the day she died. Or, like Grandma likes to say, 'since the day she went home.'"

She went *home* eighteen months ago, and I had yet to visit her grave. I couldn't bring myself to do it.

"You don't have to be sad, Mom." He added silverware to the water. "Laynee doesn't want to come back. She's happy being at home. Don't ask me how I know, 'cause I'm not good at explaining it very well. But I know. I feel it in here," he patted the left side of his chest. "Do you feel it, too?"

"I sure do, buddy," I lied and pulled him into a hug. "I feel it, too."

Chapter Eight

Summer 1982

Living with Aunt Ginger wasn't all bad. As long as I obeyed the rules, minded my tongue, and stayed out of her way, we got along great. Most days, she'd still be asleep when I left for school and gone when I came home. She'd return after midnight, but there was always someone with her. I never got to see who it was because they'd go straight to her room.

One Friday night, she told me she would be hosting the Friday night gatherings again. Before I could ask what a "gathering" was, she told me about her girlfriend's daughter, Molly. She said Molly and I were the same age and could hang out in my room on those nights. She warned me again not to venture out of my room. When I asked if she had told Molly about that rule, she laughed and said I didn't have to worry about Molly getting curious. She already knew better.

Molly was a Godsend. That night, we realized we'd seen each other around school but had never had the chance to meet. We talked, ate snacks, and watched TV, but I couldn't focus on being friendly because of the horror outside my bedroom door.

Screams filled the air. Against Molly's objections, I quietly opened the door to get a peek at what was happening.

A group of people dressed in black robes and hoods

chanted and laid something on top of what appeared to be a makeshift altar. The room was filled with smoke. One of the men turned and caught me looking at them. Two intense, bright green eyes stared back at me.

I gasped, and my whole body shook.

Molly quickly closed the door.

"What in the world is going on out there?" I asked. My voice shook as hard as my body.

She blinked at me. "They're worshipping Satan."

I froze.

She sucked in a deep breath and inched the door open the same way I had before. "There's something else you should know. You see that guy over there?" She pointed to the one who'd caught me staring. "That's Garringer. Stay away from him. He's evil." She let the door slip back into place. "And never be in a room alone with him." She swallowed before continuing, "Trust me, you'll regret it for the rest of your life."

Smoke drifted under the door. "They're making sacrifices," she said. "So far, it's been bats, rats, and small stray cats." She chuckled at the phrase but then turned serious again. "But one day, Jan, it'll be me or you up there. Mark my words."

~

Present Day

"I don't know, Janny." Ted slid into the driver's seat and then put on a pair of shades to block the morning sun. We were on our way to meet with Cody and the youth ministers.

"The research suggests Anna may have a mild form of schizophrenia. However, being my father's son and all, the first thing that came to my mind was demonic possession."

"There's a big difference between the two, Ted."

"I know." He turned the ignition. "The paranoia Anna displays says one thing, but … did you see the damage done to their house? Anna's a tiny girl. Where did she get the strength to toss that heavy oak dining table like she did? She would've had to have superhuman strength to do that by herself. And did you see what she did to the baby grand piano?"

"No." After Olivia and I left, I knew I couldn't go back into that house. "We went for a walk and then called you guys."

He pressed the button for the windows. They rolled down half an inch, then stopped. Cool, crisp air flowed inside. "Still," he said. "There's something about this whole thing that doesn't add up. I doubt it's schizophrenia, and the doctors Olivia talked to agree. The things she's witnessed with Anna barely make the list for the mildest form of schizophrenia. So that leaves the other. But why would Anna get involved with demonic spirits like that?"

Ted was well aware of my past, but I'd yet to tell him about my run-in with Ruin at Olivia's. Things were going great between us now, and the last thing he wanted was for me to go down that road again. He'd also try to protect me, but I was done being victimized. By humans or non-humans. And that included God as well.

He started the car and pulled away from the house. "You know," he ran his fingers through his hair. "I may just have to consult my dad on this one."

Ted's father, Rev. Hank Eller, was known as the *go-to* man if you had a demon, suspected you had a demon or had questions about demons. His Tabernacle deliverance meetings were legendary. He was now ninety years old and still active in that ministry, though as more of a consultant these days.

We turned right onto the main road that led to the small city of Crater Lake. Doris's idea about the spicy taco casserole had hit the jackpot. Cody agreed to meet with her, but only at the Baxters' house and only if Ted, John, and Norah were allowed to moderate the conversation.

Ted asked if his friends, Lieutenant Ike Dodge and Sheriff Dan Glass, both of the Habakkuk Police Department, could meet us there afterward. Olivia wanted to see if the youth ministers or anyone in their circle knew anything about the group of kids Anna had previously hung out with.

When we arrived at Baxters', Doris was in their driveway, sitting in an older model Toyota Camry. She joined us as we walked up the porch steps.

Norah greeted us at the door. She then led us to a large recreation room. Pool tables, dartboards, and video game equipment filled the massive space. Cody, John, and Stephanie sat at a nearby table stacked with snacks and sodas. Olivia was at a table next to them. We greeted her, and she pointed to the two empty chairs next to her. Ted pulled them out, and we sat.

Cody stood to hug his grandmother, then sat next to Stephanie again. Doris continued to stand.

"Okay." Norah slapped her hands together. "We have chips, salsa, soda, tea, and a bunch of other stuff to munch on, so help yourselves. We also have coffee brewing and lemonade in the back. But, first things first." She turned to Doris. "Cody would like to talk to you about something. Well, a few things, actually, but they won't be easy for you to hear. He asks that there won't be any name-calling or—"

"He wants me to behave."

Norah smiled. "Yes."

"Fine. Get on with it."

Cody sipped his soda and then placed it back on the table. "Grandma, I love you, and I know you love me. I also know you want the best for me, but I'm not a kid anymore. You and Grandpa have taught me everything I need to know to make wise decisions. Have faith in the work the two of you have put in. Stephie and I are getting married soon and hope to spend the rest of our lives together. I know you're not okay with that decision, but I ask that you respect it."

"And if I don't?"

"Stephie will be a part of my life whether you accept it or not. We're a couple. A team. If you can't accept or even try to get to know her, you and I will never be able to reconcile. Is that what you want?"

Doris pinched her lips together and then looked away from Cody.

He leaned forward on the table. "Can you at least give it a try before we walk away from this? I don't want to part ways with you, Grandma, but if I have to, I will."

She snapped her head toward him. "You'll cut me out of your life, is that it? Like your mom and the rest of the spoiled brats that are supposed to be my kids. Is that how you're going to treat me, Cody? Like an old bag, you no longer have any use for?"

"That's not what I'm saying."

She sat at the table next to him. After a few moments, she reached for Cody's hand. "She's not a Christian."

I groaned. What was Doris doing? I'd already told her that Ted had led her to Christ.

John Baxter scooted closer to the table. "Actually, she is. Cody and I tried to tell you, but … let's just say you weren't interested in hearing her name at the time."

"And how do you know she didn't agree to do that so Cody would marry her?"

"Doris," Ted interjected. "I believe it's genuine."

"I don't."

"Well, all we ask is that you take her word for it until you do."

"Fine." Her hand slapped the table so hard it shook. "I'll do what I have to do. It'll be a cold day in Hades before I let another loved one be led astray by some good for nothing—"

"Doris," Norah laid a hand on her arm. "Remember, no name-calling."

She yanked her arm away and faced Stephanie. "The reason I haven't got to know you is because I don't need to. I know your type. I know what you want and why you want it." She leaned back in her chair and exhaled. "But if this is the only way Cody thinks this can be worked out, so be it. Be at my place tomorrow morning. Ten a.m. Don't be late. You'll ride with me while I deliver meals to the sick and shut-ins. You okay with that?"

Stephanie smiled. "Yes, ma'am. I'll be there."

"And be prepared to pull your own weight. I'm not a babysitter." She grabbed her purse and stood. "Cody, I'll see you at home." She narrowed her eyes. "You are coming home, aren't you?"

"Yes, but you should know that Stephie and I are looking at apartments. For after we're married, of course."

"Of course." Doris rubbed at her temples. "I guess this bully session is over then. But I'm warning you …" She pointed one of her long fingers at John. "If I'm right about this girl and all of you are wrong, you'll wish you never met me." She tightened her grip on her purse and marched out of the room.

Ted followed her. "I'll make sure she's okay."

A door slammed in the other room, and Olivia blew out a breath. "Oh, my word, that woman." She quickly slapped her hand over her mouth and looked at Cody. "I'm so sorry. I shouldn't have said that."

"My grandmother's not a bad person. She's been through a lot, and it affects the way she relates to people," he reached over and hugged Stephanie. "But if you make it past that, you soon realize that she's someone you'd want to have in your corner."

John patted him on the back. "That's a nice thing to say about your grandmother."

"She means well and—" He was interrupted by the doorbell. When Norah went to answer it, he turned his attention to me and Olivia. "John said there was something you ladies wanted to talk to us about."

I glanced at Olivia and nodded.

"Is it about Anna? Stephie and I haven't seen her around lately. Is she okay?"

Olivia spoke first. "Anna's visiting her aunt and uncle in Montana. We wanted to know if you guys had any information about the group of friends she was hanging out with. These weren't the type of kids that would go to youth group, and they were slightly older, but we were hoping one of you might have some information about them."

Stephanie looked up. "Would you happen to know what they looked like?"

"That's just it," Olivia stood and paced around the table. "I've only seen them once, and I don't have any names. But there were about eight to ten of them. More boys than girls. They wore long black coats—even inside the house. And black hats, they all had on hats. Dark make-up around the eyes, and they didn't talk much. When I entered the room, they just stared at me, all creepy-like. And they smelled bad. Not body odor or marijuana bad. More like rotten eggs."

The glass of lemonade I held almost cracked under my grip. There was no doubt about it now. Ruin was here.

Sheriff Glass walked into the room and greeted me first. "Lieutenant Dodge is talking outside with Ted." He turned to Olivia. "Ms. Jensen, our guys have been looking for that group you called about earlier. No luck so far." He reached into his pocket and pulled out a small notebook. "A couple of the young people we interviewed mentioned seeing them around once or twice, but no one knows where they came from."

Olivia nodded. "Well, thanks for checking."

"They might be related to someone locally or are holed up somewhere," he put the notebook back in his pocket. "It's not our top priority, but we'll keep looking into it. A group that size can't be too hard to find."

Cody turned to Stephanie. "Your camera. Go get your

camera."

Stephanie's eyes widened. "Oh, the photos," she said, running out of the room.

"Sheriff, Stephie's been taking photography classes at the community college. We were at the lake a few weeks back, trying to catch the sunset. I think the group Ms. Jensen described was there, black hats and all. The guys wore black jackets with *Legion* written in red across the back. They sat on the rocks and talked. When the sun set behind the rocks, Stephie turned her camera there and continued to shoot.

"One of the guys confronted us. He was about twenty-one or twenty-two. He thought Stephie was taking pictures of them, and he grabbed the camera. I wrestled it back from him, handed it to Stephie, and told her to wait in the car. The guy and I tussled and exchanged words, but that was it. A couple of days later, when we returned to get additional photos for her project, they weren't there, and we haven't seen them since."

"And you think she may have gotten a shot of them in the photos?"

"Yeah, but I don't know if the pictures are still there. Her professor erased some of them when she turned in her camera the next day. He only kept the good ones."

Stephanie hurried back into the room and handed her camera to the sheriff. "There are about fifty photos still on there. Feel free to flip through them."

He took the digital camera and sat at the table. Olivia and I stood over him. He flipped through the photos quickly using the camera's navigation arrows. The first couple of pictures were of Stephanie lounging by the lake in a swim top and shorts, followed by pictures of Cody and the sunset at various stages.

"Is this the group you were talking about?" the sheriff asked, pointing at one of the photos.

Cody and Stephanie nodded.

I sighed. It was a great group shot, but the best we could

see of their faces was a side profile or two.

"There should be one more that gets a little closer than that." She reached for the camera and continued flipping through the photos. "Here it is." She handed the camera back to the sheriff.

"I think we have something," he said.

Olivia and I leaned in to get a closer look. The group of kids in the photo sat on the rocks in a circle. In the center, looking towards the camera, was a man. Tall, with jet-black hair, a long black cloak, and a matching Fedora.

The sheriff tapped his finger on the photo. "Cody, is this the guy that confronted you?"

"No. I don't remember seeing that guy at all. He must've walked off when the other guy—"

"Wait." I held up my hand. "Sheriff, is there a way to get a close-up of the guy in the center?"

He pressed a couple of buttons on the camera. "Yeah, but that's about as close—"

I snatched the camera from him. Cold, bright-green eyes pierced through me from the digital screen. Eyes from the past.

"Jan?" Olivia placed her hand on my shoulder. Norah and Stephanie took hold of my arms. Cody's hand was on my back, and someone led me to a nearby chair. Only then did I realize I'd stopped breathing.

"Here, drink this." Norah poured water into a glass and handed it to me. She placed the pitcher on the table and whispered to Cody, "Go get Ted."

~

Sheriff Glass stared at his phone.

"Everything okay, Sheriff?" Ted let go of my hand and stood.

Sheriff Glass looked at him, then looked at the floor. His hands rested low on his waist. "One of my guys sent additional info from the station. I'll let you know if it's worth looking into."

John handed printed photocopies of the group to the sheriff. He took them and stepped out of the room.

Ted crouched next to my chair. "Jan, do you know the guy in that photo?"

I bowed my head and nodded.

He lifted my chin with his finger and looked me in the eyes. "What's his name?"

I opened my mouth, but no words came out.

He kissed my hand. "It's okay, love. I'm right here."

I'd completely drained the water Norah had given me earlier. She'd refreshed the glass with sweet tea. My hands shook as I sipped it. The overly sweetened drink went down as bitter as the name in my mouth. I placed my hand over my lips to stop the tea and the name from spilling out.

"What were you about to say?" Ted asked.

"Garringer." I placed the glass on the table and grabbed a napkin to wipe up the tea that spewed out along with the vile images associated with the man and the memories. "He's back."

Ted's brows furrowed. "Garringer? It can't be. He's dead."

"How can you say that? He was in Habakkuk a couple of years ago. We saw him."

"No, honey. *We* didn't see him. Other people said they did. And none of those sightings were confirmed. They were likely just rumors."

"I saw him the night I was leaving Resurrection Church, remember? After Kite and Eve's baby showers? I told you all about that, Ted."

Like my friend Mary, Kite and Eve were also good friends of mine. And one night, after celebrating their new babies at their church, I spotted Garringer. It was at a distance and across a busy road, but it was him.

"I remember you telling me," Ted answered. "But that was years ago, and it was dark outside. That could've—"

I grabbed him by the shoulders. "I'm telling you, it's

Garringer. That photo proved it. If there was ever any doubt, there isn't now. I'll never forget the brutality in those eyes. The coldness." I shuddered and sucked in a breath to calm my heart. It pounded hard and fast and threatened to beat out of my chest. My eyes darted up at Olivia.

"And he didn't come alone."

Chapter Nine

Winter 1983

Molly and I were inseparable. She was three months older, and I looked up to her as the big sister I'd never had. Not only did we hang out on nights of the gatherings, but at school as well—the only place Aunt Gingie let me go alone. She wouldn't even let me visit Molly's house without going with me. Which was okay because it didn't take long for me to figure out that the whole town of Corinth was strange. I never dared to venture out any further than Aunt Gingie let me. I was terrified I'd come across the people who were once again in the next room, sacrificing who knows what.

I sat on my bed and chatted with Molly while we painted our finger and toenails bubble gum pink. When I reached for Molly's left hand to apply a second coat, the bed rumbled beneath us. The quiet chants of Aunt Gingie's friends gathered in the other room increased in intensity and volume. Rancid smoke filled the bedroom. We coughed and jumped off the bed as a crack formed on one of the white wooden bedposts and snaked its way to the bottom. Dresser drawers opened and shut, and curtains blew wildly in a nonexistent wind.

The chants from the other room grew louder, and the smoke thicker. A sinister presence filled the room. Molly and

I gripped each other in horror and then clawed at our necks to remove the invisible hands strangling them.

A powerful force pulled Molly toward the ceiling. She dangled mid-air and screamed when she dropped to the bed like a rag-doll. She rolled off, but the presence slammed her back against it.

The bedroom lamp flickered sporadically, and a chorus of voices came with each flicker. Unseen fingers slid away from my neck and stopped over my heart. The beats increased when one of the many voices whispered, "Ruin would like to introduce himself."

~

Present Day

"Ted, Jan," Sheriff Glass looked at the paper he was holding. "There's something you ought to know."

I stood. "Is it about Garringer?"

Ted placed a hand on my shoulder.

"Garringer?" Sheriff Glass placed the paper on the table next to him. "Who's that?"

"The tall guy that was in the picture." Olivia handed him the camera. "Jan knows him. And he's talking to that group, which means he knows those kids. We need to find him. I want to know what they did to Anna."

He raised a brow. "You know that guy, Jan?"

I nodded. "From years ago, when I was a teen. Up until recently, I thought he was dead." Flashbacks from that horrific night played before my eyes. The memory of his fury forced me to catch my breath.

Sheriff Glass's mouth twisted back and forth like he wanted to say something. After several moments, he said, "I think the two of you should sit down."

"Sit down for what?" My tone was sharper than I'd

intended, but if he had something to say about Garringer, I wanted to be able to move quickly. "If you have information on Garringer, you need to act fast before he hurts someone. Anna may already be one of his victims."

He picked up the piece of paper. "For over a year, we've had this sketch on file. Holton Jacobs, who was seven years old then, gave us the description. Do you guys know him?

"Yeah," Ted said. "Rick and Keri's little boy. They go to our church, but what does Holton have to do with Garringer?"

"Holton was at a backyard party," the sheriff said. "An incident happened with one of the kids. His parents brought him down to the station later that night, and he gave our sketch artist a description of a guy he saw walking around the pool." He handed the sketch to Ted. "But we could never corroborate his story with anyone else at the party."

"This looks like …" Ted stared at the picture. I leaned over to get a better look. Hate-filled eyes stared at me from the parchment.

"It's Garringer," I said. "But what has this got to do with—"

"Jan, please," the sheriff put up his hand. "Sit down. What I have to say—"

"Dan," Ted wrapped an arm around my waist. "Just say it."

Beads of sweat dotted his forehead and slowly made their way to his chin. He pulled a handkerchief from his pocket and dabbed at his forehead before it slipped through his fingers and fell to the floor. He then wiped his chin with the back of his sleeve.

"Holton said," he cleared his throat before continuing. "He said this guy lurked around the pool while everyone else was inside." He focused his eyes on me. "The same pool where Laynee's body was found."

Ted pulled away from me. "Are you talking about *our* Laynee and the pool at my brother's house?"

Dan nodded.

Olivia, Cody, Stephanie, and the Baxters blended in an odd kaleidoscope of colors as the room spun around me. I stepped back to lean against Ted, but he wasn't there. The room spun faster as I slid to the floor. Strong arms caught me from behind. A flash of red hair identified the arms as belonging to Cody. He carried me to the leather sofa. Nora fussed with the pillows, and Olivia's lips moved while she held my hand, but I heard no words. Only one sound echoed within my skull, and it told me one thing.

Garringer had killed my daughter.

~

Dan thrust out his arm to keep distance between him and Ted. "I know you're upset, but if you calm down, I can explain."

Ted's chest heaved. "Calm down? Are you kidding me?"

John and Cody elbowed their way between the two. Ted pointed a finger at Dan. "You had a suspect in the death of my daughter, a death that *your* department declared an accident, and you want *me* to calm down?"

The coolness of the couch leather and the wet cloth Norah had placed on my forehead had helped stop the room from spinning. But the pain in my husband's words threatened to propel the room back into motion.

"But that's just it," Dan said. "It *was* an accident," he moved Cody aside. "Ted, listen to me. When the Jacobs stepped forward, we sent every guy we had out on this case. We scoured the entire city for this guy," he held up the sketch. "But remember, Holton was only seven and talked on and on about this guy having scary green eyes. Monster eyes, he called them. We turned the town upside down but never found anyone fitting that description." He stepped closer to Ted. "When the medical examiner concluded it was an accidental drowning, I went to her office and examined Laynee's body myself.

"There were no bruises or marks that suggested she was held underwater against her will. No unidentifiable DNA under her fingernails or clothing and no evidence of a struggle." He pulled out his phone and tapped it. "The ME's findings were conclusive—death by asphyxia due to aspiration of fluid into the lungs and air passages. No evidence of foul play." He slid the phone back into his pocket. "Ted, it really was an accident."

"No one mentioned anything to us about foul play," Ted shouted. "You did all that investigating but never said anything to Jan or me other than it was ruled an accident." His hands balled into fists. "Laynee was our daughter! And I thought you were our friend. Why are you just now telling us this?"

Dan straightened. "Because Holton's parents admitted he had an overactive imagination, and I saw no point in upsetting your family more than you already were. Especially when I didn't have anything to back it up."

"That wasn't your decision to make." I heard the struggle in Ted's voice as he choked back tears.

I removed the cloth from my forehead and glared at Dan. The badge on his uniform caused my stomach to burn. "Laynee did not accidentally drown. She was murdered."

"At the time, there was no evidence to support that. But now that we know you knew this guy, and he was spotted by the pool the same day Laynee died, we can bring him in for questioning."

I'd had enough. "Ted, let's go home."

Olivia helped pull me up from the couch.

Dan lifted up both hands. "I take full responsibility for everything that happened, but please don't leave yet. If you think he had something to do with Laynee's death, you need to come down to the station. And if you had a bad history with this guy, that speaks to motive. We can use that and

Holton's sketch to re-open the case."

I waved him off and looked at Ted. "Please, let's go."

He nodded and clasped my hand.

"But what about Anna?" Olivia's eyes pleaded with us. "What if this guy is the one responsible for her violent behavior. Or what if he plans to do to her what he did to Laynee?" Tears filled her eyes. "Please go with the sheriff. You can help bring him in."

I wanted to help Olivia, but if I didn't leave now, I was going to explode on someone or something. The longer I stayed, the louder the bomb ticked. "I can't right now, Olivia. I need to leave."

Ted led me out of the room. John and Norah jumped ahead of us, and we followed them to the front of the house, where they stood holding the door. John gave Ted a sympathetic touch on the shoulder, and Norah and I hugged.

As we walked to our car, I made a decision.

An irrevocable one that would change the course of my life forever.

And I welcomed it.

Chapter Ten

Winter 1983

I dropped to the floor and rifled through the belongings that had been tucked away in my dresser drawer before they'd been scattered by the presence that had filled the room.

I searched for the tiny address book Mrs. Gibbons had given me. I never told Aunt Gingie I had it. I'd hidden it by folding it up with my underwear.

I crawled across the floor to a pile of stuff near the closet. Underneath the pile was the small book. I hugged it against my chest and flipped it open.

"What is that?" Molly asked. Our bodies shook from the frigid chill left in the room by the entity that had mysteriously vanished.

"Where's the nearest phone?"

"Shhhh." Molly placed her hand over my mouth. "They can hear you."

I swallowed. "Ruin? It can hear us?"

Her lips trembled. "You know about Ruin?"

"It choked me, Molly," I fingered the tender skin around my throat. "Then introduced itself." I pointed to the fresh scratches across her arm. "And it attacked you." I held up the phone book. "I'm getting out of here. Tonight. Where can I find a phone?"

"Jan, you can't run out of here now and go looking for a phone," she glanced nervously at the door. "Besides, the

nearest one is 10 miles away."

"Are you saying that's the only phone in this town?"

She nodded, then raised a brow. "However, I wouldn't be surprised if Gingie has one in her bedroom."

I wasn't allowed in that room, so I'd never checked. And there was no possible way to make it to her room without being noticed. I couldn't chance it. I saw what my aunt could be like when she got angry. I'd take my chances out on the road.

Outside my bedroom and to the right was a hallway that led to the kitchen and back entrance. I could get down that hallway without being seen by Gingie or her friends in the living room.

I stuffed the phone book in my back pocket, grabbed my mother's picture off the nightstand, and headed for the door.

Molly ran in front of me and blocked it. "Jan, you can't run. You'll get us both killed."

I pointed to the door. "Those people are worshipping the devil himself, and tonight he paid us a visit." I grabbed her hand. "Come with me, but we gotta hurry. We have to leave this place!"

She leaned back against the door. "You run tonight, you'll get caught, believe me." Her eyes filled with fear. "Others have tried, including me. Everyone in this town is a part of this. There's no way you'll get out."

I couldn't believe what I was hearing. "What do you mean I can't get out? That's insane."

"You want to see insane?" She straightened and pulled off the shirt she was wearing. She turned so that her back faced me. Right above her bra line was a circle, and it was branded deep into her skin.

Inside the circle was the letter "G".

~

Present Day

I gazed into our firepit.

Orange and red flames blazed and glowed in the night air.

I tightened my sweater around me. The night autumn air was chilly. Perfect for the mood I was in.

Tears threatened to pour from my eyes, but I couldn't let them. Not yet.

Ted went straight to his office when we returned from the Baxters'. I'd stormed into our bedroom, the great room, kitchen, and closets and gathered everything I could find that related to God or Christianity. Every book, Bible, study guide, and piece of jewelry was tossed in a cardboard box. From the walls, I grabbed every decorative cross, tapestry, and plaque that had previously encouraged my Christian walk and dropped them on top of the heap.

From the garage, I took a shovel and work gloves and headed to the far side of the house—away from the bedroom windows and behind the mimosa trees and dug a hole four feet deep. Images of my daughter dying at the hands of Garringer fueled me to dig deeper. Not only had God not protected her, He'd allowed her to cross paths with the human incarnation of Satan himself.

My parents, my real parents, David and June Maxwell, would be ashamed of what I was about to do. But as of today, their God was no longer my God. I was done.

The cardboard box overflowing with the bells and whistles of my Christianity sat at my feet in front of the hole.

From what I'd been told, my father, like Ted's dad, had been a legend. The son of missionaries, he loved to travel and especially enjoyed the remote and tribal areas of northern Uganda. As an adult, he returned and ministered there for years. He met my Mom, who was a stewardess at the time, on a flight back to the States. When they married, she returned to the region with him and became absorbed in the lives of others, just like he did.

A couple of years later, they found out she was pregnant with me. There were complications, and the doctors in the Ugandan regional clinics suggested she return to the States for specialized care. My father agreed. He put her on a plane and promised to join her in a few weeks.

Two days before I was born, she received news from the church mission board. Tensions between rival tribes in the northern region had escalated to war. They sent planes for my dad and his team to evacuate, but my father insisted it was too early to do so. He'd asked them to tell my Mom that if he couldn't help broker peace, he'd get out before it was too late.

But it was already too late. That same day, my father, along with eleven of his co-workers, was brutally murdered in the uprising.

He never got the chance to see what I looked like.

"Hey," Ted walked up beside me.

"Hey."

He had a small cassette player in his right hand. His thumb rubbed slowly across the buttons. He looked at the hole, then said, "I came to see if you were all right. You haven't said a word since we returned from the Baxters'."

His eyes were red and swollen, and I looked away. The thought of him alone in his office, crying his eyes out, ripped at my heart. I held back the tears. This was no time to be vulnerable.

"There was nothing left to say. The sheriff stated his facts, and I stated mine. There was no need to go over it again. I know what happened to our daughter."

He shifted from one foot to the other. "He called. We spent the last hour or so on the phone. Once I calmed down, I realized a lot of what he said had some truth to it."

"What?"

He held up a hand. "Not about him withholding information from us. That was wrong, and he's apologized. He's been a good friend of ours for years, Jan. You and I both know he didn't mean any harm. In his mind, he thought he was protecting us from unnecessary heartache."

I turned my head away from him.

He continued, "We need to help him find Garringer. A search party is already down at the lake. I could go by myself since Dan has the photo and the sketch, but you're the only one who will be able to give a positive ID. You've seen that psycho in person. Ride with me to the lake. Let's find him so the police can interrogate him."

I shook my head. "What good will asking him questions do? He's a liar, and his father is the father of lies. We'll never get the truth."

"I know," his thumb rested on one of the cassette player buttons. "But we have to start somewhere."

I reached for the player. "What's on here?"

He handed the device to me and blinked away tears. "It's Laynee. I kept the tape of her singing, *It Is Well With My Soul*, from the church play she was in a couple of years ago. After I hung up with Dan, I listened to it." He swallowed. "Several times."

I gripped the recorder and looked into the fire. *Garringer will pay.*

"Dan would also like to ask you some questions. He wants to know how you and Garringer crossed paths and what made you think he was dead. And if he had any reason to want to harm Laynee."

I nodded. "I'll do it, but not tonight."

"Jan—"

"Listen," I inhaled a shaky breath and blew it in his direction. "You know my entire sordid history with Garringer and his evil minion, Ruin. If you'd like to fill Dan in, then go ahead. You might also have him check with the Corinth Police Department. They may have something on Garringer from the early nineteen eighties. I'll stop by the station tomorrow and talk to him. But tonight, I can't."

He looked deep into my eyes. "I don't want to condemn

a man before I have all the facts, but my gut is telling me something's not right, and I won't rest until we have answers." He glanced at his watch. "But I'm not going to leave you here alone either. Dan sent two guys from the precinct over to watch the house. They're out front in an unmarked car. And Libbybelle called. She's on her way over, too."

Just what I needed. The over-protective presence of my adoptive Mom and the police. I needed to come up with a way to get rid of them.

He pointed to the hole in the ground and the cardboard box at my feet. "What are you doing?"

"Nothing important," I lied.

He kissed me on the forehead. "Don't wait up. It'll likely be very late when I get back."

I watched him walk back to the house. When he pulled out of the driveway, I pressed the play button on the tape player.

Laynee's soft, melodic voice filled the night air. I turned up the volume and placed the device in my sweater pocket. Scents from the feathery, fragrant flowers of the Mimosa trees comforted me.

I crouched in front of the hole and removed the lid from the box. Everything in it, at one time or another, represented my journey with God. I reached inside and pulled out my Mom's Bible. The pages were crinkled and the leather worn, but it smelled the same as when my Mom read it to me as we snuggled in her bed. It originally belonged to my father. When he died, my Mom used it as her own. I flipped through the pages. My Mom's and my dad's personal thoughts and notes were written next to many of the verses. Notes that spoke of new insight, revelations, and prayers.

My hands trembled. This was all I had to remember them by. An old book full of words I no longer believed. This bible was once my lifeline.

I held it close to my chest. It used to make me feel close

to my parents and gave me the courage to face another day. I squeezed it one more time and tossed it in the hole. A soft thump echoed around me as it hit the soil below. Laynee's angelic voice continued to filter through my sweater pocket. *When peace, like a river, attendeth my way, When sorrows like sea billows roll; Whatever my lot, Thou has taught me to say, It is well, it is well, with my soul.*

I gave in to the tears, grabbed the cardboard box, and dumped the rest of the items into the makeshift grave. My relationship with God was done. The funeral took place in my heart when I realized Garringer was responsible for Laynee's death.

Now, it was time for His burial.

Because nothing was well with my soul.

~

"Jan?"

Libbybelle.

I wiped the tears and pitched the last shovelful of dirt into the hole. I turned the shovel over and then patted and smoothed the area. I then tossed the work gloves and the shovel behind the trees. The last thing I needed was Libbybelle worrying about me.

"There you are," she rubbed her hands over the fire. "What are you doing out here?"

I shrugged. "It's a nice night. Thought I'd take a stroll." The lies were getting easier and easier to tell.

"A stroll, huh?" She reached for my hands. "Your hands are cold as ice. You've been out here much longer than the few minutes it would've taken to stroll around this yard."

The tape player in my pocket clicked and restarted again in continuous play mode. I quickly pulled it from my pocket and hit the stop button.

"Was that Laynee's voice I just heard?" She reached for the player, but I held on to it.

"No. Just some music I listened to as I walked around

the yard."

"Now that's the second lie you've told. You think I don't know Laynee's voice when I hear it? I'm going to ask you again. What were you doing out here?"

I lowered my eyes.

She gently lifted my chin. "Ted told me about Garringer and how you no longer believe Laynee's death was an accident."

I pulled away from her. "I *never* believed it was an accident."

She nodded. "I know, but you don't have to deal with this alone, Jan. We're your family, and we're all in this together. Stop pulling away from us."

"Have you checked on Adam?"

She sighed. "Yes. He's sound asleep, and you're still pushing me away."

That's because if you knew what was on my mind, you'd try to stop me. "I'd rather Adam not know about this until we know more." *Like after I've killed the person who murdered his sister.*

She nodded, and we walked back to the house. I locked the door behind me. We've never locked the door to our backyard. But tonight, I wasn't taking any chances. Garringer was still out there, and what if he decided to come after Adam?

I frowned, then thought of the shotgun in Ted's office. If Garringer stepped one foot in this house, I was going to blow him back into the pit he came from.

Part of me wished he'd try.

"Ted mentioned that the two of you haven't eaten yet," Libbybelle walked to the kitchen counter and slid a rectangular-shaped dish from an insulated tote. She placed it on a dish towel and removed the lid. The smell of homemade lasagna wafted in the air. The cheese on top still sizzled. "I know it's late," she said. "But you really do need to eat something."

I had no appetite, but if I told Libbybelle that, it would only lead to an argument, and I didn't have the strength for one. She was a firm believer that food nourished the soul as well as the body. But my soul was in question, and my body longed for revenge. And the latter I planned to take care of tonight.

"Just a little bit, please."

"That's fine. Ted'll be starving when he gets back." She pulled the dish towards her. "I made enough to last you guys a couple of days. Hopefully, that's all it'll take to get this Garringer mess sorted out." She tilted her head to the side. "I know you're a lot more upset than you are letting on. But like I said earlier, I'm here if you wanna talk."

I took a seat at the counter. "I'll be all right. Tonight's been an emotional roller coaster. Maybe I'll feel more like talking in the morning."

She didn't respond but instead pulled three plates from the cabinet and heaped large helpings of lasagna on two of them. She then grabbed another kitchen towel and retrieved several pieces of garlic bread from the oven. She placed them on the plates and then filled two bowls to the rim with a salad she'd removed from the fridge.

"Mom, what are you doing? Adam's already eaten, and I can't eat all of that. And who's the other plate for?"

"These aren't for you, honey. They're for the two nice men outside watching the house."

Blast it. The police. I'd forgotten about them.

"I was going to hand them a couple of bottles of water with this, but it's awfully cold out. I'll make them some hot tea instead."

"Don't worry about it, they'll be fine." I stood and handed her a tray to place the food on. "And you're giving them too much food. We pay enough taxes to ensure they don't miss any meals."

She frowned at me, then left to take the food to the officers. By the time she returned, I'd already dished out and eaten a small portion of the lasagna. I left the plate on the counter for her to see it.

"I've been thinking," she placed the plate in the dishwasher. "I don't like that Garringer's still on the loose. You and Adam should stay with me for a while."

She was right. Adam wasn't safe here. "That's a good idea. I'll go pack a few of his things."

She waved her hand. "No need. He has plenty of clothes at my place. But what about you?"

My hands trembled. The emotions of the day and the hole-digging were starting to affect my body, but rest would have to wait. "Mom, I can't. They're some things I need to take care of."

She placed a hand on her hip. The look in her eyes told me she had a vague idea of what I was planning. "You're going after Garringer, aren't you?"

Nope. I was wrong. She had more than a vague idea.

She shook her head. "Jan—"

"I don't want to talk about it, okay?" My voice had risen, and we looked up the stairs to see if I'd awaken Adam.

We heard him tossing around in his bed, and I turned to face her again. "I'm sorry, Mom," I sucked in a breath to calm my nerves before reaching for her hand. "I didn't mean to yell. But tonight's … not a good night for me to talk about anything. Could you please just wake Adam and go? I'll be okay, I promise, and I'll call you tomorrow."

She tightened her lips and then turned to go up the stairs. After a few moments, I heard her and Adam talking quietly.

I lowered my head. *Did I just scream at Libbybelle? The only Mom I've known for the past thirty-five years?* I couldn't go on like this. I needed to pull it together. I balled my fingers into fists, so they'd stop trembling. I was determined to see my plan through, but there was no need to upset my family in the process.

Footsteps on the stairs startled me, and I turned to look without lifting my head. Libbybelle headed towards the front door, but Adam walked over to me. "Grandma says I have to stay with her for a while," he placed a hand on my back. "Are you okay, Mom?"

The concern in his eyes fueled my resolve to do what I had to do. The thought that one day, I'd have to tell him about Garringer and the murder of his sister angered me. I stood and kissed him on the forehead. I wasn't going to answer his question about me being okay, but if I didn't say something, he was going to worry. I cupped his chin. "There's a dangerous guy in our area, and the police haven't found him yet. We think it'll be safer for you to stay at Libbybelle's until they do."

"But what about you?"

I wrapped my arms around him and squeezed. He smelled rustic, like Old Spice cologne. He must've gotten that from his dad. "No need to worry about me. Your dad will be back soon. In the meantime, I need you to look out for Grandma Libby, okay?"

He smiled. "She's safe with me."

I followed him to the front door. When Libbybelle looked at me, tears filled my eyes. "I know I already apologized, but I really am sorry. Please forgive me."

"I'll wait in the car, Grandma," Adam said, closing the door softly behind him.

Libbybelle's eyes were full of love. "There's nothing to forgive. We're all emotional right now, but we'll get through this," she gripped my shoulders. "But I want you to think about what you're planning to do. Think about the consequences. You may be willing to face them, but what about Adam? He's already lost his sister. He doesn't need to lose his mother, too." She sighed heavily and then pulled me into a hug.

What most people didn't realize about Libbybelle was that a hug was not just a hug. Every hug she gave came with a silent prayer. She held me tight and cried softly in my ear. I didn't hear any words, but I knew she was bombarding heaven with prayers for me. And there was no doubt in my mind that she was also calling on God to intervene divinely on my behalf and to send an army of angels to watch over me.

But I didn't need a host of angelic protection.

I needed a pistol.

Chapter Eleven

Winter 1983

"Molly!" I stared at the circle on her back. "What have they done to you?"

"Garringer did this. He tied my arms to my bedpost, then used a hot branding iron to mark me."

He'd branded her?

She pulled her shirt back on. "What I'm trying to tell you is that I tried to escape. It was on the night of one of these gatherings—except at my place. I tried to slip out through our basement window. I didn't make it ten feet before I was dragged back inside the house by one of Garringer's henchmen." She pressed her lips together, then continued, "They were going to kill me. And no one in this town would've done anything about it." She leaned against the door and traced the flower design on her jeans with her index finger. "If my mother hadn't intervened, they would've killed me." She straightened. "But her pleas weren't enough. Garringer said I had to pay a penance for my disobedience. So for six months, he used me as his personal slave."

"What does that mean?"

She shook her head. "I'm not going to tell you. The details would destroy your innocence, and I don't want to do that to you."

"Molly, I have to know what's going on around here. Keeping me in the dark isn't going to help me."

"All I'm going to say is that he made me do things with him." She looked at the floor. "Bad things."

"You're not talking about—"

"I am," she continued looking at the floor.

"Molly, you're only fourteen!"

"I was twelve at the time."

I blinked away tears. What had Aunt Gingie gotten me into?

Molly cleared her throat and flicked her eyes up at me. "I still have to remain at his beck and call because of the 'severity of my crime.' Those are Garringer's words, not mine. But it doesn't change the fact that I have to be available to him whenever he wants me. The last time was two weeks ago."

"Two weeks ago?" Her words hit me like a rock. "You've been going through this all this time? Why haven't you said anything? And how can you go on acting so normal?"

"Right now, I'm doing what I have to do to survive. The time will come for us to plan an escape, but tonight's not the night." Her eyes turned cold. "But it's gonna happen soon. Real soon, because that monster is not putting his hands on me again. Ever. I'll kill him first."

~

Present Day

I walked to the unmarked police car in front of our house and tapped on the driver's side window.

The window rolled down, and heat warmed my face. I needed to make this quick. They were obviously quite toasty in there, and the night temperature had dropped.

"I came to collect the dishes and to see if I can get you guys anything else."

The officer on the passenger side retrieved the dishes from the back seat. "The lasagna was delicious," he handed me the plates and bowls. "But we're good, thanks for asking."

I nodded. "Oh, and I'm getting ready to go for a quick drive. Just wanted to let you guys know."

The officer behind the steering wheel glanced at his watch and shook his head. "That's not a good idea, ma'am. It's almost midnight."

"It's okay. I do it all the time."

"Ma'am, we're out here for a reason. But if you insist on going, an officer will have to go with you."

"You mean you guys will have to tail me?"

"Not us," he motioned to the police radio. "We'd call dispatch, but you'd have to wait until another car arrives."

Ted's car pulled into the driveway, and my teeth clamped together. I could've possibly talked the officers into letting me leave, but there was no way Ted was going to let me go anywhere tonight with or without the police tailing me.

I needed another plan, and I needed one quick.

I followed Ted into the house and placed the dishes on the counter.

The look on his face told me they'd had no luck in finding Garringer.

I warmed up Libbybelle's lasagna and fixed him a plate. He ate a few bites and pushed the plate away.

"I'm sorry, honey," he said. "I'm so tired, I can barely keep my eyes open."

"Why don't you go on to bed," I wrapped the leftovers and placed them in the refrigerator. "I'll be up in a few minutes."

I washed the remaining dishes and wracked my brain for a plan that would let me leave the house without upsetting my husband or involving the police.

I came up with nothing.

I switched off the kitchen lights, went to the bedroom, lay next to Ted, and closed my eyes, once again hoping to devise a plan.

The doorbell rang. My eyes popped open, and I looked at the clock. Five a.m. I didn't even remember falling asleep.

Ted was lying on his stomach, still asleep. I grabbed my bathrobe, quietly closed the bedroom door, and made my way down the stairs. I peeked through the front window.

Doris.

I yanked open the door. "I thought we made it clear," my tone was harsh, but I whispered the words so I wouldn't wake Ted. "You're not to show up at our home this time of morning unless it's an emergency. And I swear, Doris if this is about Cody and Stephanie again, I'm going to—"

"Shhh!" She glanced over her shoulder and pointed her thumb at the unmarked police car. "Just let me in before the coppers over there start asking questions."

Coppers?

She carried a large *I Love Lucy* bag on her shoulder. She patted the canvas tote, then said, "You don't want them asking me questions."

I grabbed her wrist and pulled her inside. "Doggone it, Doris. What is it this time?"

She shook loose of my grip, pushed the door shut, and locked it before placing the heavy bag on the floor. "I came to see you."

"I don't have time for your nonsense this morning. You have no idea what Ted and I are going through right now."

Her eyes softened, and she reached for my hands. "Cody called last night and told me everything."

I rubbed my temples. My imagination was playing tricks on me because I thought I'd surely caught a glimpse of compassion in her eyes.

"He told me all about that creep Garringer and how the sheriff and his crew came up empty-handed last night. I'm not surprised. We're talking about the Keystone Kops here. They have no idea how to track this guy or any of his posse. But none of that matters now because I'm here to help."

My ears were playing tricks on me as well. Did Doris

just use the word *posse*?

She stepped closer and lowered her voice. "I just want you to know that I know people, who *know* people, who know *people*, who can take care of this problem for you. By this time tomorrow, nothing could be left of that Garringer dude but a bad memory."

I took a step back. I wasn't sure what disturbed me more, that Doris boasted of having mob-like connections or that I was considering her offer to help.

"Um, thanks, but that's okay. I'll find Garringer myself."

She narrowed her eyes. "You said *I'll,* not *we.* As in a solo mission. You're planning to take him out yourself, aren't you?"

"Whatever I'm planning is none of your business."

"Uh-huh," she licked her lips and nodded. "Like I said, you're going after him."

She reached down into the Lucy bag on the floor. The back of the bag was solid black, but the front sported a huge black-and-white photo of Lucille Ball. Doris rummaged around in the bag. "If you're going to go after Garringer alone, you're going to need this," she pulled out a gun and thrust it toward me.

I jumped back and stifled a scream. "What are you doing, pointing that thing at me like that! Is it loaded?"

"I'm not pointing it at you. I'm handing it to you. And it's not a thing. It's a Glock 38. It's accurate and automatic. And yes, it's loaded. Who carries around an unloaded gun?"

I stared at her in disbelief.

"The safety's on. I could drop this on your hardwood floor right now, and it wouldn't go off. So, here. Take it."

I shook my head.

"Haven't you used a gun before?"

"No."

"Doesn't matter. Just point and shoot, but make sure you get that scoundrel, okay? A couple of shots from this baby, and he won't be messing with anybody else's kid. Ever." She grabbed my hand and placed the gun in it.

I stood motionless as the cold, heavy metal rested in my palms and images of Garringer's demise danced in my head.

"Oh, you're gonna need this too." She reached back into the bag and pulled out a cell phone. She flipped it open and turned it on. "This is a burner phone. I already had them program it for you, so it's totally untraceable by the cops."

"Them? Who's them?"

She waved away the question. "I got one for me, too, and I've added the phone number from that one to this one," she held a matching flip phone. "If you're ever in a pinch, press the number five, hit send, and I'm on my way."

"How will you know where I am?"

"I had them install a special device on my phone to track yours."

I sighed. "Doris, again. Who is *them*?"

She tilted her head back and gave a sly grin. "The less you know, the more you can deny. My mission is to take this guy down, and if you won't let me or my anonymous friends help, then I need to make sure you're prepared to do it."

I looked down again at the gun. Last night, I'd hoped to secure one, but I'd had no idea how. Now, one had literally been placed in my hands.

The reality of its lethal power made my heart race. "Why, Doris? Why are you doing this?"

She folded her arms across her chest. "Because Laynee was my friend," she paused and blinked away tears. "That little girl, *your* little girl, was as precious and sweet as the day is long. Sundays, after service, while you and the pastor performed boring meet and greets in the hospitality room, Laynee would come to sit by me. She was always so pretty and dolled up, and I always teased her about the yellow ribbons she wore in her hair like there was no other color of ribbon." Doris chuckled and continued. "She'd scoot next to me on the pew, and we'd talk about everything, from her learning to write in cursive to why zebras wore stripes, though we mostly talked about flowers. I'd planted a flower garden in my backyard. She loved daisies, and I had plenty of them. We talked about her riding out with her dad to come see it," she shrugged. "But you know how we are. With little ones, we think, there's always tomorrow." She stopped blinking away the tears. I watched as they fell uninterrupted onto her rumpled silk blouse. "I loved that little angel something fierce. And when Cody told me you were sure this Garringer guy was the one responsible for her death, I couldn't stand by and do nothing, so I made a few phone calls to my acquaintances, and now I'm here." She sucked in a deep breath and huffed it out. "We can't let him get away with what he did to Laynee."

I thought I knew everything there was to know about my daughter. I always knew she had a heart as deep as the ocean, but I had no idea she'd invited Doris to swim in it. It represented her character and broke my heart, knowing someone like Garringer lived, and she didn't.

My lips quivered as I handed Doris back the gun. "Thanks for telling me how much Laynee meant to you, but I can't let you get involved. This is something I have to take care of myself."

She pushed the gun back towards me. "And you will. I just wanted to make sure you had the proper tools." She pulled the *I Love Lucy* bag onto her shoulder. "That gun is yours. I have a couple more, just like it at home. It's unregistered but brand new and has never been used. To release the safety mechanism, just pull the trigger.

"There are eight rounds in there, so you have a few to target practice with if you need it." She turned to open the door. "I have to go meet with that nut job, Stephanie. But remember to put that burner phone in your purse. Mine will be on me all the time. I get one ring from you, and I'm on my way, armed and ready. Got it?"

I nodded and accepted the fact that this seventy-plus-year-old grandmother had just made my job a lot easier. She gave me the tools I needed to end Garringer's reign of terror. My hands itched to make good use of them.

"Thanks, Doris."

"The only thanks I need is reading about that freak's death in tomorrow's paper," she looked me straight in the eyes. "We got a deal?"

Oh, yeah. We had a deal.

~

"Did someone just leave?" Ted asked from the top of the stairs.

I opened the foyer closet and secured the Glock and burner phone in my purse.

"I thought I just heard someone at the door," he descended the stairs, and I shoved sweat-laden hands into the pockets of my bathrobe.

"Yeah, that was Doris. Cody told her about Garringer. She came over to offer her support."

His disheveled hair and wrinkled pajamas highlighted the pain on his face. I hated that we had to go through this. Hated it, hated it, hated it. Laynee was a daddy's girl if there ever was one. They were super close. When the authorities told him that Laynee's death was an accident, he'd been able to make peace with that.

Now, that peace had been shattered.

My blood boiled. Ted was a great husband and a wonderful father who loved a God who kept letting the bad guys win and the good ones lose. My husband deserved better.

I followed him into the kitchen. "Would you like a cup of coffee?"

He sat at the center island. "Yeah. And make it as strong as you can, please."

I started the coffee and let it percolate. I stood behind Ted's chair and placed my head on his shoulder. "Don't worry," I said. "We're going to get through this."

He spun the chair around and looked at me with a slight smile. "Did *you* just tell *me* we'll get through this?"

"Of course I did." I pretended to be insulted. "Why?"

"Because it's usually me telling you that and not the other way around. And, because you like to handle stuff on your own." His eyes turned serious. "But to be honest, you're making me nervous. You found out that Garringer's in town and may be responsible for what happened to Laynee, and you're so … calm."

I rubbed his shoulders and smiled. "I'm learning that it's not what happens to you in life. It's how you respond." I was tempted to add the words, … *and it's best to respond with wrath so severe, it's never before been seen by mankind*, but decided that admission would slow down my plans to seek out Garringer. "Besides," I added, "I'm all cried out and tired of being angry. Dr. Schultz talked about letting go and letting God. You know how I feel about that, but she made me think about how I react to things."

He kissed my forehead. "Good, because I have some troubling news. Dan called this morning. The police chief is giving him grief about the amount of resources he's dedicated to finding Garringer. The chief said that our eyewitness—to Garringer being at the scene—at best is circumstantial and, at worst, speculation. With a lack of physical evidence to tie him to Laynee's drowning, he's threatening to pull the plug on the time and money needed to continue the investigation. He may not even re-open the case at all if we can't come up with something more concrete."

I removed two mugs from the cabinet and poured coffee into them. I dipped a spoon in to taste the strength. "The chief's probably afraid of a lawsuit or some garbage like that," I sat next to Ted and handed him one of the mugs. "It's all about what they can *prove*."

He gently laid his hand on top of mine. "Honey, if you follow it logically, the chief's right. We have no proof. Dan told us that at the beginning. But when we heard Garringer's name, we assumed the worst."

"No, I didn't assume the worst; I experienced it. Garringer's evil. I know for a fact he's murdered once. And don't forget, he also tried to kill me and nearly succeeded. I still remember the heat of his grip around my neck and the look in his eyes when he was getting ready to snap it." My mind filled with the memories, and I shivered. "No one will ever be able to tell me that Garringer being spotted in Habakkuk is a coincidence. And the first time someone caught a glimpse of him was on the same day my daughter died? That's all the proof I need."

Ted stared into his coffee for a long moment, then said, "Dan's been given enough room to bring him in for questioning, but if we don't find him, or if we do find him, and he doesn't confess, we're back to where we started." He gripped my hand. "I don't know how any of that will work out, but I want you to know that no matter what the chief decides, I'm not stopping until we find him. We need answers. And I'm not going to stop until we get them. No matter how long it takes."

I gave his hand a reassuring squeeze.

I didn't have the heart to tell him I planned to get to Garringer first. And I wasn't going to require proof, confessions, or answers.

Just his life.

Chapter Twelve

Winter 1983

Molly picked up my bed pillow from the floor and tossed it on my bed. "For the past two years, I've been working on a plan to get out of this town," she said. "I'm leaving and taking my mother with me."

I plopped down on the bed. "I don't want to hear anymore." I wiped away tears with my sleeve.

She knelt beside me. "The three of us will have to escape together. Staying here will be too dangerous for you if you don't. And if you escape before we do, I'll be tortured into telling them everything I know, and we'll be watched twenty-four-seven. My mom and I will never be able to get out of here."

No way was I leaving Molly behind. Not after what she told me about being Garringer's slave and the circle branded onto her back.

"Does Quiggy know about your plans?" Quiggy was the name Molly's mother went by. Everyone in this town, including my Aunt Gingie, used code names. After everything Molly shared, I began to see why. I wasn't even sure Molly's name was Molly.

She shook her head. "I haven't told her, but I'm not leaving here without her."

"If only I could get to a phone."

"Who would you call?"

"Mrs. Gibbons." I pulled the small address book from my jeans pocket. "She was a good friend of my mom's. Before she left me here with Aunt Gingie, she gave me this," I handed the book to Molly. "She told me to call if I ever needed anything."

"There are a lot of phone numbers in here."

"She included the phone numbers of everyone in the church my mom and I attended. Anyone in that book would be willing to help me."

"You're sure?"

I nodded. "They all stepped up to help take care of me after my mom died. I love and miss them terribly and know they feel the same."

"Who would you call first?

"Mrs. Gibbons."

"Does Gingie know about this book?"

"No."

"Then we can't let her find out about it. It'll end up in the garbage dump for sure." She flipped through the book slowly, then smiled. "This may be your ticket out of here."

"Our ticket out of here," I corrected her.

"Do you think they'll be willing to help us, too?"

"Absolutely."

She sat next to me. "I hope so. Getting my mom out won't be easy. She knows too much. And Garringer thinks he owns me," she scooted closer, and we slid into a hug. "But don't worry, nothing's going to stop me from coming up with a plan to get us out of here. The only thing that'll stop me is death. Which is what would happen if Garringer ever found out about any of this."

"Molly, please don't talk like that," I buried my face deep in her shirt.

"I've already settled it. If I have to kill to get out of here, I will. And if I'm killed in the process, so be it. I'm willing to

pay that price for my freedom."

~

Present Day

"Good morning, Jan," Sheriff Glass said as he entered Ted's office.

I nodded at his greeting but remained seated in the chair across from Ted's desk. Sheriff Glass sat in the other one next to mine. Ted slumped into his chair and folded his arms on top of his desk.

Sheriff Glass called earlier to ask if I'd mind if he stopped by to ask me some questions. I did mind and told him I didn't see the point, but I agreed anyway. If I refused to participate in the investigation, it would have caused Ted more heartache, and I didn't want to add to his pain any more than I had to.

Sheriff Glass pulled a spiral notebook and pen from his pocket and swiveled his chair in my direction. "Thanks for agreeing to meet."

"What would you like to know?" I asked.

He gave a slight chuckle. "Eager to get this over with, I see."

"Yes."

"Okay. When and where was the first time you met Garringer?"

"Hasn't Ted already filled you in on that part?"

He nodded. "But for investigative purposes, I'd like to hear it directly from you."

I sighed. "I first met him when I was—"

His phone buzzed. "Excuse me, a second."

He pulled out his phone and scrolled. A second later, he stood. "That was a text from the tip line. The group Cody and Stephanie saw at the lake has been spotted on Fern Water

Road."

"The opposite direction of the lake area where Ted and the officers looked the other night."

"Good luck trying to get any information out of them," I said.

He stuffed the notebook in his pocket. "I'd still like to talk to them."

"I'm going with you," Ted pushed away from his desk and pulled on a jacket. "Give me a second to grab a few things."

The sheriff grumbled. "Let me and my boys handle this."

"Let him ride along with you," I said. "He'll just drive over to Fern Water Road on his own if you don't."

Sheriff Glass looked at me with sorrow-filled eyes. "Jan, I'm really sorry about all of this. Ted was right. I should've brought Holton's sketch to you guys as soon as I found out about it. I was trying to protect you, but that wasn't my decision to make."

The doorbell rang, and I rose to answer it. "Yeah, well, you guys better get going while the tip is still hot."

The sheriff nodded and lowered his gaze. If he hoped I'd accept his apology, he was dead wrong.

The bell rang a second time, and I hurried to answer it. Olivia rushed in.

"I just got off the phone with Anna and saw the sheriff's car outside. Is he here?"

"Yeah, is everything okay with Anna?"

"Her uncle told me she's doing much better and has even started going to church with them," she flicked her hand at me. "But that's not why I'm here. When I asked to speak to her, the first thing she told me when she got on the phone was where that group she was friends with liked to hang out."

"Where?"

"At Crater Lake, where Cody and Stephanie had seen

them, but she said there's a hidden cove further down the shore where the group meets up. She also said it's easy to miss, and there's only a small, narrow hole at the entrance to climb through. She joined them there several times after school, but they always tried to get her to come back after midnight. That was when all the 'good stuff' happened, they'd told her."

It was before midnight when Ted and the group of police officers he was with had searched the area. That could explain why they didn't find anyone. And I bet they didn't go further down the shore like Anna mentioned.

"Is the sheriff in Ted's office?" she asked. "I want to let him know what Anna told me."

"Yes, but he and Ted are headed that way now," I lied. "They received a tip a few minutes ago."

She blew out a breath. "Good. If they don't find anything, tell them to return after midnight. Maybe stake the place out."

Ted and the sheriff bustled out of the office and straight toward the door.

"Oh, there they are, Sheriff," Olivia said.

I grabbed her elbow. "Let's not hold them up. If Ted calls and says they still couldn't locate the group, I'll let them know then."

She agreed, and we stepped aside to let them through. When the sheriff's car pulled out of the driveway, I noticed that there was only one instead of two officers in the unmarked car watching the house. This was my chance. Thanks to what Anna told Olivia, I could head down to Crater Lake while Ted and the sheriff were off on a bogus tip. But I needed to go now, so I'd be able to find it. I've been to the lake before at night. No way would I be able to find a hidden entrance in the dark.

"Did Anna remember hearing anyone in the group talk about Garringer?"

Olivia shook her head. "I had Stephanie email her a

copy of his picture. She didn't recognize him, but she did say the group always talked about a Father G and how they never wanted to cross him."

"That's one of the code names he uses."

"A code what?"

I grabbed my purse and sweater from the foyer closet. "Olivia, I'm sorry, but I have to run."

"I was hoping to talk to you."

"Sure. I'll stop by your place when I get back."

"No," she folded her arms and stared at me. "It has to be now."

"What is so important that it—"

"Ruin," she took a step toward me. "We need to talk about Ruin."

~

On the patio, Olivia watched me nervously move teacups and saucers around the small wrought iron table. The cloud-filled sky promised rain.

"If it rains," I said. "We'll head back inside."

She furrowed her brows. "Of course, we'll head back inside. But right now, I want to know about Ruin."

I sat and stared at an empty cup. "How … how do you know about Ruin?"

"Anna. Before she tried to set herself on fire and I shipped her out to her uncle, Ruin had told her to give you a message."

I swallowed. "What was the message?"

"That he says hello. *Again*."

My mind raced back to the terror-filled night Molly and I were in my room at Aunt Gingie's. The first night Ruin appeared.

She leaned forward on the table. "Who or what is Ruin? What Anna shared has me frightened to the core, but honestly, I don't know what to believe. Anna says that Ruin is here because of you. Before yesterday, I would've said that was nonsense. But now, we have a guy from your past, who you'd previously thought was dead and who is now suspected of your daughter's death. And today, I learned that somehow, *my* daughter is mixed up in all of this. Jan, I need you to tell me what's going on."

"I don't know where to start."

"The beginning would be nice."

I leaned back in my chair. Concern for Anna was etched along Olivia's face, but I didn't have time for this. My window of opportunity for tracking down Garringer dwindled by the second. I could try to make a quick departure, but Olivia was a former athlete. She'd catch up to me in a matter of seconds. She wouldn't let me leave without finding out if Anna was in danger, and I didn't want to tussle with my friend. The best way to get rid of her was to tell her everything quickly.

"Ruin is a demonic spirit. I first encountered it years ago when I lived with my Aunt Ginger. She was a high priestess in a satanic cult.

"They gathered weekly at her house, where they chanted and performed small animal sacrifices. But they were also in contact with the spirit world. When they wanted something major done, like causing problems for a local church, they called on Ruin—the most powerful spirit they could summon. All sorts of havoc were wracked upon the town when it appeared."

"A demonic spirit? she asked. "A spirit that knows you *personally*?"

"Ruin visited me several times when I lived with my aunt." I massaged the back of my neck. "Sometimes, it showed up when my friend Molly was there, but most of the time, I was alone. It attacked me twice. Molly and I were in a room together the first time it happened."

"And the second time?"

"The second time was when it ordered Garringer to sacrifice me at an altar. Garringer was the cult's priest."

Olivia's mouth popped open.

I continued, "Two cult members broke into my aunt's house one night. They grabbed and dragged me deep into the woods. Garringer waited beside an altar he'd made from rough-hewn stone. He'd also laid sugar cane stalks on top of it. He then lit a torch and called on Ruin. The men had bound my arms and legs with leather straps. I wanted to run but couldn't escape the leather bands on my legs.

"The men placed me on the altar," I paused as memories of the sugar stalk razor-sharp leaves cutting into my back surfaced. I shook my head and applied mental filters to the horrific nightmare. "Anyway, my Aunt Ginger rescued me. I found out later that Garringer had sent her on an errand hours away. After she left, that's when he had his men kidnap me from her house. Thankfully, one of her friends, who was also a cult member, told her what was happening.

"My aunt showed up with a large blade, freed me from the straps, and told me to run.

"I ran, but I could still hear her curse Garringer. She then called on some goddess of the spirit world to strip him of his power. I don't know if it worked or not, but from that night on, he made my life miserable. That is, until …"

Olivia leaned in further. "Until what?"

My hands shook. No need to go into that now. "How did Anna come in contact with Garringer's crew?"

"Millie's Mercantile." Olivia slid her teacup toward me. "You know the place?"

"Yeah," I lifted the teapot from the warmer and poured some into her cup. "I used to take Adam and Laynee there after school for root beer floats. We used to see Anna there all the time, doing her homework. Sometimes, we even sat with her."

"She said one day, Whisper, one of the girls in the group, struck up a conversation with her after you and the kids left. They soon became friends, and after a couple of weeks, she introduced Anna to the others in the group. They called themselves Legion. Anna admits that the whole group was strange, but she overlooked that because they'd always had so much fun together.

"Then they started sneaking into her school, asking her to skip class and meet them at the lake, so she did. They were all in that cove I told you about earlier. Inside there, they drank alcohol, lots of it, and popped pills. She didn't ask what they were. She just took them. There were also … intimate activities, though Anna denies participating in those. Then she said they'd sit in a circle, chant, and summon spirits, similar to what you said took place at your aunt's house.

"That's how she met Ruin. At first, she just thought it was fun and games until she started feeling its presence everywhere. At school, the mercantile, at home. She noticed her behavior changing but didn't know how to fix it. She now believes Ruin took control of her thoughts. The more she skipped school and met with them in the cave, the worse it got."

"How is she doing now?"

"Better. She told my brother-in-law and his wife everything. They talked to their pastor in Montana about it, and he suggested Anna see a counselor on staff at another church. Becca, the counselor, has experience with satanic cults and has been a huge help to Anna." Olivia paused, then asked, "Do you think Anna was targeted?"

"What do you mean?"

"She said Whisper, the girl she met at Millie's, asked a lot of questions about you. The group saw you stop at Anna's table with the kids, so they knew you were friends."

"You think they used Anna to get to me? That doesn't make sense. You said before that Anna brought them to your house to watch movies. It wouldn't take a rocket scientist to figure out I lived right across the street. Why not come right at me?"

"I don't know, but Ruin did tell her to give you that message."

"Ruin paid me a visit the last time I was at your house. It could've told me then."

"*What?*"

"It was there the day you showed me the damage from Anna's rampage. It made sure I knew that."

Olivia's face turned pale. "An evil spirit in my house? But I haven't noticed anything strange happening. Do you think it's still there?"

I stood and glanced at my watch. "Yes, I do."

"Where are you going?"

"I told you I have to go."

Her eyes blazed. "You tell me there's a demon in my house, a demon *you* brought here, and you're just going to leave?"

"Olivia—"

"Get that thing out of my house!"

I thought about the feverish grave-digging from the night before. "I can't do that, Olivia. I no longer have the authority to do so."

"Authority? What are you talking about?"

"The power to cast out demons, in Jesus' name. I no longer have that type of authority."

"Then who does?"

"You're a Christian. You can do it yourself."

"I wouldn't know where to start," her eyes narrowed. "Jan, if you can't get that thing out of my house right now, find me somebody who can."

My first thought was Ted, but I didn't want him to get involved. Not when his heart had been ripped open anew. But I could ask his dad.

"Ted's father will do it. Freeing people from demonic activity was a huge part of his ministry. I'll give him a call. You're welcome to stay here until then."

"No, I'll book a hotel room in the city." She ran her fingers through her hair. "Do you really think your father-in-law will be able to take on Ruin? I mean, years ago, sure, but

I met Hank. He's an old man."

Images of the senior Pastor Eller in action flashed through my mind. Age couldn't deter that level of faith and passion. "Yeah, I'm sure."

She nodded, and we walked the cobblestone path leading to the front of the house. She stopped and bent over when we neared the mimosa trees.

"Oh, look. How pretty."

I turned to see what had caught her attention. In her hands was a silver butterfly hair barrette embedded with Swarovski stones.

"Is this yours?" She handed the hair clip out to me, but I didn't take it.

"No, it was my mom's. A friend collected her things and gave them to me after she passed away. I must've dropped it last night as I was going through some of her things out here."

She gingerly ran her fingers across the clip.

"You okay, Olivia?"

She sniffed and used her shirt to wipe her nose. "It just seems so unreal, you know? Satanic priests, high priestesses, and demons. I feel like I've lost my grip on reality." Her lips quivered before she added, "I fear for Anna's safety. I can't live in my house. I don't know how any of this is going to end. I'm scared, Jan. Really, really scared."

I placed a hand on her arm. "I wish there was more I could do to help."

"There is," she grabbed my hands in hers. "Pray with me."

My heart pounded. We were close to the burial site of my faith. I remembered the words I'd said the night before about God never being a part of my life again. Olivia's eyes pleaded with me, but there was no way I could pray with her. I could fake it, but she deserved better than that.

I slowly removed my hands from hers. "If you want answers from heaven, stop by the church and talk with Miss

Flora. Do you know who I'm talking about?

"Older lady, petite, gray hair, and flawless brown skin?"

I nodded. "She volunteers there during the week. Miss Flora's a prayer warrior if there ever was one. You'll want to take on Ruin yourself when you're done praying with her."

She chuckled. "Sounds like a great idea. Will you come with me?"

"I can't."

"That's right, you have to be somewhere." She handed the silver filigree barrette to me. I waited until she crossed the street and got into her car before looking down at the ornate clip in my hand. It used to sparkle like diamonds against my mom's ebony waves. I'd worn it in my hair the day I married Ted and planned to give it to Laynee on her wedding day.

I twisted the barrette in my hands. No matter what I did to Garringer, it would never bring Laynee back to me, or her wedding day, or the children she could've had.

I leaned against a tree. The chance of locating Garringer on my own and making him pay for the pain he's caused my family was slim to none. For the first time in twenty-four hours, I doubted if I had the strength or the courage to see it through. But my family would never be at peace unless I stopped him. And that's what I planned to do.

Or die trying because my gut told me that nothing would go as planned.

Chapter Thirteen

Spring 1983

"Jan!"

I sat straight up in bed. My heart raced. A hysterical Aunt Gingie grabbed my shoulders and shook them.

Her right eye was purple, black, and swollen shut. There was a slash on the right side of her face. Blood dripped off her cheek and onto my pajamas.

"Wake up, Jan," she continued to shake me. "Wake up!"

I inched away from her. "I'm awake, Aunt Gingie. What happened?"

"I don't have time for questions. I have to leave, but I need you to stay here. Don't go to school today."

I sat up straighter. "But I have to go. Molly and I entered our project at the science fair, remember?"

"Molly!" Aunt Gingie fell back against the wall and slid to the floor. Her hands trembled over her face. "Oh, Molly, Molly, Molly," she sobbed. A second later, she stood, wiped her face, and shouted at the floor, "Molly! Why'd you have to do this? May you burn in hell for all the trouble you've caused!"

I threw back the covers and ran to my aunt. "Did something happen to Molly?" I grabbed her arms and forced her to look at me. "Aunt Gingie, say something!"

She took hold of my hands and held them gently. "Just stay here and forget about school. Molly won't be there."

My heart stopped. "Aunt Gingie, you're scaring me."

"Good." She wiped at the blood on her face and opened the bedroom door.

"Because right now, we all need to be scared."

~

Present Day

I weaved through the cars at Habakkuk Hills Mall and parked in front of Lighthouse Springs, my favorite home décor store.

I leaned back against my seat. A walk from here to the lake would take five minutes. The fresh air from the walk would clear my head, but I also suspected Garringer and his crew knew what kind of car I drove. I wanted to approach the lake—and their secret cave—with a degree of anonymity. A gray hoodie and dark shades would make up my disguise.

The early morning clouds had disappeared, and the noon sun shone bright through the windshield. The outdoor mall bustled with activity, and I watched enviously through the window as everyday people went about their lives.

A young couple passed before me with two screaming toddlers trying to climb out of a double stroller. The couple hurried to a nearby bench, where each parent grabbed a child. Twin boys. One quietly sat on his mother's lap. The other wiggled out of his dad's arms and toddled along the brick pavement, letting out a yelp whenever the father tried to scoop him up.

Not far from them, a middle-aged couple shared an ice cream cone as they sat on a wooden ledge under one of the many trees that shaded the sidewalk.

Two teenage girls, laden with shopping bags, emerged from a store on my right. They giggled their way down the walk and met up with two more girls at a dress shop on the corner. One of them pulled a bright red purse out of one of the bags, and the quartet shrieked in excitement.

When was the last time my family had been that joyous and carefree? I blinked away tears. We used to be that way all the time.

My phone chimed. I hit the answer button. "Hello?"

"Mom, where are you?" It was Adam.

He didn't have a cell phone, so I checked the number he was calling from. He was calling from the landline at our house.

"Why are you at home? Why aren't you with Grandma Libby at her place?"

"Grandma's here with me. We stopped by to talk to you about Saturday."

My mind drew a blank. "Saturday?"

"Yeah, my birthday. Number fifteen." He chuckled into the phone. "What's the matter, Mom? Did you forget?"

I smiled as I remembered the blunder that became a family "tradition." It started when I forgot Ted's birthday and didn't remember it until days after.

I went on a shopping spree and bought every gift that I imagined Ted could possibly want and apologized profusely at the meager celebration I had been able to pull together that night.

Ted was so excited about the gifts that I received instant forgiveness. Laynee and Adam looked at all the gifts I'd given their dad and bemoaned how they wished I would've forgotten their birthdays. From then on, Ted and I pretended to forget their birthdays while secretly stockpiling gifts for them.

But this time, I wasn't pretending. My son was quickly turning into a young man, and I'd completely forgotten that his birthday was days away. More tears stung my eyes. I swallowed and tried hard to match his playful tone. "Nope, I didn't forget. I'm at the mall right now searching for the perfect gift." I pushed away the guilt of telling yet another lie to my son and made a mental note to shop for him when I returned from the lake.

"Mom," Adam said with alarm. "Please let Dad buy my gift. I already have enough books and sweater vests."

"I'm not shopping for books or vests. From what I hear, bow ties are the latest rage."

He groaned. "Mom."

"What?" I teased. "I think you'll look quite handsome in one."

"How about a gift card? Dad says I'm old enough to shop for my own things."

"How about you put Grandma Libby on the phone?"

"Okay, but remember what I said about the gift card." He whispered something to Libbybelle before she took the phone.

"Jan, where are you?" she asked.

"At the mall."

"The outdoor mall by Crater Lake?"

"Yes." She knew what I was up to. I closed my eyes, shifted nervously in my seat, and waited for the rebuke.

None came.

"Mom, you still there?"

"I'm here." I imagined her shaking her head back and forth at my stubborn refusal to let go of the hunt for Garringer.

"Listen," she said. "You and Ted have a lot of things on your plates right now. Adam and his friends are welcome to celebrate his birthday at my house. He doesn't want a party, but I haven't met a teenager yet who's said no to pizza and soda with friends."

My head fell against the headrest, and my heart reeled from the fact that I hadn't made plans for my son's birthday. "Thanks, Mom. This helps a lot."

After a few moments, she added, "Listen. Celebrating my grandson's birthday at the farm on Saturday will be easy. What won't be easy is having to explain why his Mom isn't there. And you know what I mean."

I glanced at my purse. The gun's weight forced it to lean heavily against the passenger seat. Yes, I knew what she meant.

The thought of Libbybelle telling Adam on his birthday that I'd disappeared or had been injured or killed churned my stomach. I placed a hand over the cell's mic and sobbed.

Sheriff Glass was right. I should let the police handle this. Part of me wanted to run home, grab Adam, and flee the country. Another part wanted me to end Garringer's reign of terror today. He was never going to leave me or my family alone. I was stuck.

"Jan, are you still there?"

"I'm here."

"Good," she said. "I'm putting Adam back on the phone."

Before I could protest, Adam said, "Don't forget, Mom. Gift cards are awesome birthday gifts."

I cleared my throat. "I'll think about it."

"Are you okay? Sounds like you've been crying."

I cracked the window and breathed in the cool air. "I'm okay," I lied. "You know me and this weather. Allergies."

"Okay." The word came out slowly, and he didn't sound convinced. "Grandma attached our bikes to the car," he said. "We're heading up to Jacob's Trail to meet her friends for a bike ride. You wanna come? I'll grab your bike from the garage, and we can pick you up on the way."

I cleared my throat again. "That sounds like fun, but Grandma's friends are waiting on her, and I'll just slow the two of you down. But you, me, and Dad can tackle the trail Sunday after church. I'll make sandwiches, and we can have a picnic."

"But I'll see you guys on Saturday, right? On my

birthday?"

I swallowed. "We'll be there."

"Uh oh, Grandma's grabbed her purse. Gotta go. Love you, Mom."

"Love you, too." I tapped the phone off.

I reached for my purse and pulled open the magnetic snaps. The sun's rays beamed through the windshield and straight onto the Glock. The gun shone like an angel of light.

I needed to get going. I wiped my face with a tissue and stared at the cell phone Doris gave me. My initial plan was to walk to the lake, find the hidden cave Anna had told Olivia about, and hope to find Garringer there.

Plan B had been to go there after midnight when Anna said the group typically gathered there and demanded they tell me where to find him. I'd planned to threaten them with the gun, even though I knew that could quickly go awry, and I was prepared for that.

But I'd just told Adam I'd be there for his birthday, so neither was an option anymore. Instead, I'd find the hideout. If it was empty, I'd search for something that could lead us to Garringer. I'd turn it over to the sheriff's office if I found anything and let them take it from there.

I promised my son I'd be there on his birthday.

I needed to keep that promise.

~

I placed my hands on my hips and sighed.

After thirty minutes of walking along the shore, there was still no evidence of the hideaway Anna mentioned. And the more I walked, the more remote and rugged the terrain.

Families enjoying the lake were a mile behind me, and the last few people I ran into were couples who'd sought privacy behind the large rocks. But I hadn't seen a single soul for the past ten minutes.

I sat beside a huge rock, set my purse next to me, and

thought about my options.

It was a long way back to the main area of the lake, where the water was clear and the beach clean. Here, the water was dark, and debris littered what little was left of the shore.

I removed my shades and scanned the rock formation about thirty feet away.

Could that be what Anna meant by a cave?

That's when I saw it.

Tree branches, the same color as the rocks, were tied together by a netting that camouflaged a small opening. I grabbed my purse and ran over to take a closer look.

The branches were an arms-length above my head. I jumped up and grabbed one, and several smaller ones fell down with it.

I secured the purse around me like a crossbody and found a secure place for my foot in one of the crevices. I hefted myself onto the rock ledge and climbed through the hole.

Cool air greeted me, and a quick look around showed no one inside.

Below the opening were several wooden crates stacked together for makeshift steps. I took the first couple, then jumped to the dirt floor.

In the middle of the cave was a large stone circle. Ash had been spread throughout the circle, and the bones of what I hoped to be a large animal lay on top.

Recently slept-in sleeping bags and blankets were scattered about. Alcohol bottles and drug paraphernalia had also been strewn across the cave floor. Large ceremonial candles stood in a corner, though none appeared to have ever been lit.

A noise came from the back of the cave. I turned and saw that the cave floor sloped and the rock walls narrowed into a long tunnel. I pulled the gun from my purse, flipped off the safety, and walked slowly down the dim passageway until the path opened to what appeared to be an office.

Water flowed down the stone walls and puddled on the floor, making the same sound I'd heard earlier. The small office area was darker than it was inside the cave. On top of an upside crate was a tall battery-operated lamp. I flicked it on and froze.

A pile of 8 x 10 photographs was on a huge wooden slab. And on top was a picture of me.

I quickly sorted through the rest of the photos.

There were pictures of our house, cars, and a few others that showed me picking Adam and Laynee up from school. My heart stopped at a close-up photo of a smiling Laynee in her favorite yellow dress. A dress I knew she'd only worn to church.

I studied the picture. In the background behind Laynee were the all too familiar Noah's Ark-themed walls that decorated the halls of our children's ministry. Someone had taken this picture from inside our church!

I knew Garringer had killed Laynee, and now I had proof. His fingerprints would be all over these photos.

I shoved the pictures and the gun in my purse and ran back into the tunnel. I intentionally left the lamp on so Garringer would know I'd been there.

I jumped over the blankets and bags on the floor in the main area and headed for the crate steps, taking them two at a time. I wiggled back through the opening and dropped onto the beach.

A sharp pain radiated through my ankle.

I ran to get back to my car at the mall parking lot. My ankle screamed in protest.

The sound of heavy breathing startled me, and I fell. I looked around, but nothing was there. I scrambled up and ran faster. The breathing started again before turning into soft laughter and morphing into maniacal high-pitched shrieks.

I rocketed down the shore but came to a screeching halt

when shrieking came toward me.

I turned and ran in the other direction. The screams grew louder. I ducked behind a large boulder that backed up to the water.

Silence.

I peeked around the rock and prepared to resume my run when the heavy breathing made its way down the back of my neck. I whipped my head towards the water but saw nothing.

I searched my pockets for my cell phone. Then I remembered I'd placed it in the passenger seat after my conversation with Adam. I snatched open my purse and pulled out the cell phone Doris gave me. I dialed the number five and was about to hit send when a dark shadow fell on the rocks around me. I dropped the phone and wrapped my fingers around the gun.

I stood and made it halfway around the boulder before being slammed against it. The gun fell, and my body shook with pain. I braced myself against the rock and looked up at the dark figure towering over me. Familiar green eyes penetrated my soul. And as always, they blazed with fury.

But this time, so did mine.

Chapter Fourteen

Spring 1983

Aunt Gingie never answered my question about what happened to Molly, and the blood from the cut on my aunt's face smeared my hands.

The doorbell rang.

I opened the bedroom curtains. Several police cars were in front of our house. Two officers were at the front door, and several more walked around to the back.

I ran to Aunt Gingie's bedroom and knocked on her door.

No answer.

"Aunt Gingie," I called, not bothering to disguise the panic in my voice. "You've got to come out now! The police are here."

She yanked the door open and ran down the hallway. I followed, glancing around her to see out the small window near the door. She pulled me to her side. "Did they see you?" She asked, her eyes wild.

"Yeah, I think they did."

The doorbell rang again, followed by a loud knock.

She finger-combed the tangles from her hair, then turned to me. "This is what we're going to do. First, I'll do the talking. Not one word from you. Got it?"

"Yes."

She'd changed from the shorts and T-shirt she'd had on earlier to a nightgown and robe. The gown was lacey and extremely short. So was the robe, and it was tied loosely around her waist.

Another loud knock echoed down the hall.

She rounded the corner and then shouted, "All right, already. I'm coming."

She snatched the door open, and I walked up behind her. Only one of the officers was in uniform. The other wore a pair of khakis and a white button-down shirt with a dark blazer. He spoke first. "Are you April Lorraine Rainwater?"

She tossed her hair back and scoffed, "Nobody calls me by that name anymore."

"So you are April Rainwater?"

"What do you want?"

The uniformed officer grabbed Aunt Gingie by the arm and slapped cuffs on her. "You're under arrest."

"No!" I cried. "Please don't take her away." I gripped her robe. The officers stared at the grip I had on Aunt Gingie.

There was blood on my hands.

~

Present Day

Garringer flung me onto the cave floor.

A cloud of putrid dust landed in my mouth.

He prowled silently around me. Prints from his black steel-toe boots made a chalkless outline around my body.

I spit the dust from my mouth and flipped over to face him. "You monster. You killed my daughter!"

I braced for the kick, but the pain still knifed through my side. I blinked away the glaze threatening my vision and scrambled toward the stone pit near the cave's center. He grabbed my ankle and yanked me back toward him.

"Why did you do it?" I screamed and inched my way back to the stone circle. I only needed one, just one stone to bash his head in. "What did Laynee ever do to you?"

He stood over me and grinned. His movie-star good looks forever tainted by the evil that oozed from his pores.

I blinked again to clear my vision. He looked the same way he did on that horrific night all those years ago. Jet-black hair, tanned complexion, prominent cheekbones, and a six-foot-three frame. And just like back then, that frame looked down on me now, ready to devour. Fury boiled in my veins as his tongue played across his lips. His lust reminded me all too well of the malevolence I was dealing with.

"What? No hello?" He frowned and then crouched close to my face. "Not even a *'How've you been'* for your master?"

"You never were my—"

The slap stung, and a bone cracked. Blood pooled in my mouth and dripped onto the dirt floor. I glared at him and repeated the phrase he didn't let me finish. "You were *never* my master."

His face darkened. "You despicable witch. You haven't changed a bit. Always daring to defy me."

I ducked the oncoming blow and grabbed one of the stones. It made contact with his skull and blood spewed from his temple. Hatred fueled another strike to his jawbone. I scrambled to my knees to deliver another blow, but he grabbed my wrist. The pain from the snap dropped me into the dirt.

He stood, eyes ablaze, and struck me with the back of his hand. I soared across the cave floor. The rancid smell of the dirt, the pain, the dizziness, and the blurred vision converged. My stomach clenched and blood and lunch poured from my mouth and onto the floor in front of me.

Garringer seized my ankle again and dragged me away from the pit. I dug my nails into the dusty ground and clawed my way back to the pit for another stone.

The grip on my ankle ceased. Garringer hurried toward my head, and with the heel of his boot, stomped my right hand into the ground.

My screams echoed off the cave walls.

He then grabbed a fistful of hair and dragged me deeper into the cave.

Darkness played at my eyes as my left hand pried at his grip. He yanked me off the ground and threw me against the stone wall.

I slid to the ground, and regret pierced me to the bone.

Garringer was about to get what he'd waited thirty-five long years for.

My demise.

Chapter Fifteen

Spring 1983

I chewed my bottom lip.

A female officer escorted Aunt Gingie into the dingy interview area where I waited. The stone-faced policewoman pointed, and Aunt Gingie sat stiffly on the wobbly aluminum chair beside me. Hours had passed since I'd last seen her. She still wore the short, lacy gown and robe, but now a pair of oversized jeans and ratty-looking tennis shoes completed her outfit.

"What's going on?" I whispered.

"Shhh," Aunt Gingie nodded toward the huge man walking toward us. "Remember, I will do all the talking."

"Ms. Rainwater," the man pulled out a chair and sat. "I'm Detective Bruce Cheatham, Homicide."

"Homicide?" I blurted out before I could catch myself.

Aunt Gingie snapped her head towards me. "Quiet!"

The detective picked up a sticky note from his desk and nodded towards me. "Family Services are on their way to pick her up," he slapped the note on a stack of papers. "But one of my officers will question her before she leaves."

"Family Services?" Aunt Gingie chuckled. "I don't think so. I'm her legal guardian, and she's going home with me." She thrust her cuffed wrists toward the detective. "Undo these. I'm outta here."

He smiled. "Yeah, I've heard about you. I've been told

you've been arrested for all sorts of crimes in this town, then a phone call comes in, and you're out before the ink dries on the paperwork." He pointed to his chest, "But this time, I'm in charge, and you're not going anywhere."

She continued to hold her wrists out to him.

"You're being charged with arson," he said. "Four eyewitnesses picked you out of a line-up. You set fire to Holy Trinity Church on Route 7. That's ten years hard time."

She lowered her wrists and tossed her hair over her shoulders. "I'll be out of here within the hour."

He leaned forward. "Ms. Rainwater, like I said, I'm a homicide detective. I can help you with this arson charge if you cooperate with me. All I'll need from you to do that is information. I want to know about the murder of Terese Katherine Fitzhugh. Her family says she also went by the name Quiggy. Ms. Fitzhugh's body was pulled from a river eighty miles north of here. You know anything about that?"

My heart pounded in my chest. Quiggy, Molly's mother, was dead?

Aunt Gingie stared at the detective. "I've never heard of anyone named Quiggy."

I turned and stared at my aunt. She'd just been told her best friend was dead. How could she deny that she knew her?

The detective reached into his desk and pulled out a yellow notepad. "She also had a teen daughter named Molly. Do you know anything about her?"

"No. That name doesn't ring a bell either."

Tears rolled down my cheeks. I bowed my head and remembered the chilling words Molly had spoken months earlier. "They were going to kill me ... and no one in this town would've done a thing about it." I swallowed, looked at the detective, and ignored Aunt Gingie's icy stare.

"Detective Cheatham? Ask me if I know a girl named Molly."

~

Present Day

Cold water stung my face, and I jolted awake.

I lifted my hands to wipe my eyes, but they wouldn't move. Every part of my body cried out in pain. I blinked away the water. A blurry Garringer stood over me. In one hand, he held a rope. In the other, a knife.

My legs wouldn't budge, either. He'd tied them and me to a wooden chair laden with blood and slime.

He stepped towards me. "Tell me where she is."

"Get away from me!" The bones in my face were on fire, and I shook from the pain.

"I said, where is she?"

"Where is who?" I quietly breathed out the words instead of screaming them. I'd hoped that would minimize the agony.

It didn't.

"Speak louder," he tossed the rope to the side and kneeled in front of me. The knife in his right hand gleamed. "I can't hear you."

"I don't know who you're talking about," I said quickly. "All I know is that you killed my daughter."

He stood and circled my chair. "One. More. Time. Where is—"

"I don't know who you're talking about!" Pain shot through my skull and threatened to send me back into unconsciousness. "Ted's not going to let you get away with this. He'll hunt you to the ends of the earth for what you've done."

He stopped behind the chair. "You mean *Pastor* Ted? Ha. What's he gonna do? Hit me over the head with his Bible?"

"Rot in hell."

"I plan to," he grabbed my hair and yanked my head

backward. "Now tell me where she is."

"Who is *she*?"

He loosened his grip and walked in front of me. "Three seconds to tell me where she is, or you'll be just as dead as your ditzy little daughter."

I spit in his face and then struggled against the rope binding my wrists.

He pulled a blood-stained cloth from his pocket, wiped away the spit, and then forced the filthy rag deep into my mouth.

"You will tell me where Molly is," his breath heated my face. "Then you will die."

Molly?!

He straightened and calmly walked to the back of the cave. When the sound of his steps disappeared, I rocked the wooden chair back and forth and tried to wrestle my wrists free from the rope, but my right hand was useless.

Blood from the rag seeped down my throat, and my whole body constricted. I looked around for a sharp stone or pebble. I needed something to slice the ropes, or I was going to suffocate.

I rocked the chair harder until it slammed against the ground. I spotted a thin piece of slate and scooted the chair close enough to grab it with my left hand, but it disintegrated into ash against the thick rope. Garringer would be back soon. I had to think of something fast.

"Mom?"

Startled, I looked up toward a side entrance to the cave. *No! Not Adam.*

He jumped down, ran to me, and removed the rag from my mouth.

"Adam! What are you doing here?"

He sat the chair upright and then worked on the ropes binding my hands.

"Adam, you have to— "

"We went looking for you at the mall. When Grandma

Libby saw your car was there but you weren't, she was afraid you came to the lake by yourself and might be hurt. While she was on the phone with Dad, I jumped on my bike to come look for you."

"Adam—"

He continued loosening the binds. "People on the beach said they saw you come down this way. When I was outside, I heard voices, so I came in through that side hole."

My heart raced. "You need to get out of here. Now."

"I can get through these ropes."

"Adam, stop! Look at me." His fingers hesitated on my wrists before he pulled himself away to stand in front of me. Tears stained his face. "Mom, who did this?"

"Buddy, listen, that's not important right now. What I need for you to do is get out of here fast. You hear me?"

He bent over and worked on loosening the ropes that secured my legs to the chair.

"Son, I need you to go get Dad and Sheriff Glass. Will you do that for me?"

"I'm not leaving here without you, Mom."

Heavy footsteps made their way up from the tunnel. I leaned over and whispered in his ear. "He's coming, Adam, and I don't want anything to happen to you." Tears streamed down my face as I stared into his eyes. "If you leave now, you can make sure the man who did this to me and Laynee won't get away. But you need to leave now. He needs to pay for what he did to your sister."

My heart broke. I'd just spewed out the only words I knew would ever get my son to leave my side. He searched my eyes for confirmation. I nodded in the direction of the entrance he used. "Go."

He shot up and ran towards the opening. Garringer emerged carrying a small dead animal. He spotted Adam, dropped the animal, and bolted after him.

"You monster, leave my son alone! Run, Adam! Run!"

Chapter Sixteen

Spring 1983

Quiggy was dead. Molly was missing, and Aunt Gingie was going to jail.

Detective Cheatham wanted me to answer three questions. Did I know Molly? When was the last time I saw her, and did I know where she was?

I swiped at the beads of sweat that dotted my forehead. The heat emanating from Aunt Gingie's scowl made me second-guess talking to the detective. But the thought of not being there when Molly needed me scared me more.

"Yes, Detective Cheatham," I cleared my throat and continued, "I know Molly, and I knew her mother, Quiggy. Terese Katherine, I think you said her real name was."

The detective shot a look at Aunt Gingie. She tilted her head to the side and stared back at him.

He wrote something on his notepad. Without looking up, he asked, "And the last time you saw them?"

"At our house, Friday night."

"Did you see them leave?"

"Yes."

"Alive?"

Shocked, I turned to look at Aunt Gingie. She smirked at the detective.

"Jan," he said. "Look at me, please."

I looked at him. "Detective, of course, they were alive. I watched them walk out the door and down the road."

He wrote something else on the notepad. A uniformed officer walked up to his desk. The name on the badge said Sgt. Mordell.

"Cheatham, Family Services is here to take the girl."

Aunt Gingie quickly turned to me and jerked her head toward the officer. "Go."

I grabbed her arm. "Aunt Gingie, please don't send me away. I just wanted to help them find Molly!"

She reached for my hands, the noise from the shackles startling us both. Sergeant Mordell stepped closer. He looked oddly familiar.

"It's not like that," she said. "It's going to be okay. Just go with the officer."

She gave Mordell a stern look and said, "You better make sure nothing happens to her on the way to Family Services," the last two words came out tight and clipped.

I squeezed her hands. "But what if something happens to you?"

She leaned over and whispered, "I'll be okay, trust me. But more importantly," she glanced at Mordell before returning her gaze to me. "Trust your gut. I'll be out of here soon, I promise."

The officer took me by the elbow and led me through the waiting area to a narrow corridor. It was quiet and empty, and a huge metal door marked the exit. Next to the door was a keypad. He punched in a few numbers and then pushed the door open. A light gray sedan waited outside.

He pushed me towards the car.

The driver's face was covered with tattoos, and he wore a black skullcap and matching turtleneck.

The rear door opened.

Two more men stepped out wearing the same thing. I backed away from the car. "They don't look like they're from Family Services."

Sgt. Mordell grabbed me by the shoulders and shoved me into the backseat. One of the men quickly sat beside me and put his hand over my mouth. The other entered on the left side and shut the door. Mordell vaulted into the passenger seat, and the car sped off.

I bit the hand covering my mouth and screamed.

The man on the left picked up a roll of duct tape from the floor. "This is going to be fun." He ripped off a piece of the tape and smiled.

I screamed again.

~

Present Day

My heart stilled as Adam climbed through the main cave entrance.

Garringer grabbed the back of his jacket and yanked him down. He then hoisted Adam off the floor and into the air. My heart resumed its frantic thud.

Adam's face turned ashen. "Let go of me!"

"As you wish." Garringer lifted Adam higher and then threw him in my direction. He landed inches away from my feet with a sickening crunch.

"Adam!" I scooted my chair closer to him, but Garringer lunged forward and pulled Adam up by the collar.

I couldn't take anymore.

"Garringer, please don't hurt him," I cried. "I'll do anything you say, I promise." My mind reeled. I couldn't believe this was happening.

He tightened his grip on Adam. "Tell me where she is."

I continued to sob.

Garringer swore and strengthened the chokehold. Adam's face went from colorless to beet red in a matter of seconds.

"I don't know where she is." Desperate tears dropped onto my bloodied blouse. "I'm telling you the truth. The last time I saw Molly was the last time I saw you. The night of the fire. The night you died."

He reached into his pocket and pulled out the knife he had earlier. "The night you *thought* I died." He wrapped his arm around Adam's neck. "Well, that's too bad. You could've saved the life of this sneaky little imp."

Adam pulled free and kicked Garringer hard in the stomach. Garringer lost his balance and fell, slashing his leg with the knife.

I leaned forward. "Adam, get out of here, now!"

He ran to my chair and worked again to untie the ropes.

Garringer stalked toward us with the knife.

Adam freed one of my legs. When he reached to undo the other one, Garringer yanked his head backward. Adam's neck was completely exposed.

"You have one more chance to tell me where she is."

I shook my head. "I'm telling you the truth. I don't know."

He pulled Adam's head back further and placed the sharp blade against his skin. Adam grabbed at the knife and tried to stand but Garringer forced him back to the floor with his boot. He placed the knife against Adam's throat. Blood streamed across the blade and down Adam's neck.

"No!" I used my free leg to maneuver closer to Garringer. He kicked my chair over with the steel tip of his boot.

"Please!" I begged. "Don't do—"

"Let my son go. Now."

Ted!

The Glock Doris had given me was pointed straight at Garringer's head.

With the knife still at Adam's throat, Garringer turned to Ted and snickered. "Well, if it isn't the preacher man himself. Perfect timing. Now, you'll be able to watch both your son and your wife die."

"I said let him go," Ted tightened his grip on the gun.

Garringer raised the knife in the air. "And I say, go stand over there by your wife. One wrong move, and I'll thrust this blade straight through your son's fiendish heart."

Ted lowered the gun and slowly made his way over to where I lay on the ground. He grabbed the chair as if to sit it upright, but then he nodded to Adam, who wrestled free of Garringer's grip and lay flat against the ground.

A shot rang out.

Garringer dropped to the dirt floor. Blood flowed from his chest.

Adam scurried toward me. Ted ran to Garringer.

Sheriff Glass and Doris stood near the entrance that Adam had used earlier. Sirens wailed in the background.

The sheriff stomped over to Ted and grabbed the gun from his hand. "You were supposed to wait for us." He handed the weapon to one of his deputies. "What happened?"

Adam freed me from the chair and helped me stand. He then glared at the sheriff. "My dad stopped that man from killing me and my mom. That's what happened."

Doris smiled and made her way over to Adam. "Come on, son. Let's get you out of here. Your grandmother's worried sick."

Adam nodded and reached for my hand.

One of the younger officers, who'd also entered the cave, approached us. The name on his uniform read McGee. "Paramedics are on the way," he used a handkerchief to wipe away the blood on Adam's neck, then looked at the wound. "The medics will have this fixed up in no time." He turned to me. "Would you like some help out of here, ma'am?"

I nodded and leaned against the officer. Every muscle in my body weakened by the second. "Adam, Doris is right. Please find Grandma Libby and let her know we're all okay.

I'll join you in a few minutes, I promise."

Doris wrapped her arms around Adam and said, "Come on. Libby's gonna have a heart attack if she doesn't see one of you come out of here soon."

The young officer tightened his hold on me and prepared to follow them.

"No," I jerked my head toward Garringer, "I want to go over there."

Officer McGee placed my arm around his shoulders. Every step sent waves of pain throughout my body. When we finally made it to Garringer, I saw that Ted, who was still kneeling beside him, had removed his jacket and placed it on top of Garringer's gaping chest wound.

My husband had put a bullet in Garringer's heart.

"Hold on," Ted said as he squeezed Garringer's hand and applied pressure to the wound. "An ambulance is on the way."

Garringer opened his eyes and glared at Ted. "They know what you've done. This isn't over."

"*They*?" Ted asked. "Who are you talking about?"

Garringer coughed.

Ted applied more pressure to the wound, but blood continued to flow through the jacket and onto his fingers. He closed his eyes and asked, "Garringer, did you kill Laynee?"

Garringer looked up at me. "Sure."

"What does that mean?" I screamed and stepped closer. "Tell us what you did to her!"

He coughed again and a thin red line trickled down the side of his mouth.

Ted reached for his hand and placed it in his. "It doesn't have to end like this. Your eternal life now hangs in the balance." He shook his head and then looked deep into Garringer's eyes. "It's not too late for you to repent and accept Christ as your Savior. All you have to do is ask."

Garringer tried to pull his hand away from Ted's grip, but he continued, "God's word says that your sins are as far as the East is from the West. He's already done the hard work. Even for a soul as black as yours."

"You'd like to believe that, wouldn't you, pastor?" He moaned, then added, "But the flames of hell are already licking at my feet." Blood mixed with saliva gurgled from his throat, and then his body went limp.

"Garringer?" Ted gripped his hand tighter. "Garringer!"

Officer McGee took Garringer's wrist and then shook his head. "He's gone."

A tear rolled down Ted's cheek and onto Garringer's hand.

EMTs rushed in and asked us to step aside. But like Garringer had said, it was too late. I took one last look at his face. Vacant eyes stared back at me.

My vision clouded, and my knees went weak. Officer McGee caught my head before it hit the stone floor, and Ted rushed to my side.

I smiled at him. "Thank you for saving Adam."

He murmured something, and a flurry of activity surrounded me as blackness descended.

But once again … it was too late.

Chapter Seventeen

Spring 1983

"Trust me," Aunt Gingie had said.

Tears rolled down my face as duct tape covered my mouth, wrists, and ankles. I sat in the backseat of a car barreling down a dark road in the middle of nowhere between two men I'd never seen before.

All because I wanted to help Molly.

I had no idea what might've happened to her, but was I on my way to a similar fate?

If only I knew what that was.

Mordell motioned to the driver. "Turn left, here."

The car drove down a long gravel driveway and stopped in front of a small, dilapidated, windowless cabin. The door opened. Two men dressed in the same black skullcaps and turtlenecks as my travel companions walked up to the car.

Mordell rolled down his window. One of the men looked at me, then at Mordell. "Garringer said to take the girl back to Gingie's," the man said. "He wants her there within the hour," then his eyes narrowed. "Unharmed."

The man sitting on my left uttered a deep guttural sound. I looked at him, and he winked.

A cold sweat made its way down the back of my neck. Either way, I was doomed. Return to Gingie's and face the wrath of Garringer or spend the night in a dark cabin with six men. And that included the one foaming at the mouth next to me.

Mordell yelled at the driver. "You heard the man. Let's go!"

When we pulled up to Aunt Gingie's, all four men exited the car. Two stood guard on the porch. Mordell climbed into the backseat and removed the duct tape from my legs and wrists. Now I realized why he'd looked so familiar. He was one of the men who'd attended Aunt Gingie's gatherings. On those nights, he wore a black robe. But tonight, he wore the uniform and badge he had on when he kidnapped me from the police station.

He grabbed my chin and forced me to look at him. "One sound from you, and you're dead. You understand me?"

I nodded, and he ripped the tape from my mouth. I muffled a scream as he pulled me out of the car and walked me up to the front door. He followed me inside and then locked it behind him.

He pointed to the sofa. "Sit."

"Is my aunt here?"

"Sit," he repeated.

I swallowed and pointed to the room across the hall. "My bedrooms right there. I'm tired. Can't I just lie down and go to sleep instead?"

He threw open the door to my bedroom and stepped inside. Seconds later, he came back out. "Okay, but if you're thinking about escaping through that window, think again. Pal and Ridge are guarding the front, Simon and me, the back." He grabbed the front doorknob and laughed. "Your decision."

He slammed the door behind him, and I ran to lock it. Garringer would be on his way. I had to find a way out.

I went to my bedroom window and opened it just enough to hear what the men outside were saying. When Mordell's voice joined them, I went to my dresser and pulled out the drawer where I kept the small phone book Mrs. Gibbons gave me, but it wasn't there. I emptied every drawer onto the floor. Nothing.

I glanced at the clock on the nightstand. Midnight. I was running out of time. I searched everywhere I could think of, but it was of no use. My ticket out of here—as Molly had happily stated— was gone.

Tears stung the back of my eyes. Aunt Gingie must've found it.

I fell backward onto the bed. She and Molly were the only two people I cared about in this town. Now, it appeared she had something to do with Quiggy's death and Molly's disappearance. I shook my head as I remembered the cuts and bruises on her face when she came into my room this morning. The one person left in this town for me to trust had betrayed me and set me up to die.

I stared at the ceiling. "God, please help me."

Heavy footsteps made their way into my bedroom. I sprung from the bed and cowered in the corner. The framed picture of my mother on the nightstand stared back at me. I grabbed it, put it under my shirt next to my heart, and closed my eyes. I swallowed and did the only thing I knew how to do. Something my mother had taught me. I called on the name of Jesus.

"Get up!"

I opened my eyes. Garringer.

He pulled me up by the arm. The picture of my mother slid from under my shirt and onto the carpet.

He grabbed it off the floor and flung it across the room. The dresser mirror cracked from the force.

He tightened the grip on my arm. "You've been shooting your mouth off to that new detective in town. Talking to him about my Molly." He twisted my wrist. "Gingie should've taught you better. It's too late now because she's no longer a problem. My men made sure of that. And since Molly ran out on me," he grabbed my other arm and threw me onto the bed. "I'll take from you what I should've gotten from her. The only difference is, you'll be dead when I'm done."

I screamed and rolled off the bed. He grabbed me and then put his hands around my throat. "Go ahead and fight," he lowered his face closer to mine. "I'll still get what I want. I'll just be entertained while getting it."

He reached for the buttons on my shirt, and the room exploded. The force of the blast blew me into the corner of the room.

I ran to the window. Garringer's and Mordell's cars were in flames. I looked down and saw Garringer at my feet. A piece of metal protruded from his temple.

I ran towards the door, but it was blocked. Molly stood there with a can of gasoline in one hand and a small satchel in the other. Standing next to her was Aunt Gingie.

I stumbled backward. "Molly!"

Her eyes locked on Garringer.

"Jan," Aunt Gingie ran to me. "Are you all right? Did he hurt you?"

"He was about to, but then there was this explosion and—"

"I know," Molly said. "That was us."

I looked down at my blouse and swallowed. Fear gripped me as vivid images of Garringer pulling at the buttons played in my mind.

"Aunt Gingie, he was going to—"

"I know what he was going to do, silly girl." She ran trembling fingers through my hair. "Just thank your God that we got here in time."

"Jan," Molly stepped closer to Garringer. "It's time for you to leave."

"Why?"

Inches from an unconscious Garringer was the heavy wooden dresser. His blood coated a corner of it. Aunt Gingie tossed me a sweater from one of the drawers. "Put that on and then escape through the back."

"Mordell and his men are at the back door."

"Not anymore," she said.

I slid the sweater on and asked, "What's going on? Molly, everybody's been looking for you. I didn't know if you were dead or alive. And Aunt Gingie, I thought you'd sent me here to die."

The sound of cars speeding down the road gripped our attention.

Aunt Gingie put her arms around my shoulders and pointed toward the back of the house. "Your only chance of getting out of here alive is dwindling by the second."

"If our lives are in danger, we all need to leave." I said and stepped around her. "Come on, Molly. Let's go."

"I can't. I've got a score to settle." She set the satchel and gas can next to Garringer, and Aunt Gingie tossed her a book of matches.

"Molly, don't!" I ran towards her. "He's too badly hurt to come after us."

"I don't want him badly hurt. I want him dead."

"Aunt Gingie, stop her, please. She doesn't have to do this. There's still time. We can all leave together."

Aunt Gingie shook her head. "You still don't get it, do you? I can't go either. This goes way deeper than what you see here in this room. This is the end of the line for me." She walked over and cupped my face in her hands. "No, how could you get it? You're so far beyond the nightmare we've created here that there's no way you'll ever be able to understand it." She sighed and looked into my eyes. "But understand this. I killed those two men outside for your freedom. Your mom took care of me, and I promised myself that I would take care of you. My goal was for you to leave this house as pure as you were when you walked in it." She wiped away a tear. "But Jan, if you don't leave now you'll never make it out of this town alive."

Her touch was warm, and her voice was soft. So were her eyes. She resembled the picture of my mother.

Car doors slammed outside.

I grabbed Molly's sleeve. "Please come with me."

"I'm not leaving until he can look me in the eyes. He killed my mother, Jan. He beat, tortured, and set her on fire before tossing her in the river." She tilted the gasoline can and poured its contents onto Garringer. "Tonight, when he gets to hell, I want him to know that I was the one who sent him there."

Fists banged on the front door. I ran into the hallway. Molly and Aunt Gingie had barricaded it with the large oak table from the kitchen, but it wasn't enough. Whoever was on the other side was close to pushing through the door.

It was now or never.

I went back into my bedroom and fumbled through the clothing on the floor until I found my mother's picture and her Bible. I then ran to the back of the house, flung open the door, and dashed down the steps and into the woods. Seconds later, I heard male voices shouting at Aunt Gingie. Then gunshots.

Lots of them, and then everything went silent.

I stopped running and waited to hear something, anything from Aunt Gingie or Molly.

More silence.

I turned to look back at the house, and my heart sank to my knees.

It was on fire.

~

Pained green eyes pleaded with me through the outer darkness.

Burnt flesh permeated my nostrils, as I floated in the nothingness.

The eyes continued begging for help.

The darkness shook, and the familiar green eyes morphed into bone and flesh. A face formed.

Garringer.

He called to me through lips that didn't move, and the

darkness shook again. More eyes appeared. More faces.

The stench was unbearable.

"Help me!"

I ignored Garringer's voice and floated higher.

Mournful wailing erupted below me. I turned and watched as thousands of angry, gnashing teeth headed towards Garringer.

The darkness behind him burst into a furnace of flames as the gnarled teeth sank into his skin and ripped at his seared, burnt flesh. His mouth opened, and a high-pitched scream sent bolts of lightning through my body.

The electric shocks to my floating body stopped, and Garringer's audible cries suddenly ceased.

But his eyes were still screaming.

~

Present Day

Bright lights filtered through my eyelids.

"Jan? Can you hear me? I need you to wake up, sweetie. It's me, Ted."

I opened my eyes and blinked at the fuzzy image sitting next to me on the bed.

My right wrist and hand were bandaged, so he gingerly lifted my left one. "You were having a nightmare, but it's okay. You're awake now."

"No."

"No, what?" He brushed a strand of hair away from my sweat-laden forehead.

"It wasn't a nightmare." Tears flowed down my cheeks. "It's all my fault. Will God ever forgive me?"

"Honey," he kissed my hand. "You're in the hospital. You've been here a couple of days." Tears filled his eyes. "I'm just glad you're okay. You've been through a lot."

I glanced around the room. Flowers decorated every available inch of space, and the vibrant colors contrasted starkly against the sterile white walls. A monitor beeped in the distance.

"I'm in the hospital?"

He nodded then pressed a button on a device attached to the bed. A lovely-sounding voice came through the speaker. "Yes, Mr. Eller?"

Ted smiled at me. "My wife. She's awake."

"I'll send her doctor right in." The small box clicked, and the kind voice was gone.

Flashbacks of Garringer holding a knife to Adam's throat flooded my mind. I grabbed Ted's wrist. "Adam. Where is he? Please tell me he's okay."

"Adam's with Libbybelle, and he's fine."

"But his neck … it was bleeding. I saw Garringer—"

"EMTs took care of that cut at the scene. He had a few other cuts and bruises on his body, but he's recovering well."

"But he," I leaned forward, and my head spun. I tightened my grip on Ted's wrist.

He eased my head back onto the pillow. "Take it easy. Like I said, you've been through a lot."

I reached up and touched his face. "I'm so sorry."

"For what?"

"For putting our children in Garringer's crosshairs. For lying to you. For keeping secrets. For not seeking help when I needed it."

His brow furrowed. "Secrets?"

I nodded. "I've been keeping secrets from you for a long time. Doris was right. I'm a phony. I'm not fit to be anyone's wife. Let alone the wife of a pastor."

"I don't understand."

"I married you under false pretenses, Ted. I led you to believe I was a Bible-toting, Scripture-quoting, Spirit-filled woman of God. Truth is, I don't even like Him."

"Jan—"

"You knew I blamed Him for a lot of things, but you have no idea how deep it goes. For a while, I told myself I'd be okay if I just read the Bible more, devoted myself to prayer, and spent more time with Him. That worked for a while, but Laynee's death fractured all that. And when I heard about Garringer's involvement, I couldn't do it anymore, so I buried God beneath the mimosa trees."

He chuckled and patted my hand. "I think the pain meds have messed with your mind a little bit."

"I haven't had this much clarity in my whole life, Ted." My heart thudded in my chest. "Please take me seriously. I need your help before it's too late."

"Ah, so it's true," Dr. Horace, our family physician, walked through the door. "My patient is awake and talking too, I see. All good signs." He reached into his pocket and pulled out a silver pen light. Ted scooted off the bed as the doctor approached.

"She's been talking ever since she woke up, doctor, but not everything has made sense." He swallowed and then asked, "Is it possible she suffered some type of brain injury?"

"No. Her brain scans are normal. More than likely, it's the medication. Each patient reacts differently to them." He lifted the penlight and leaned over me. "This may be a little bright," he said, pushing a button on the pen. He pointed the light in my right eye and then the left before flicking it off and sitting on the bed. "How do you feel?"

"Stiff. Sore. Slight headache."

"I know it might not sound like it, but that's good news. You have fractures of the cheekbone, right hand, and wrist. Not to mention the lung contusions and hematomas. If stiffness and soreness are all you're feeling right now, then your medical team here at St. Matthew's is doing a fantastic job."

I touched my face and winced.

"There's been minimal displacement of the left cheekbone," he said. "Surgical intervention isn't needed at this point, and as I'm looking at it, it's barely noticeable. I suggest we continue monitoring it and I'll prescribe something for the pain. After a few weeks, the pain and swelling should be gone. Cosmetically, if you'd like the displaced bone to be put back in its correct position, a surgeon will be able to manually do that under general anesthesia."

I widened my eyes.

Ted grabbed my left hand again. "Honey, Dr. Horace is right. It's not really noticeable, so you don't have to worry about a surgeon fixing it."

"Good, because that sounded painful."

They chuckled, and Dr. Horace added, "Your right hand and wrist are healing well, and so are your lungs, but the orthopedic and pulmonary specialists will still be in to check on you later."

"I want to go home."

"You're not quite well enough for that yet, but I'll meet with the other doctors in a couple of days to discuss your going home then."

"What about visitors? I want to see my son."

Dr. Horace looked at Ted, then patted my hand before quietly exiting.

My heart thudded, and I stared at Ted. "You told me Adam was fine."

"He is." He sat in a chair next to the bed. "But I don't think it's a good idea for him to see you right now."

"Is he mad at me?"

"No, he's not mad at you." Ted reached into a bin on the table by the bed and pulled out a small mirror. "Here."

I snatched the mirror from his hands, and my mouth popped open. Stitches lined the left side of my swollen face. The other side was bright red and bruised. My eyes sported matching colors— black, blue, and purple."

"You told me I looked great."

"I … didn't say that. I said the fracture on the left side

of your face wasn't really noticeable."

"How can you tell? It's covered with stitches."

"That's because you also had a nasty cut on that side, but trust me, when you're all healed up, you'll barely notice it."

I shook my head and moaned.

"I didn't want Adam to see you until some of the bruising faded and the swelling went down. I don't think he's slept at all the past few days, and I didn't want to make it worse by him seeing you like this. But now that you're awake, I'll let you decide."

"How long have I been here?"

"Four days."

"I've been out of it for four days?"

"You were in a lot of pain, sweetie, so you were heavily medicated."

"I want to call him."

Ted's brows shot up. "Of course. What have I been thinking? Everyone's waiting for an update." He grabbed his cell phone off the table and then stood quickly. "Let me get Doris."

I looked at him. "Doris?"

"Yeah. Right now, she's in the waiting room, but she's been coming here every day."

Surely, I hadn't heard him right. "Did you say, *Doris*?"

"Yes, and she's been a great help. She knew Libbybelle wanted to focus on Adam, so I have clean clothes, a toothbrush, and homemade soup thanks to her."

Now, it all made sense. "Well, she's always thought highly of you, Ted. I can see why she'd be here supporting you."

He shook his head. "She's here because she's concerned about *you*."

"Maybe."

"Well, I'll let her know what's going on, but first we need to call home." He dialed the number and then placed the phone in my left hand.

Libbybelle answered after the first ring.

"Mom?"

"Praise the Lord, Janny! It's so good to hear your voice. I've had every prayer warrior within a two-hundred-mile radius praying for you."

I smiled as a vision of Libbybelle doing her "Thank You, Jesus" happy dance popped into my mind.

"Hold on," she said. "Someone needs to talk to you." I heard her call for Adam through the phone's speaker. Seconds later, he was on the phone.

"Mommy?"

He hadn't called me that since he was four years old.

And it was music to my ears.

Chapter Eighteen

"Ted, really, I'm fine."

I eased onto the sofa and set the wicker laundry basket on the floor beside me. My left hand and arm ached. My right hand was still bandaged, and working without it took some getting used to.

"You were just released from the hospital yesterday. You're trying to do too much, too soon. Dr. Horace said your body needs to rest. So please, go upstairs and lie down. I'll fold the laundry." He pulled several of Adam's sweatshirts from the basket.

I took one of the sweatshirts from him. "I spent eight days in the hospital. The last thing I want to do is lie down," I patted the seat next to me and smiled. "But folding laundry is always more fun when you have company." I lifted my right hand. "Besides, I could use your help."

He plopped down next to me. "I just don't want you to overdo it."

"I know." I rolled up a pair of my socks and playfully tossed them at him. "But you've treated me like one of Libbybelle's porcelain doll figurines. I'm not that fragile. I'm tougher than you think." I bent over the basket to grab another pair of socks and winced. "Okay, maybe not that tough, but I promised to ask for help if needed, right?"

"Yes."

"Well ..." I kicked the basket closer to him. "Get to folding."

He laughed. "Sure. But there's one more thing."

"What?"

"Adam's surprise party tomorrow."

"Come on, Ted. We discussed this. It's my fault Adam couldn't have the initial birthday celebration he wanted, so I want tomorrow's surprise party to be special. One he'll never forget."

"You've only given everyone a day to pull this off. It's too ambitious. Dr. Horace said it's important for you to take it easy." He held up his hand before I could protest. "And I know how you are. You'll want to be directly involved in every aspect of it. I'll agree to the party only if you let me, Libbybelle, Doris, and Olivia do most of the work. How does that sound?"

"Can I help hang the decorations?"

"That would be difficult to do with one arm."

"Blow up the balloons?"

"Your lungs are still healing."

"Ted—"

"How about micromanaging everyone so the party goes off without a hitch? You can do that from the comfort of a padded chair."

Oh, that sounded very queen-like and fun.

"Deal." I scooted across the sofa and into his arms. "But no whining when I'm in charge. Got it?"

He laughed softly in my ear. "Got it."

"Enough about me," I straightened to face him. "What about you? How are you doing?"

"What do you mean?"

"You killed a man, Ted." I snuggled closer to him. "I know that's been hard on you, so don't try to deny it."

When he didn't respond, I said, "It's okay if you're not ready to discuss it. I just wanted you to know that I understand."

"Yeah," he sighed. "I've replayed that incident over and over in my mind, trying to figure out if there had been any other way to stop Garringer." He shook his head. "But he was going to kill Adam. There's no longer any doubt in my mind about that. I saw it in his eyes. I just thank God I stopped him before he did."

"Where'd you get the gun?"

"I think it fell out of your purse," he let out a slight chuckle. "So, I guess the real question is, where did *you* get the gun?"

"From Doris. She gave it to me the day I went looking for Garringer. But I dropped it when he slammed me against the rocks at the beach. How did you get it?"

"Adam found your purse, the gun, and a cell phone on the beach when he went looking for you. He dialed the only number programmed on it, and Doris answered. She told him not to touch the gun and to wait there. She then called Sheriff Glass and me and told us the phone Adam had found had a tracking device on it. She got there before we did, but Adam was already gone by then.

"Doris had her own weapon, so I grabbed the one by your purse, and the three of us split up to look for you guys. What slowed us down was that someone messed with your footprints and Adam's, making them hard to follow. Thankfully, I was able to pick up Adam's again and followed them to the cave."

I shuddered. What would Garringer have done to me if Adam hadn't found that phone and Ted hadn't grabbed that gun?

"You know," I said. "I haven't even thanked Doris yet. If it wasn't for the GPS on that phone, you never would've been able to find us."

"Libbybelle and I have thanked her plenty. She says you and Adam are alive and well, and that's all the thanks she needs. She only wishes she could've done something to save Laynee."

I stood and walked into the kitchen. Ted joined me and pulled two coffee mugs out of the cabinet. I leaned against the counter.

"You know," I blinked back tears. "Garringer never really admitted to killing Laynee."

His brow furrowed. "You have doubts?"

"It's just that he never actually confessed to doing it, and that's not like him. He always liked to boast about the evil acts he committed."

"What about the photos you found in the cave?"

"Oh, he definitely stalked our family, but I'm not convinced he killed Laynee."

"Jan—"

"I believe it's just what the M.E. said in the beginning— an accidental drowning."

He stepped toward me. "And if it wasn't?"

"Then Garringer or someone in his crew is an evil psychotic murderer who killed our baby girl in cold blood…" I sucked in a breath and let the tears flow, then added, "And I forgive them."

Ted's head jerked to the left, and he stared at me with slightly parted lips, but no sound came out of them.

Tears streamed down my face. "Ted, God taught me so much during this ordeal." I shook my head. "I didn't want to hunt Garringer down and kill him solely for what happened to Laynee. I wanted him dead for all the things I experienced in the early 1980's. I was never able to completely get him out of my head. I was so consumed with it being all about me that I never considered it being about him."

Ted narrowed his eyes. "About Garringer?"

I nodded. "I had this dream." My heart stopped for a moment, then I said, "At least I hope it was a dream."

I wrapped my arms around me and looked down at the floor. The black and white square tiles blurred together and created an image resembling billowy gray smoke.

"In the dream, Garringer was lost in the darkness, and

he pleaded with me to help him escape it. I didn't. Then, the darkness erupted in flames. He continued begging me for help, and I continued ignoring him. Even though I knew the hounds of hell were about to devour him. And they did. But did I help him? No. I ignored his cries and floated away from the darkness."

Ted placed a hand on my shoulder.

"Don't you see?" I probed Ted's eyes and face. "I could've helped him. If I had been serious about my relationship with God, I could've helped him. Garringer was once an innocent little boy who'd somehow lost his soul. God placed him in my path, and what did I do? Nothing. I never said one prayer for him. Ever. It's my fault things ended up like they did," I sobbed. "I hated him so much, and now he's eternally lost."

"That was a decision Garringer made, Jan. He could've died instantly, but God gave him a chance to redeem his lost soul, and he rejected it with his last breath. His own words condemned him. Not you."

I shook my head. "I should've tried to help him years ago when I had the chance." I lowered my eyes. "And the faith."

He lifted my chin. "You think God wanted you to witness to Garringer when you were fourteen years old and surrounded by Satan worshippers? Or maybe you think He wanted you to share the gospel with Garringer before he burned you alive on his altar?"

"I don't know," I shrugged. "Perhaps."

He kissed my hand. "I think you're doing exactly what you said you didn't want to do, and that's making it about you again. Our God is an awesome God. A merciful God, so rest assured, you were not the only person God put in his path. But in the end, the responsibility of Garringer's salvation—or the lack thereof—depended on him and no one else. God would've welcomed him with open arms. All he had to do was ask. But as he said, he'd made his decision long ago. And it wasn't for God."

I chewed my bottom lip. Could that be true? That, in the end, Garringer's eternal fate had rested solely on him? If so, why did I feel so guilty?

Ted dampened a paper towel and handed it to me. I wiped my face and said, "Regardless, I don't want to live like that anymore. I don't want a phony relationship with Christ. I want a real one. I want to make a difference in the lives of the people He places in my path."

Ted smiled. "That's good because, unlike Garringer, you still have time to make the right decisions. It may be too late for him, but it's not too late for you."

The words *too late* echoed in my head.

He wrapped his arms around my waist. "If you're serious about wanting a real relationship with Christ, then repeat after me."

He prayed, and I repeated the words I'd heard since childhood but never quite believed. Now, the words weren't just coming out of my mouth. They were pouring from my heart.

When we finished praying, he said, "On behalf of our Father, I'd like to say, welcome *back* to the family."

I smiled. "It feels good to be back, but there's something else I'd like to talk about too."

"Okay, what?"

"Our marriage."

He frowned. "What about it?"

"Do you remember the things I confessed to you when I woke up in the hospital?"

"You mean the conversation about secrets and burying God under the mimosa trees? Yeah, I remember."

"I lied to you for a long time," I reached down and pulled an invisible piece of lint off my paisley pajama pants. "I guess I just need to hear from you that we're still going to be okay."

No response.

I looked up, and a faint smile played on his lips.

I blinked at him. "Are you trying to figure out a nice way to say you're divorcing me?"

"What? No. Never."

"Then what's going on? I know how much you hate being lied to."

He rubbed his chin. "I do hate it, but it also hurt hearing how you suffered silently for so long. That's not the type of marriage I thought we shared. And I was upset that you never came to me so we could talk about those things." He let out a shaky breath. "Then I realized the ugly truth. I never allowed myself to think about it, but I knew you struggled with your faith. When Laynee died, I was forced to think about it because you talked about it often. I chalked it up to grief, but deep down, I knew it was more than that. My inaction almost caused me to lose you twice. Once, by your own hands when you drove up to Jacob's Peak to speed off of it, and the other by Garringer's. I won't risk losing you again, but we need to make some changes.

"You've been unhappy for a long time, Jan, even before Laynee's death. But now that you've decided to walk *with* God and not in the other direction, the three of us can work through those changes. I was smiling because I felt like we were getting a second chance. However, there'll be no more lies and no more secrets this time."

I smiled. "I love you, and thank you for the second chance."

"We're both getting second chances. We can make this work as long as we're honest with ourselves and each other."

"I'll be up front and honest, I promise."

"And so will I." He cleared his throat. "But there is something I'm confused about. What did you mean when you said you buried God under the mimosa trees?"

"You mean God's funeral?" I laughed at the futility of such an attempt. "Next time we're in the yard, I'll show you."

He smiled and pulled me towards him. The feeling of his heart beating next to mine provided a warmth that I'd long forgotten. He kissed me, and heat flooded my body, which ignited a passion that set both our bodies on fire.

He scooped me up and headed toward the stairs.

I knew what he had on his mind.

And every bone in my body, including the broken ones, trembled with anticipation.

Chapter Nineteen

"Doris, that's not what I'm saying."

I grabbed the leftover plates and plastic cups from Adam's party with my only usable hand and tossed them into the large trash bag she held.

"I know exactly what you're saying. You're saying that watching Garringer die has made you feel pity for him and his soul. But you wanna know what I say? Good riddance. I'm glad Ted put a hole the size of Texas in his chest. If it were me, I would've added a couple more just for fun."

"You don't mean that."

She stared at me with steely gray eyes. Okay. She did mean that.

Libbybelle waltzed into the kitchen. "Ladies, I'll clean up the rest of this mess later. Right now, I want everyone to join me in the living room. Janny, I have a surprise for you."

"A surprise for me? What for? It wasn't my surprise party, it was Adam's."

"Good grief, I know that." She gently pushed me toward the living room sofa. "Sit here."

"Are you going to tell me what's going on?"

She pointed to the sofa. "Sit. Trust me, when you see who's on the other side of that door, you're gonna be glad you were sitting."

I plopped down and looked nervously at the front door.

Olivia, Doris, and Miss Flora, the elderly onyx-skinned woman whose powerful prayers had caused Ruin to screech and flee Olivia's house, joined us in the living room and stood behind the sofa. Ted rushed in from the garage. He was smiling. I had a sneaking suspicion that he was in on this, too.

Libbybelle walked to the door. "Ready?"

I had no idea if I was ready. I chewed my bottom lip and nodded at Libbybelle.

The door opened.

Three women stood behind it. An elderly one, a middle-aged one, and a younger one that looked to be in her thirties.

But it was the one in the middle that caused my heart to skip.

It couldn't be!

She stepped into the foyer. I stood and slowly walked toward her. With every step, I prayed to God that my eyes weren't deceiving me.

"Molly?"

She placed a well-manicured hand over her mouth and nodded. Tears flowed from her unmistakable caramel-brown eyes. "I go by Marjorie now. But yes, Jan. It's me, Molly."

I shook my head. "But it can't be. I saw the house on fire. I heard the screams. I watched it explode …"

She stepped closer. "Gingie and I made it out before the explosion. Barely, but we made it. I escaped with a few minor injuries, but Gingie suffered serious burns to her legs. However, Gingie's alive and well. She relocated to the West Coast for a few years but has been back in Missouri for at least fifteen years."

I swallowed. "My aunt's alive?"

Molly nodded. "And she's married, too. She also teaches religious studies to high schoolers at a private school not too far from here, if you can believe it."

I ran and hugged her so tight that I was sure I'd squeezed every available breath from her body. This whole time, I was sure she and Aunt Gingie had died in that fire along with Garringer. I was wrong on both accounts.

We held each other and rocked back and forth like we did when we greeted each other as teens. That's when I looked closer at the elderly woman standing behind her, wiping her eyes.

I sucked in a breath and pulled away from Molly. "Mrs. Gibbon's, is that you?"

The elderly woman nodded. We'd kept in touch over the phone for years, but this was the first time I'd seen her in over three decades. I let out a soft cry and folded into her arms. They were just as warm and loving as I'd remembered them.

Molly put her hand on my shoulder. "And this …" She pulled the young lady standing behind her to her side. "… is my daughter, Leah."

Leah had long dark hair and beautiful green eyes.

Familiar green eyes.

"Molly, her eyes. They remind me of—"

"I know," Molly said. "They remind you of Garringer. And they should. He was her father."

A loud gasp erupted behind me. I turned. Doris stormed into the kitchen and mumbled something about getting her purse.

I looked back at Molly. "I … I don't understand."

"Garringer killed my mother because she found out I was pregnant by him. She then arranged for me to live with my grandparents in New York. Gingie helped my mom find a hiding place for me until they could figure out a way to get me out of Corinth safely.

"When Garringer couldn't find me, he went ballistic and demanded answers from Gingie and my mom. Gingie was furious that I'd let myself become pregnant—she and my mom had given me something to prevent that, but it made me sick, so I quit taking it. Nevertheless, neither of them told him anything. One of his men beat up Gingie, but when my mom continued to refuse to tell him where they'd hidden me, he killed her." Molly looked over at her daughter. "Leah has never met her father. And trust me, she's nothing like him."

She didn't have to tell me that. Although Leah was a younger and much prettier version of her father, there was a peacefulness about her. The kind that made you want to reach out and embrace her.

Libbybelle handed out tissues. "No need to figure all of this out right here in the foyer." She ushered everyone into the living room. "There's a lot for you ladies to get caught up on. Have a seat, and I'll start the kettle for tea. Olivia and Flora," she motioned toward the kitchen and continued, "Let's give them some privacy. Ted, you too."

Doris bustled from the kitchen, clutching her purse. She walked up behind me and whispered, "Don't think for a minute that girl's not here to seek revenge for her father. Don't be fooled by that pretty face. I'll be in that chair by the window, with my best friend loaded and ready in my purse. Just say the word, and I'll blow Garringer's mini-me back into the pit she came from."

"Doris, that's not what's going on here."

She shook her head at me and sat in the chair, still clutching her purse. Doris may have had her doubts, but I didn't. My gut told me that Leah was just as Molly said. Nothing like her father.

Then it hit me.

Back in the cave, he thought I knew.

"Molly, did Garringer know you were still alive?"

"I'm not sure. The night I set him on fire was the last time I saw him. Immediately after that, Gingie and I ran out of the house. We both thought he died in the explosion. It wasn't until Mrs. Gibbons contacted me and told me what happened to you that I realized he'd somehow survived." She placed a hand on her daughter's shoulder. "Leah attended Kingdom University, a Christian college about two hundred miles from here. Her research paper was on spiritual warfare, so she traveled several times to Corinth and interviewed a few of the older cult members. Those who remembered Garringer also thought he died that night. Even Leah's older half-brother, Liam."

I blinked. "Garringer has other children?"

"Yes," Leah answered. "Five of them and they all still live in Corinth. Their mothers, like my mom, were abused by him at a young age."

I scratched my forehead. "When Garringer and I were in the cave, he demanded that I tell him where you were. Of course, I had no idea you were even still alive. So, I guess he was looking for you and Leah."

Libbybelle walked in and placed a plate of freshly baked scones on the table. Olivia followed, carrying a tray with a teapot, teacups, and saucers. After filling them, she and Libbybelle disappeared back into the kitchen.

Molly took a sip of her tea. "Only a handful of people knew I was pregnant and had managed to escape that night. We knew Garringer would go on a rampage when he couldn't find me, so I took the small phonebook you'd hidden in your bedroom dresser at Gingie's. I didn't want Garringer to find it.

"After the explosion, Gingie and I knew we had to separate. I hitchhiked my way out of town and found a payphone. I called the number you had highlighted in the book, Mrs. Gibbons. I told her what happened, and she picked me up that night. We drove around for hours looking for you. She filed a missing persons report with the Corinth police, but of course, they never contacted her. I was able to stay with her for a couple of days until my grandparents came for me. Besides Gingie, Mrs. Gibbons, and my immediate family, no one else knew I survived."

Mrs. Gibbons chimed in. "Except for that time when Leah returned to Corinth for her research paper. Didn't you tell Liam that you were his sister?"

Leah nodded. "That's right. I'd forgotten about that.

Liam's a nice guy, and we still keep in touch. I didn't see any harm in telling him, since everyone thought Garringer was dead."

I took a deep breath and tried to process all the information thrown at me. Then, another realization hit. I looked at Mrs. Gibbons. "So, this whole time, you knew Molly and my aunt were alive, and you didn't tell me?"

She nodded. "Gingie said it would be safer for you that way. She also told me how deep that town's corruption and cultic activity was. They lost a lot of people that night, and she feared that when her and Molly's bodies weren't found in the rubble, they'd come looking for all of you. She said the less you knew, the better off you'd be."

"How did she even know I'd made it out of town alive?"

"She's known for quite some time. Ever since Libbybelle and Papa George legally adopted you. She never shared how she'd found that out, but she knew you were safe and in good hands. She even caught a glimpse of you working at their diner once. Of course, she snuck away before you could see her. Her concern was always for your safety."

I closed my eyes to try to stop the spinning in my head.

For years, I'd blamed God for what I thought I'd lost. And the whole time, besides my parents, I hadn't lost anything.

"Jan," Doris said. "Who are these creeps standing outside and staring at your house?"

I stood and headed for the window and almost ran into Olivia, who came from the kitchen with a fruit bowl. She followed our gazes and looked out the window. "What's going on?"

A group of young people dressed in black cloaks stood on the road in front of our house. In front of the group were two older-looking adults, one male and one female, also dressed in black.

Olivia stepped closer to the window. "I don't know the

younger ones in the back, but I definitely recognize the two in the front. They were at my house when Anna had her movie night. She called them Whisper and Thwart."

"Okay," I said. "But what are they doing *here*?"

Molly and Leah joined us at the window.

"It's Liam!" Leah said with glee and pointed to the older male in the front.

I turned to her. "Who?"

"Liam. My brother."

Olivia shook her head. "No, I definitely remember that face and the name. Anna called him Thwart."

"Well, maybe that's the name he goes by here, but I'm telling you, that's my brother." She moved towards the door, but Molly grabbed her arm. "Where are you going?"

"To say hello to my brother."

Molly tightened her grip. "Absolutely not. He's probably here because of what happened to his dad. If Garringer was looking for me, he was also looking for you. He knew about my pregnancy. Every doctor in Corinth answered to him. And no doubt that Liam, Thwart, or whatever his name is, told his dad that he'd talked with you in Corinth. So his being here is not a good thing."

"Jan, maybe we should call the police." Olivia pulled out her cell phone.

Doris shot out of her chair and tried to grab the phone out of Olivia's hand. When Olivia refused to give it to her, Doris said, "Who needs the police?" She patted her purse. "I have everything we need right here to shatter those vermin to smithereens."

"Ted!" I shouted. I needed him to intervene before Doris took the situation into her own hands.

He and Libbybelle ran in from the kitchen. "What's wrong?"

I pointed out the window.

He shook his head. "I don't get it. It's just a group of kids."

"The older one in front," I pointed out the window again. "Is Liam. Garringer's son."

"What does he want?"

"I don't know. They're just standing there staring at the house."

"I called the police," Olivia said. "They're on their way." Doris rolled her eyes.

Ted shook his head once more. "I don't get it. Why call the police on a couple of young people? The worst that can be said is that they're trespassing. I'll go talk to them."

"Ted, wait." I looked at Leah. "The girl standing next to your brother. Do you recognize her?"

"No. I've never seen her before." She reached into her jeans pocket and pulled out a cell phone. "Hold on, I just got a text from Liam."

"Let me see it," Molly said.

Leah handed the phone to her, and Molly's face went pale. "It says, 'Leah, I know you're in there.' What does he mean by that?"

Leah asked for her phone back. "I don't know, Mom, but I can call him and find out."

"That's not a good idea."

"Mom, he already knows I'm here. Besides, I want to know why he's acting so weird." She looked at Ted and me. "I'm telling you, he's not this Thwart you guys are talking about or some freak. Liam's not like that." She dialed a number and then activated the speaker. It was answered after the first ring.

"Liam, what's going on?" Leah asked. "You're frightening these people."

"Leave this town, now." A deep, gravelly voice responded.

Leah's head jerked back, and her stance stiffened. "I don't understand. Why do you want me to leave? I just got here."

"Because when I bring the powers of perdition down on

this abysmal city, I don't want you in it. They're going to pay for what they did to our father."

I wrapped my arms around my stomach and closed my eyes.

I should've known better. This wasn't over. Not by a long shot.

I opened my eyes and stared into the faces of Liam and the mysterious young woman standing next to him and reminded myself that God was in control. This time, I wasn't going to respond with anger or fear. I grabbed Ted's hand. I was going to respond with faith.

"There's more," Liam's voice thundered through the speaker.

Leah placed a trembling hand over her chest. "And what's that?"

A chorus of sinister voices reverberated through the phone. And they all said the same thing.

"Pastor Ted must die!"

Chapter Twenty

I opened the mailbox and froze.

I placed the happy anniversary card, the one I'd planned on mailing to Ted's parents, under my arm. I then reached for the note that someone had already stuffed in our mailbox and opened it.

Pastor Ted will die.

The crude black and white letters had been pasted onto thick, blood-red colored paper. I leaned against the mailbox to steady my body and my heart. I sucked in a deep breath. Two sentences were pasted on the paper, and I'd only read one. I looked at it again.

Pastor Ted will die.

In 40 days, before the noon hour.

I stepped away from the mailbox. First, a verbal threat, and now a written one?

It had been several days since we'd last seen or heard from them, but there was no doubt in my mind that Garringer's son and his group were responsible for the note.

I glanced around the neighborhood. The sun had just risen, and everything was still quiet. Colorful leaf-covered yards were all I saw.

I looked at the note again. The note had to have been placed in our mailbox while we were sleeping. Ted and I had grabbed yesterday's mail when we returned from the grocery store last night. The grisly note wasn't in there then.

They wanted to kill my husband.

I closed my eyes. Sheriff Glass had taken statements from everyone still at the house after Adam's party. Leah told him everything she knew about her brother, Liam. He then accessed Liam's arrest record, which was a mile long, and several warrants were out for his arrest in Ohio, Kansas, and Oklahoma.

He was indeed following in his father's footsteps.

I closed the mailbox and engaged the steel latch before looking around the subdivision again. In another hour or so, the neighborhood will be full of activity. Joggers, school buses, dog walkers. But for now, the subdivision slept. Or at least it appeared to, because I couldn't shake the feeling that I was being watched.

I walked back to the house and placed my hand on the doorknob. Wait a minute. It rained last night. I put the anniversary card on top of the note and returned to the mailbox.

Two huge footprints, too large to be Adam's and too narrow to be Ted's, were pressed into the mud surrounding the mailbox. Several more muddied prints had crushed the mums Libbybelle had planted along the driveway. The prints continued toward the house.

I ran back to the house and put the note and the card for Ted's parents on the foyer table. I grabbed my cell phone from where I'd left it on the sofa and ran back outside to the footprints. We were expected to get more rain this morning, and there was a chance the prints could get washed away.

I tapped the camera icon on my phone and took several pictures. Water droplets dotted my phone. I looked up. Smoke-gray clouds had already filled the sky. I snapped a few more before returning to the house and double-checking the locks on all the doors.

"Jan?"

I jumped and placed my left hand over my chest.

"Molly, you scared me."

She descended the stairs and grabbed my hand. "Are you all right? You look pale."

"Yeah, I'm fine. No, I'm not. Not really. I mean, I am … sort of." I shook my head and walked to the kitchen counter. "Molly, I have no idea what I'm talking about right now. Would you like some breakfast?"

She smiled. "Same old Jan. So easily rattled." She pulled a chair out from the table. "No breakfast, thank you. Just coffee. Then pour yourself a cup and come sit next to me. Tell me what's going on." She sat in the chair. Confident brown eyes stared back at me.

If I were the same old Jan, she would definitely be the same old Molly. Always calm under pressure. Images from our time at Aunt Gingie's flashed before me. Whether it was the two of us being tossed around the room by Ruin, glares from Aunt Gingie, or threats from Garringer, Molly always remained stoic. I was always the one who flipped out.

Molly and Leah had decided to stay at our place for the past few days. However, Leah was flying back to her job as a worship leader in Georgia later this morning. Molly vowed not to leave my side until the matter with Garringer's son was dealt with.

I smiled. Same old Molly was right.

She pulled out the chair next to her. "Sit."

"I will, but I want to show you something first."

I grabbed the cryptic note from the foyer table and sat beside her. I handed her the note.

She read it and glanced at the calendar on the kitchen wall. "Forty days from now. Is that an important date or something?"

I scooted from the table, walked to the calendar, and counted out forty days. Then I counted again. What kind of sick games were these kids playing?

Molly's voice pulled me from my trance. "Did you count it out?"

I nodded. "In forty days, it'll be Christmas."

"As in, the actual Christmas Day?"

I returned to my chair. "Yes."

She looked at the note again. "So, according to this, they're planning to kill Ted by noon on Christmas day. Have you called Dan?"

I jerked back in my chair. "Dan?"

She tilted her head. "Yes. Dan. Dan Glass."

"You mean *Sheriff* Glass, Ted's friend?"

"Well, he thinks of you as his friend, too. However, he explained why you've been acting icy toward him. He withheld important information about Laynee's case from you and Ted, so I get why you're angry with him."

I knew Molly and the sheriff had spent a lot of time together the past couple of days. Still, I had no idea they'd gotten to know each other well enough to be on a first-name basis. I definitely didn't think they'd gotten close enough to have conversations about me.

"Jan, did I do something wrong?"

"No. When the two of you spent time together on his day off, I suspected there might've been a spark between the two of you, but it all seems to have happened so fast. I'm a little shocked, is all. Especially that I came up in the conversation."

She leaned back in her chair. "When we were having coffee the other day, I asked him why every time you looked at him, you had fire in your eyes."

I chuckled. "According to my husband, that's because I'm harboring unforgiveness toward the sheriff." I winced. Ted also pointed out how I distanced myself from my prior friendship with Dan by now referring to him as *Sheriff* instead of Dan, which was probably a sign that he was right about the unforgiveness part. I needed to fix that. Otherwise, how would I ever be able to move forward?

I cleared my throat. "I said Sheriff, but I meant Dan. Now that I think about it, how is it possible that I can forgive

Garringer for everything he did but not forgive Dan?"

"Maybe because Dan was a friend," Molly said. "With your enemies, you expect the worst, but with friends, you expect more."

I nodded. "Deep down, I really do believe he thought he was helping us, but the part I'm struggling with is that I can't help thinking that everything Adam went through at the hands of Garringer could've been avoided if he'd just told us what he knew."

Tears filled my eyes. Molly clasped my hands. "I'm sorry you're having to go through this, Jan."

I wiped at the tears. "Scenes from that day still haunt me, and I know they haunt Adam too, though he'll never admit it. I thank God every day that he's safe and thriving at Libbybelle's and is not giving us a hard time about staying at her place until this Liam mess is dealt with. But Ted's right. When it comes to Dan, it's just plain unforgiveness. I'm working on it. I really am. And I thought I was doing a good job until you mentioned my icy acts and fiery stares toward him."

She laughed. "Well, I knew something was wrong. Which is why I told him I can't see him again."

"What do you mean?"

"Not in regards to helping with the investigation into Liam, but in a personal way. You were right when you said there had been sparks between us."

"So now you're not going to pursue that?"

"Jan—"

"No, Molly, wait. I've known Daniel Glass for over ten years, and Ted has known him longer than that. The whole reason we moved and started a church here is because of Dan's family. His dad and Ted's dad are good friends, and that's how we knew about the need for a new pastor in this area. Dan's a good guy. He made a bad call regarding Laynee's case, and I'll probably have issues with that for a while. But that's something God's dealing with me about, so it'll be impossible for me to stay mad at him forever."

She let out a small laugh.

"Molly, listen." I placed my hand over my heart. "From the deepest parts of me, I want you to know that I don't have any problem with you continuing to see him. In fact, I highly encourage you, too."

"Well," she leaned forward and placed the foreboding note on the table. "I'll see him again whether I want to or not." She reached into the pocket of her thick pink robe and pulled out her cell phone. "Call him. He needs to know this was placed in your mailbox."

I stared at the phone but didn't take it. "Not yet. I can't tell Dan about the note before I tell Ted, and he's still asleep."

Molly blinked and looked at me as if I had two huge antennae sticking out the side of my head. "Jan, you have to wake him. He needs to know what's going on."

I pushed away from the table and walked to the kitchen window. I stared at the rivulets of rain streaming down it. "There were also footprints leading from the mailbox to Ted's office window. Heavy drapes are closed over it, so no one could've seen inside, and the house alarm would've gone off if anyone had tried to open it, but still …"

Molly sidled up next to me. "Jan, the rain's gonna wash those footprints away."

"I took photos. I'm not going to wake Ted. He'll be down for breakfast in a little while anyway. I'll show him the note after that. Then he can be the one to call Dan."

"The longer we wait, the harder it's going to be—"

"I'm not going to wake him up, Molls."

This time, the look she gave me told me she thought I'd completely lost my mind.

"Molly, you don't understand. Ted's been through a lot in the past couple of months. First, he had to deal with my fragile mental state after Laynee's death. Then he had to search for me and Adam, resulting in him having to kill a man. Then, after sitting by my hospital bed for weeks, he now has that man's son threatening his life. He deserves to sleep peacefully. I'm not going to disturb him."

She pulled me into a big hug. "If you say Ted needs his rest, then so be it. But I can't help hoping he wakes up soon. We need to act quickly."

"The last time I rushed into things, it ended badly. What I need to do right now is pray and keep my emotions together. I don't want to rush into things again and put someone else's life in danger or do something stupid."

"Seeking justice for your daughter was not stupid," she breathed out. "But I understand about not wanting to go off half-cocked. Would you like for me to pray with you?"

"No. I'll just grab my Bible from the office and read it at the kitchen table until Ted wakes up." The automatic coffee pot beeped, and I lifted the carafe. "But I'd love to share a cup of coffee together before I start."

She looked at her watch. "It's after six, and Leah's flight is at eight. If she isn't up already, I need to remind her that we need to leave soon. But if you'd like me to stay, I can tell her to drive my car to the airport, and I'll pick it up later."

I pulled two stainless steel thermoses from the cabinet and filled them with the freshly brewed, dark Colombian liquid. "No, enjoy this time with your daughter." I handed her the thermoses. "And take these for you and Leah. By the time you get back, Ted and I will have talked, and Dan and some of his officers will still be here. I'll definitely appreciate having a friend here then."

She gave me another hug and ran up the stairs with the steaming hot mugs. "I'll be back before you know it."

I leaned against the counter, sucked in a deep breath, and said, *"Lord, give us wisdom on how to deal with this new threat. Guide us, Father."*

I turned to replace the carafe when a knock at the patio door startled me. A hooded figure dressed in all black stared at me through the glass.

I froze.

"What are you gaping at? Open the blasted door."

The hood shifted, and strands of flaming red hair darted out like lightning strikes.

"Doris," I slid the sliding door open. "What in heaven's name—?"

"Listen," she dashed in and was about to lock the door when Molly and Leah bustled down the stairs.

"Good morning, Doris. How are you?" Leah's cheerful greeting was met with a grunt from the hooded Doris. Molly ignored her and led Leah by the arm toward the foyer.

"Leah, wait." I sidestepped her wheeled suitcase and hugged and kissed her on the cheek. "We've enjoyed your stay here. I can't believe it's time for you to leave already. We're going to miss you."

She returned my hug and smiled. "If it wasn't for the Christmas musical rehearsals at my church, I wouldn't be leaving now. However, several e-mails from the drama ministry director reminded me that the worship leader really needs to be there. And auditioning soloists virtually was not as easy as I'd thought it'd be." She tightened the grip on her luggage handle. "Let me know if anything new comes up with Liam. I'd still like to help. I'll even fly back if I have to if that's okay with you."

"You're welcome here anytime, whether the investigation is ongoing or not. Like I said, we enjoy having you here.

A gagging sound came from the red-headed, hooded figure standing in the kitchen.

Leah looked over my shoulder and waved. "Bye, Doris."

Silence.

I touched Molly's arm. "The airport is over an hour away. You guys should probably get going." Molly glared at Doris. I knew she only held her tongue out of respect for me and Ted. She'd mentioned more than once that she had fantasies about punching Doris in the throat.

I walked her and Leah to the front porch and stayed until they pulled out of the driveway. Afterward, I stormed into the kitchen.

"Doris, that is the last time you'll treat one of my guests that way."

"Uh-huh," she pulled out a chair. "Sit. I got something to show you."

That's when I noticed the Lucille Ball tote bag she was holding at her side. I also noticed she had on a pair of black jeans. She never wore jeans, and she never wore black. But today, from the hoodie that covered most of her face to the tennis shoes on her feet, she was wearing it.

I sat as she rummaged through the now all too familiar bag. A minute later, she pulled out a black smartphone, swiped at the large screen, then slid it across the table in my direction.

"There."

I picked up the phone. The screen displayed a map of Habakkuk's streets and highways. A red dot blinked non-stop on the screen on one of the main streets about five miles north of us.

"What's this?"

"The location of Twerp."

"Who?"

"The chump who threatened Pastor Ted."

"Oh, you mean Thwart." I looked at the screen again. "I don't get it. What does this have to do with him?"

"That's where he's located. Or at least where his car is located."

I shook my head, still not sure what she was getting at.

"That's Twerp's car," she huffed and pointed to the phone. "The red dot is telling us where it's located."

I narrowed my eyes. "And you know this how?"

"Because I'm the one that put it on his car."

"Put what on his car?"

"The tracking device."

I straightened. "The what?"

"Why are you looking so shocked? I told you before that I know people, who know people, who know people. And the people I know knew some people who knew how to hook me up with a tracker."

Did she just say "hook me up"?

"And they also told me where to find him. So this morning, while it was still dark, I jogged over to the address they gave me, which was about five miles from here. I didn't drive in case someone spotted me and called in the plate number. I also didn't want to walk the streets dressed like a criminal, so I cut through the woods."

My brows shot up.

She continued. "The woods led me to the tree line across the street from the address they gave me. Twerp was standing outside the car with a girl and two guys. All dressed in those long black coats. After a few minutes, they went inside, but the girl kept coming back out, carrying weapons and duffel bags and putting them in the trunk. On one of her trips to the house, I slid under the car, stuck the device on the metal frame, and rolled back out. Then I came here."

I shook my head. Who was this woman? "Doris, you could've been killed!"

She blinked. "Or not. I'm here, aren't I?"

I scooted from the table and paced the kitchen floor, trying to digest everything she said. "So basically, you're telling me you know where Thwart is?"

She grunted. "I told you I was just there, didn't I?"

I glanced at the clock on the wall. The smart thing to do would be to wake up Ted, fill him in on the note, the footprints, Thwart's location, and call Dan.

But a lot of what Doris said didn't make sense. I turned to her. "If you knew where Thwart was, why didn't you just call the police?"

"For what?"

"To arrest him. He's wanted in three states. And if he's

in jail, he can't harm Ted."

"Arresting him won't stop them from killing Ted."

I stopped pacing and stood in front of her. "What do you mean?"

"His people, his cult, his crew, or whatever they call themselves. The people I know told me there are some really bad dudes in that group. The worst kind of bad. Cruel and evil. And that girl he's always with? Whisper? From what I hear, she's the worst one of them all."

Chapter Twenty-One

Doris blackmailed me.

She threatened to keep the device and Thwart's whereabouts from me and the police if I told them she'd put the device under his car.

According to her, Sheriff Glass couldn't tell his head from a hole in the ground. And that if he was any good, he would've found Thwart's car before she did.

Crime in our area had decreased since Dan became sheriff, so he wasn't bad at his job. However, perhaps he needed to befriend some of Doris's shady sources.

When she left, I woke Ted and filled him in on everything, including Doris' tracking device. He immediately called Dan.

When he arrived, neither of us told Dan about Doris. We just showed him the note and the pictures of the footprints on my phone. He took my cell and stepped outside to talk with one of his deputies.

Now that we were alone, Ted asked, "Why did Doris place the device on Thwart's car if she didn't want the authorities involved? What was the point?"

I bit my lip, hesitant to reveal the rest of the details of Doris's outrageous plan. There was no guarantee Ted wouldn't change his mind and tell the police. She'd successfully blackmailed me into silence, but Ted was a different story.

"She said if we tell the police about the device, they'll use it to locate and arrest Thwart, throw him in jail, and forget about the threat to our family. According to her sources, that won't stop his group from following through on his threat to kill you. Her sources also told her that Thwart's crew is involved in various criminal activities. Her plan is to tail them for a couple of days, uncover the illegal activities they're a part of, and then call the cops when she has them dead to rights."

"Dead to rights?"

"Those were her words, not mine."

He nodded. "So her plan involves sending them all to jail, not just one."

"To completely eliminate the threat, yes."

He retrieved his jacket from the foyer closet. "Where is she now?"

I shook my head. "I don't know. The church office, I guess." Ted had been so impressed with how Doris managed things at the church while he sat with me in the hospital that he'd hired her as his assistant.

I followed him to the door. "Where are you going? You're not going to tell Dan, are you?"

"No. I'm going to the office to talk Doris out of tailing Liam. If she won't listen, then I'll tell the police."

"Ted, you know how hard it is to talk Doris out of something when her mind is made up. She'll figure out a way to do it one way or the other."

"Then she'll have to figure out how to do it from a jail cell. Because I'll have her arrested before I see her get hurt."

"Arrested?"

"What she did was illegal."

"Ted, she did that to protect you. You can't have Doris arrested. You just can't." I stepped backward. Did those words just come out of my mouth?

He grabbed my hands and gently rubbed them with his

thumb. "I can't have Doris getting mixed up in this and putting her life in danger. And I definitely can't have her doing that for me."

The door opened. Molly, the sheriff, and one of his deputies stepped inside. Molly patted Dan on the arm and then stood next to me.

"Did Leah make it to the airport on time?" I asked.

She nodded. "Barely, but yes, we made it."

"I'm glad."

"Dan," Ted turned to the sheriff. "Did you find anything?"

"We looked for fingerprints around your office window, but the rain washed most of those away along with everything else at the scene." He grabbed a clear bag from the officer behind him. On the inside was the note I had found in the mailbox. "This is our best lead right here. However, in my experience, when people cut out letters and paste them together in a note like this, there's very little DNA because they likely wore gloves. But the state lab will be able to track down what type of glue was used, where the paper was sold, and even what type of fibers or latex the gloves were made of," he handed the bag back to his deputy.

I rubbed the back of my neck and blew out a few short breaths. The muscles in my chest tightened, and the room whirled around me in varying shades of gray.

Ted grabbed my arm. "Jan, are you all right?"

I shook my head. Dan grabbed my other arm, and they led me to the sofa in the living room. Ted lifted my feet so I could lie down, and Dan placed a decorative pillow under my head. He then asked Molly to bring me a glass of water.

She nodded and then disappeared into the kitchen.

"Honey," Ted brushed the hair off my face and tenderly placed it behind my ear. "What happened?"

"I got a little lightheaded for a second," I leaned forward on my elbows. "I think I'm okay now."

Ted eased my head back onto the pillow. "No, you're

not. Your body has been through a lot, and you've only been out of the hospital for a couple of weeks. Remember what Dr. Horace said at your last check-up? Just because you're home doesn't mean you've healed."

Molly returned and handed Ted a glass of water. He lifted my head, and I took a few sips but put my hand up when he tried to give me more. "I just needed to catch my breath for a bit. It's been a crazy morning."

"And I'm afraid it's about to get even crazier," Dan's gaze left me and traveled to Ted. He motioned for Ted to follow him into the other room.

I grabbed Ted's arm. "No. I'm fine now. Whatever it is, I can handle it." When I laid back down, he nodded to Dan. Molly turned to leave.

"Molly, don't go," I patted the plush arm of the sofa by my head. She sat and waited for Dan to begin.

Dan sat on the edge of the recliner across from the sofa. He dismissed his deputy and then lowered the volume on his police radio. "We have additional information on Liam," he pulled a notebook from the inside of his jacket. "In Kansas, he's wanted for questioning. He's a person of interest in a murder case."

Molly grunted and reached for my hand. I grabbed it and held on tight.

Dan's eyes left the notebook and looked at Ted. "The victim was a 48-year-old male whom Liam publicly threatened to kill. Five days later, he was dead."

Ted closed his eyes.

Dan continued. "There's no evidence directly linking him to the murder, but there is motive. Witnesses say Liam accused the man of killing his brother." He closed the notebook. "Garringer left behind several kids, especially in Corinth. It appears everyone in the Legion Tribe—the name the members refer to the group by—is related. The detectives in Corinth haven't confirmed they're *all* half-brothers and sisters. Still, they have confirmed a significant number of them are. Liam isn't the oldest, but he's the one in charge. Declan was the name of the brother who was killed, but the tribe called him Havoc."

Ted nodded. "Just like they call Liam, Thwart."

"And my aunt, they called Gingie and Molly's mother, Quiggy." I straightened and gave Ted a reassuring nod that I was okay. "The difference is that Legion's names sound sinister." I turned to Molly. "Did Aunt Gingie ever mention anything to you about Legion?"

She shook her head. "But remember, we cut all ties to that town. She also doesn't go by the name Gingie anymore. She didn't want anyone to be able to locate us. That's why I've been going by the name Marjorie. I had it legally changed years ago. Gingie legally changed hers, too."

Dan looked at me and said, "Your aunt's the one who introduced you to those crazies, right?"

Molly shot up from her perch on the sofa. "Hey!"

Dan furrowed his brow and stood. "Molly, I wasn't saying that you were crazy."

She lifted her chin like she was about to speak but ran upstairs instead. A moment later, the door to the guest room slammed shut.

Dan turned to Ted and me. "That's not what I meant."

I held on to Ted's shoulder and stood slowly. "Not everyone in that town was crazy, Dan. And not everyone was there by choice. Molly was one of them. And her mother died protecting her. She's mad because you referred to her mother as being crazy."

"I should go apologize." He walked to the stairs and took a few steps before shaking his head and coming back down. "I need to get going. The state lab is expecting that evidence." He raked thick fingers through dark, short-cropped hair that seemed to have more silver in it every time I saw him.

"Ted," he sighed. "There's also that other matter we need to deal with. The deadline of December twenty-fifth."

"Do you think he means it?" Ted asked.

"Hard to tell." He reached into his pocket and pulled out his cell phone. "I received a message from Detective Cheatham this morning saying there was no evidence of a note sent to the other victim."

I blinked. "Detective Cheatham?"

"Yeah, Bruce Cheatham. He's an old friend of mine and a retired Corinth homicide detective. He's helping me track down Liam. You know him?"

The name was familiar, but I couldn't place it.

Dan continued. "But just because there wasn't a note in that case doesn't mean we shouldn't take the one left in your mailbox seriously. However, we're a small-town police force. We don't have the money or the resources to provide you and your family with twenty-four-hour protection over the next forty days." Dan turned the volume on his radio back up. "Have you guys thought about leaving town until this is over?"

Ted folded his arms across his chest. "I'm not letting them run me out of my home."

Dan mimicked Ted's stance. "Okay, if I were you, I'd turn this home into a fortress."

Ted cleared his throat. Dan looked at him, his brows raised, and his eyes flicked. Then he nodded. I spun around to face Ted, but he'd already made his way to the front door.

He wasn't about to get off that easy. "Ted, what was that look about?"

Before he could answer, Dan placed his hand on my arm. "An officer will stay with you and Molly until Ted returns."

"Where is he going?"

"I'll be back soon, I promise." Ted opened the door, and they stepped onto the porch. I wrapped my arms around me. The fall rain had brought an icy chill with it.

Dan zipped up his jacket. "I'll take Ted where he needs to go. None of you should go anywhere alone. I also suggest checking in with family members every hour on the hour. And I don't mean by text message. Anyone can pretend to be a loved one via text. Call and verify you're actually talking to them. If someone doesn't respond within five minutes, call me immediately."

I nodded.

Dan continued. "Whether Thwart's playing mind games with the Christmas deadline isn't important. What's important is that we make it impossible for him to harm you." He stepped off the porch and walked to the police cruiser in the driveway. He opened the passenger door and motioned to Ted. "Ready?"

Ted gave me a quick kiss on the lips, then jogged to the car. I watched until it disappeared down the gray, misty street.

I looked at the sky. Dark clouds formed on the horizon. The longer I watched, the closer they got.

~

"It's all my fault, Jan."

Molly plopped down on the quilt-covered bed in our guest room. I smiled as I watched a bubble gum pink polished nail trace the mauve-colored patterns of the quilt. Bubble gum pink was our favorite color when we were fourteen. The bright color was far from being in style now, so I knew she'd worn it here just for me.

I joined her on the bed and grasped her hands. "It's okay, Molly. It was Dan's fault for upsetting you."

She squinted at the patchwork quilt as if a hidden mystery existed in the geometric pattern.

"Molly, there's something else going on with you. What is it?"

She shook her head. "It all comes back to me. All of it."

"What are you talking about? And why won't you look at me?"

She walked over to the window and put her hand on it. Her fingers followed the raindrops on the pane until they disappeared. "If I never tried to run away from Garringer, I wouldn't have had to be his slave. I wouldn't have gotten pregnant, my mom wouldn't have had to try to hide me, and she wouldn't have been beaten, tortured, and dumped in the river." She pulled her hand away from the window and wiped her face. "And Garringer never would've come after you to find me and Leah. Because of me, Laynee died, Adam almost had his throat slit, and Ted had to kill a man." She swallowed. "The fear, the hiding, the killing. It all goes back to the day I ran away. How could I have been so stupid? Dan was right. I was just as crazy as the rest of them."

I embraced her. "Dan was not right. And he knows it, too. I saw it in his eyes when he realized what he'd said." I looked into her eyes. "You ran away because you were scared and you were being abused. Nobody will ever blame you for that. *I* will never blame you for that, and neither will Ted. Everything that happened afterward lay at the feet of Garringer and no one else."

She nodded.

"I'll be right back." I walked to the guest bathroom for tissues. She followed and leaned against the door frame. I smiled when I saw a teasing glint in her eyes.

"So, Dan felt bad about what he said?

"Yep."

"I wish he would've come upstairs to talk to me about it."

"He started to. He climbed the steps to apologize to you, but then he stopped and turned around."

"Why?"

I shrugged.

Her eyes narrowed. "He's an idiot."

I laughed. Molly was never one to lick her wounds for long. I started to agree with her assessment of Dan but decided to hand her the Kleenex instead.

She dabbed at her eyes. "But he's a handsome idiot. A six-foot idiot with thick, straight dark hair, ripped biceps, and a six-pack."

"Molly!" The images she put in my head failed to compute with the sheriff I'd known for years. "How do you know he has ripped biceps and a six-pack?"

"Actually, now that I think about it, it may be an eight-pack."

"Molly."

"He sent me a picture."

My mouth fell open.

She laughed. "Not that kind of picture. It was that picture of him sitting in the dunk tank."

She tilted her head at my blank stare. "The tank used at the Widow and Orphan fund fundraiser last summer?" she said. "He told me you were there."

"Oh," I giggled and remembered Doris had sent him splashing underwater. Funny how I remembered that and not the ripped muscles. "*That* dunk tank."

She pulled a couple more tissues from my hand and lowered her head. "Perhaps I'm the one who should apologize. Dan knows part of my story but not all of it. Besides, if you didn't live through the horror, it's almost impossible to imagine it."

I nodded. "Yeah. It took Ted years to fully understand what I went through. And to be honest, I don't know how much of it he actually believed. That is until Garringer showed up."

She looked out the window again. "There has to be a way to end this once and for all. A way where no one else gets hurt."

I had yet to tell Molly about Doris's plan. "Well, if the police don't find Thwart soon, I know someone with a Plan B."

She turned to face me. "With this plan, is it possible that someone could get hurt?"

"I don't have all the details yet, but it sounds safe enough." Which was true. At least the version Doris told me of her plan sounded simple and safe enough. But was it really?

No, it wasn't.

A shiver crawled up my spine.

No matter which plan we went with, it wasn't a matter of *if* someone got hurt.

But who.

Chapter Twenty-Two

"You've got to be kidding me."

The large space that used to be my bedroom closet had been gutted. Every piece of clothing had been tossed on the bed or strewn across the floor. That also included my hats and handbags.

Molly and I tiptoed around the items on the floor and walked into the master bath. The white wooden shelving and wired organizers I'd painstakingly installed years ago now lay in a mangled heap in the corner of the bathroom.

"Ted, what have you done?" I marched over to him. "What did you do to my closet?"

He took a step back. "This morning, when you told me you and Molly were going to the mall, I figured this would be a good time to get some things done." He wiped at the beads of sweat on his forehead. "We finished an hour ago. Right now, I'm cleaning up." He grabbed a screwdriver off the floor.

"Who's *we*, and again, what have you done?" I tried to keep my tone light, but it didn't work. It took me years to get my closet the way I wanted. The people who'd lived in the house before us had used it for emergency food storage. Twelve metal racks had been nailed into the walls and floor, and a few smaller ones extended from the ceiling. The wallpaper behind those racks had to have been superglued to the walls because it had been almost impossible to remove.

And now this.

I tried to walk around him to see what was left of my closet. He tossed the screwdriver in the sink and reached for my hand. "You and Molly need to see this." He led us around the half-wall that separated the counter area from the shower and closet.

I couldn't believe my eyes. "Ted, what in the world?"

Attached to the wall where my large wooden closet organizer used to be were five flat-screen TVs. Each one showed different rooms of our house in full color. To the left, where I normally hung my hats and dresses, was a long horizontal concrete slab.

In the middle of the slab was a huge red button, and next to it were four cell phones, walkie-talkies, and Tasers. Next to them were several cans of bear spray and mace.

To my right, at knee level, was a small metal safe. But the biggest surprise was the door. My white six-panel wooden one had been removed. In its place was a solid gray one made of steel.

Molly stepped inside, picked up one of the Tasers, and smiled. "Ted, this is awesome. Where'd you get all of this?"

"Doris. After I talked her out of stalking Thwart, she told me about some guys she knew who could install a state-of-the-art security and surveillance system for us. I called them this morning after you ladies left for the mall." He glanced at his watch and smirked.

To his credit, he didn't mention that it was now almost midnight. After the mall, Molly and I went out to lunch, then a movie, indulged in more shopping, and enjoyed a late dinner. Dan had ensured that one of his officers was nearby the whole time.

Now I knew why Ted hadn't bugged me to come home and rest. He wanted me to stay away so I wouldn't make a fuss.

"They installed the door and all the electronic stuff," he said. "Then they gave me a list of additional things to purchase, so I went out and bought most of the gear you see here," he pointed to the walkie-talkies, Tasers, and sprays.

"Ted," Molly asked. "Did you say you had to talk Doris out of stalking Thwart?"

He nodded.

"So, she knows where he is?"

"That's a long story, Molls," I answered and placed a hand on her shoulder. "I'll explain later."

I pointed to the monitors on the wall. "What's going on here?"

"Everything in here is wireless," he said. "Including the camera." He pointed to a tiny device in the closet's upper left corner. "When that's turned on, anything that happens in here will be recorded and automatically sent to encrypted security apps Dan and I have already installed on our phones.

He placed his hand on the bright red button in the middle of the concrete slab. "This is a panic button. When pushed, it's been programmed to alert the police department and fire and rescue. Officers and an ambulance will be sent to the house immediately."

I blew out a breath. "Ted, I don't understand."

"What do you mean?"

I spread my arms and walked around the newly transformed closet. "This isn't like you." My arms dropped to my sides with a loud slap. "This isn't like you at all."

"It isn't, but I'll do whatever it takes to keep you and Adam safe. I also bought a handgun."

"Ted ..."

He placed a finger on my lips. "I pray I'll never have to use it. But I also pray that God will once again give me the strength to do so, if necessary." He lowered his finger from my lips. "There's another gun in the nightstand by the bed and one taped underneath the cabinet in the kitchen. I bought you one, also."

"I don't want a gun."

"I know, that's why there are Tasers, bear spray, and mace." He reached for one of the Tasers. Molly handed him the one she was admiring. "They're easy to use. Two clicks of the button and one charge will stop an attacker in his tracks."

Molly moved closer to Ted. "You mentioned something about a gun?"

"Yeah, Jan's gun is locked in the safe." He pointed to the heavy metal safe in the corner. "It's loaded and ready to fire. The key to open the safe is duct-taped to the back of it." He slid his arm between the safe and the wall. "As you can see, there's plenty of room to reach back here quickly." He straightened. "Chances are you'll never need it. Or the extra cell phones and stun guns locked inside with it. But if you do, I wanted you and Molly to know it's there."

Molly rubbed her hand across the metal safe. "You said *chances are* we'll never need it. Why is that?"

"Because at the first sign of trouble, I want you ladies to secure yourself in this room. This door is not only made of steel, but it's bulletproof and blast proof. And it only locks from the inside. Hit the panic button like I showed you, and help is on the way.

We tested the phones to make sure they could get a good signal, but we included the walkie-talkies for backup. And the monitors will let you see everything inside the house—how many people there are, where they're located, what type of weapons they have, et cetera. You'll share that information with the police."

I swallowed. "Why so many weapons? Molly and I will be the only ones here most of the time. We don't need all of this stuff."

"Probably not, but you never know who else might be here if Thwart's team strikes. Libbybelle or Adam could stop by, or even Olivia or Doris. Leah could also be here since she plans to spend Christmas Day with us."

He sighed. "Jan, the last thing I want is for you to be fearful. And I know that's not what God wants. Live as though there are no threats. This room is only if Thwart decides to act. And the key word is *if*. He's a wanted man and may decide to lay low instead. If that turns out to be the case, I'll pack all this stuff up and hand it over to the women's shelter if you like. Or to Doris. Something tells me she'll find a real good use for it." He wrapped his arms around me and Molly. "You ladies will remember the drill, won't you?"

We nodded against his chest, and he loosened the hug.

I walked out of my former closet and into the bedroom and stared at my belongings scattered throughout the room.

I wanted to cry over the life we now had to live, but instead, I decided to take a page out of Molly's book. She never let anything keep her down for long.

I picked my favorite blue dress off the floor. It looked like it had been run over by a Mack truck. Apparently, Ted and the installation team thought it'd be easier to walk over it than toss it on the bed.

I looked at my husband. "I don't know how much you spent on that new room, but I can guarantee you'll pay a lot more if the cleaners can't get the stains out of this dress. It's irreplaceable." I tried to scowl but instead batted my eyes. How did that happen?

He tilted his head and laughed. "And how much does 'irreplaceable' go for these days?"

"Oh, I don't know. This dress really means a lot to me." I teased and let the dress drop to the floor. "Three new dresses and seven pairs of shoes should cover it."

He furrowed his brow. "Seven pairs of shoes? But you're only buying three new dresses. Why would you need so many shoes?"

Molly scurried to my side. "She needs a new pair of shoes for each new day. Our feet take us where we want to go, but our shoes help us get there in style. Isn't that right, Jan?"

I nodded and peered around Ted to the closet door behind him. A steel-colored reminder of the grimness of our situation. And all of the feet in the world wouldn't be able to carry me where I wanted to go—a place far, far away from the madness of our lives. Ted, me, Adam, and Laynee—before the cold hearts of steeled men chased our happiness away.

Molly placed a gentle hand on my back. "You okay?"

I closed my eyes and prayed. Taking a page from Molly's book wasn't as easy as she made it look.

"It's going to be all right," she said softly in my ear. "You'll see. God's got this."

I leaned my head against hers and let the tears flow.

Because for a brief second, I'd once again begun to wonder if He really did.

Chapter Twenty-Three

"This is fun." Ted helped me out of the car and locked it with the remote.

I leaned into him. "Fun? It's the grocery store."

"I know." He hugged me closer to him as we walked inside the store. "But when was the last time we got to do this together?"

I tugged a shopping cart free from the corral. He was right. It had been a while.

When we first married, we shopped together all the time. We treated it like a date since living off a pastor's salary didn't leave much room for fine dining. But after the kids came along, we started going to the market separately. He'd pick up odds and ends after work, or I'd go during the day with the kids. Years had passed with us doing it that way, and we hadn't even noticed. He was busy. I was busy. The kids were busy. Somewhere along the line, we'd stopped doing the small things. I touched his arm. "You're right. This is fun." I reached up and gave him a peck on the lips.

He smiled. "Does that mean you'll let me buy some real food? You know, the essentials. Chips, cheese puffs, cookies, peanuts, popcorn, pizza rolls?"

I steered the cart toward the produce aisle. "Ted, you're a carboholic."

"Am I?" He chuckled and tossed a bunch of badly

bruised bananas into the cart. "How about I add fruit to that list?"

Suddenly, I remembered one of the reasons I'd stopped coming to the market with Ted. He had an annoying habit of tossing useless items into the cart. I used to get frustrated when he did that, but now I smiled at the memory.

"Fine," I removed the bananas. "But remember, you're not in your twenties anymore. Eating junk food before bed could have consequences."

He wrapped his arm around my waist. "Aw, babe. Where's your sense of adventure?"

I tossed a head of lettuce and an English cucumber into the cart. "It left twenty years ago, along with my girly figure." I gave him a playful nudge. "Hand me a tomato."

"If your girly figure left twenty years ago," he tilted his head to the left and smiled. A vintage Ted move. It was his way of making sure I'd see the one cheek that was dimpled. "Then how come I find you just as attractive as the day we met?"

My face warmed. "Behave yourself. We're in the grocery store, for crying out loud."

He handed me several vine-ripened tomatoes and winked. "All right. I'll try, but I can't promise anything." He kissed my forehead and took the cart from me. As he pushed it down the aisle, he asked, "Speaking of behaving badly, have you spoken to Doris today?"

"No, actually, I haven't talked to her in a couple of days. Why?"

"There was a situation at church today. Doris was behind it, and when I called her into the office to talk about her behavior, she got mad and ignored me the rest of the day. I thought maybe she stopped by the house and told you about it."

I slowed my walk beside him. Doris was mad at Ted? That didn't make any sense. There were times when I believed she actually thought he walked on water. "What happened?"

"She fired somebody."

I stopped and grabbed his arm. "She did *what*?"

"She fired two members of my staff."

"Was that something you told her to do?"

"No, and the worst part is that she didn't even tell me about it. They called me after it happened."

"Who'd she fire?"

"John and Norah." He took off with the grocery cart again.

Now, it all made sense. John and Norah have been on Doris's radar since they interfered with her plans to get Stephanie away from Cody. I ran to catch up to Ted and the swiftly moving grocery cart. "You can't let Doris fire them. They're great youth ministers. The teens love them, and so do I. They're doing a great job."

He continued adding random items to the cart. "Don't worry, they're not going anywhere. I also made Doris apologize to them and reminded her that only I have the power to fire someone. And that if she did that again, she would be the one getting fired."

Whoa. I know that didn't go over well. No wonder she wasn't speaking to him. "What reason did she give for trying to fire them?"

He maneuvered the cart around a festive display of holiday cookies. "Anna's moved back home with Olivia. They stopped by the church office this afternoon for a meeting with John and Norah. While waiting, Anna told Doris about her ordeal with Legion and how they introduced her to Ruin. After the meeting, Doris met John and Norah at the door with a box of their belongings. She'd cleaned out their office. When they wouldn't take the box, she pushed them out the door and told them not to come back."

I pressed my lips together. No matter how mad Doris was at the Baxters, she had no right to treat them that way.

Ted sighed. "Doris said she fired them because John and

Norah hadn't instilled enough biblical teaching in Anna. She added that if they had, Anna wouldn't have been easy prey for evil predators like Thwart and Whisper."

My mind flashed back to a conversation with Olivia about how much Anna had improved after talking with members of her uncle's church in Montana. I could see where Doris was coming from, but once again, she'd overstepped her boundaries. "That wasn't her call to make."

"That's what I told her, and she was okay with me talking to her about that part," he blurted out with a short laugh. "It was the apologizing part that set her on fire. However, after we discussed what the Bible says about humility, she called them and apologized. She stomped out of my office after that."

Ted angled the cart down the chip aisle and tossed several varieties of salty potato snacks, a couple of cans of nuts, three jars of salsa, and a large container of bacon-flavored cheese sauce into it.

"Oh, well," I said. "Knowing Doris, she'll show up tomorrow morning like nothing ever happened."

"I hope so. She's exactly what the office needs. That is when she's not firing people. But since she's been there, the place has been running like a well-oiled machine. My staff meetings have never been more organized and productive, and she's a whiz with the volunteers. Everybody shows up when they're supposed to, even in the nursery. That never happens. I don't know how she does it."

Fear probably. It wasn't too hard to imagine the tongue-lashings those poor volunteers received if they dared to show up late for their scheduled time slot. I made a mental note to check in with them come Sunday morning.

"The only other person she's had an issue with is Heather, one of the college interns from Agape Theological Seminary. Heather showed up at a meeting last week with a skirt Doris said was too short. She told Heather to leave and not return until she found something more appropriate to wear in a church environment."

I giggled. "Did Heather leave?"

"Heather said she lived too far away to go home and return before the meeting was over."

"What happened then?"

"Doris reached into her tote bag and pulled out something she called a muumuu. To me, it looked like a colorful potato sack."

"Seriously?" I laughed and ignored the stares from the shoppers around us. "Did Heather wear it?"

"Yep."

I smiled. Short skirts did not have a place in our church office or anywhere near my husband. I beamed a smile at Ted. "Well, I guess that'll teach Heather."

"She and the other two female interns have been wearing pants ever since."

Ted was right.

Doris was exactly what we needed.

~

"Finally, my brethren, be strong in the Lord and in the power of His might." Ted laid his Bible on the oak pulpit and looked over the congregation. I closed mine and laid it next to me on the pew beside Adam. He glanced at me, then looked up at his dad and smiled.

Ted continued, "Put on the whole armor of God, that ye may be able to stand against the wiles of the devil." He leaned forward and grabbed the edge of the pulpit. "Whatever God does, the devil will try and mimic. If God says He'll use those who believe in Him as His hands and feet, then know that your soul's enemy will do the same. Unlike God, Satan uses the broken, the lost, and the desperate. He romances them with lies, deceives them into doing his bidding, and then exploits them. Sadly, some of those people end up becoming threats to our lives.

"But as the book of Ephesians reminds us, our struggle is not with those Satan uses but with the principalities, powers, and rulers of the dark world that govern them. That's not to say that when we are threatened, we shouldn't protect ourselves—we should and have every right to do so. It's also important to remember that the fight didn't start here, and it won't end here. There's no man-made weapon in this world that can win that fight, but there is a divine one." He held up his Bible and crossed in front of the pulpit. "The inspired Word of God. And it tells us to gird our loins with truth, wear the breastplate of righteousness, and shod our feet with peace. Along with the spirit of faith, the helmet of salvation, the sword of the Spirit, and prayer, not only will we be able to quench the fiery darts of the wicked, we'll be able to stand when the battle's over and walk away unharmed."

He stepped down from the platform. "*Spiritually* unharmed. Satan doesn't win if we die from the flaming arrows he throws our way. He wins when we allow the arrows to wound us so deeply that they shatter our faith, kill our joy, and destroy our hope in what was done for us on the Cross. The choice is ours. We can become victims or be victorious through Christ." He held the Bible out in front of him. "And since we've been given the battle plans, the choice should be easy. Let's pray."

Adam clasped my hand, and we bowed our heads. Ted wrapped the service up in prayer and gave an altar call. I stood, ready to go stand next to him but felt a hand on my shoulder.

"Jan."

The voice was so familiar my knees buckled. Adam helped steady me. When I got my bearings, he slowly turned me in the direction of the voice.

My heart stood still.

If I hadn't known any better, I would've sworn my mother had returned from the grave. The resemblance was uncanny, but the voice had already told me everything I needed to know. The person in front of me was my Aunt Gingie.

She smiled. "Silly girl, don't you recognize me?"

To be honest, I didn't. The aunt I remembered had brassy red hair and a smile so cold it sent the temperature of a room on a downward spiral. The aunt I remembered also hated anything resembling a Bible, and now she tenderly held one in her hands.

"Aunt Gingie!" I pulled her into a tight hug. Light floral scents tickled my nose. Gone were the smells of cigarettes and peppermint. "Molly told me you were alive, but when I wasn't able to contact you with the information she gave me, I thought she was still trying to protect me from further heartache."

Aunt Gingie shook her head, and ebony ringlets danced about her shoulders. "When she told me she was coming to see you, I knew you'd try to reach out to me, so I stayed out of reach on purpose. And I still think it's bad for us to be seen together." She reached behind me and tousled Adam's hair. "But, it's been almost a year since I've seen this handsome fella." She winked at him, and I turned to Adam. Crimson filled his cheeks. "That's when I realized being apart wasn't the answer. Being together is."

I spun back to her. "How do you know Adam?"

Her eyes twinkled, and joy seemed to propel their every movement. "Not only do I know Adam, but I knew Laynee, too."

A breath caught in my throat. Did I hear her right? How would she have known Laynee?

Adam cleared away the Bibles and pamphlets on our pew and said something about going to help his dad.

Gingie and I sat.

She tucked a wayward ringlet behind her ear and placed my hand in hers. "When Molly and I escaped Garringer's guards and the fire that night, only one thing was on my mind. Finding you." She looked down, took a deep breath, and slowly let it out. "It took a couple of days, but I eventually learned that you were taken in by Papa George and Libbybelle. I'd visit their diner every other week or so, disguised, of course, but I needed to see how you were doing.

"One day, when I was leaving, Libbybelle stopped me in the parking lot. She wasn't fooled and demanded to know why I didn't want you to know I'd survived. I told her everything.

"After that, things unraveled quickly, and I ran out of places to hide. Especially after the town found out that Molly and I weren't among the dead. I knew you were in good hands, and Libbybelle and I promised to stay in touch. And we did. That's how I knew about Adam and Laynee."

Anger stirred in my veins. Papa George died over a decade ago, but how could Libbybelle not tell me that my aunt was alive? *Why* didn't she tell me?

The anger dissipated. I already knew the answer to those questions. She'd done it out of love. If I'd known my aunt was alive, I wouldn't have been able to rest until I tracked her down, and that would've put my entire family in danger. Libbybelle only wanted to protect me and let my family live in peace.

"But you didn't just know about Adam and Laynee," I said. "You've seen them before."

"Yes, thanks to Libbybelle. She'd allow me to come to see them every couple of years, but only if I disguised myself as an older lady. Then she'd take them to play at the park, and I'd join them and watch. She never introduced me as your aunt, only as her friend.

"Adam reminded me so much of you. Smart, well-behaved, kind, thoughtful," she bowed her head and laughed. "But Laynee? She reminded me of your mom. She never let one of those visits go by without asking me if I knew Jesus. I would say no, and she'd ask me if I wanted to. I'd say no again, but she still gave me the biggest hug, as if I were her new best friend. I didn't understand it then, but now I know that was her way of letting me know she loved me regardless of my answer."

Aunt Gingie sniffed and then looked at me. "Then, one day, she asked me again if I knew Jesus. I told her no, but that I'd like to, and she prayed with me." She lifted a finger and swiped it under her eyelid. "I'll never forget it. It was such a beautiful moment."

My eyes watered too as I pictured the scene. That was my Laynee all right. I loved how easily she'd related to people. And how much she loved to pray.

Aunt Gingie continued. "Your mom tried to get me to commit my life to Christ every time she visited. I can't tell you how many times I threw her out, but she kept asking. I can imagine her in heaven now, tickled pink, that it was her granddaughter who helped pull me out of darkness and into the light."

After a long pause, she placed her hand on top of mine. "I was at the funeral."

"I'm sure you were, but I was so young at the time—"

"No," she tapped my hand. "I don't mean your mom's funeral. I mean Laynee's."

I stared at our hands, then her eyes. Laynee's funeral remained a haze in my memory, but I know I would've remembered seeing Aunt Gingie there. "I don't understand."

"Libbybelle told me what happened to Laynee and where the funeral would take place. She also made it clear that was not the time or the place for you to find out that I was alive. So again, I disguised myself as Libbybelle's friend from the park." She motioned toward the carpeted area below the pulpit, the area where Laynee's yellow and white casket had rested. "I loved that little girl so much."

Heat warmed my cheeks. Part of me was still upset with Libbybelle for keeping all of this from me. And another part was thankful. For years, she kept my aunt's secrets. Still, at the same time, she made sure my children knew the one person in my biological family that my mother trusted enough with whom to leave her only child.

I let out a long breath. "Thank you for coming, Aunt Gingie. For Laynee then, and for me, now."

She leaned forward until her forehead met mine. "All the thanks goes to you, silly girl." I giggled at the moniker she'd affectionately called me since childhood. "And your mom. If I'd known when we were kids that my big sister and her daughter would change my life so drastically, I'd been much nicer to her." She laughed softly. "And I definitely would've stopped stealing all her cute clothes."

"Sorry to interrupt," Ted's voice came from the aisle next to our pew. "But if I understand my son correctly, you're the famous Aunt Gingie I've heard so much about."

We looked toward the aisle. Ted was surrounded by Adam, Libbybelle, Molly, Dan, and Doris. The rest of the church appeared empty.

Aunt Gingie stood and shook his hand. "More like infamous."

He smiled. "Nonsense. Janny's always spoken highly of you."

She turned to me, and color filled her cheeks. I noticed once again how her eyes sparkled with life. The dark, unmoving eyes of the past were gone.

Ted turned to his right. "Of course, you already know Molly." He stepped back and wrapped his arm around Libbybelle. "And apparently, you know Adam and Libbybelle as well." He smiled at Doris, who was on his left. Doris frowned and rolled her eyes.

"Doris is our church secretary," he continued. "Next to her is Dan Glass. He's a family friend and the local sheriff."

Aunt Gingie nodded toward Dan. "Did Detective Cheatham let you know we were coming?"

I turned to her. "*We*?"

"Yes. Did Molly forget to mention that I was married?"

"No, she told me. It's just that—"

"You're having a hard time wrapping your head around

it?"

"Well, yeah." There was more shock in my tone than I'd intended. Lots of men had paraded through Aunt Gingie's home when I stayed there, but rarely did I see the same guy more than once. She'd never struck me as the marrying type. Ever.

She chuckled. "Yes. Married."

I stared at her. I couldn't help it. Aunt Gingie, married?

"Actually," she continued, "I was married the whole time you were with me, Jan. Lonewolf and I married a long time ago when I was seventeen. A few years before you arrived with Mrs. Gibbons, he told me he'd had enough of the occult and wanted us to leave Corinth. I didn't want to go, so he left town without me.

"But when Quiggy and I needed somewhere to hide Molly, I called him and asked him for help."

"So, the two of you have reconciled your differences?" Ted asked.

"It took a couple of years, but yes." She turned to the sheriff. "Wolf's with Agent Cheatham, back at the motel. They knew I wanted to meet with Jan alone first."

Dan reached into his suit pocket and pulled out his phone. "Which motel?"

"The Greatway Inn, the one by the airport."

I shot a glance to Ted and then to Aunt Gingie. "Please tell me that's not where you're staying. That's not a safe place."

Aunt Gingie shrugged. "It was the first place we saw last night after our plane landed. I'll call and find another one on my way back."

"Nonsense. Ted and I have plenty—"

"That's not a good idea," Dan flipped his phone shut and glared at me. "Ted's a target, which makes everyone in that house a target. It's bad enough I can't convince you and Molly to leave. Now you want to add two more people?"

Before I could respond, Ted wrapped his arm around

my waist. "Honey, Dan's got a point. Don't worry, I'll make reservations for them at one of those nice hotels downtown."

Suddenly, Doris nudged Ted and me to the side and positioned herself between me and my aunt. "Listen, lady," she said. "You don't want to be around those highfalutin' downtown folks. You and your husband will stay with me."

Aunt Gingie looked at me, and I shook my head. I knew my aunt, and I knew Doris. There was no way the two of them staying in the same house would end well.

She smiled at Doris. "Thank you for the invitation, but I—"

"You did say you were married, didn't you?"

Aunt Gingie blinked. "Yes, but—"

"Good. Because fornicators are not welcome in my home." She turned and walked up the aisle toward the sanctuary doors. After a few steps, she stopped and frowned at Aunt Gingie. "Come on. What are you waiting for? A chariot?"

For a brief moment, the dark stillness that once took up permanent residence in Aunt Gingie's eyes flashed.

"Actually, Gingie," Ted said. "Staying with Doris isn't a bad idea. Her home is not far from us, the church, or Libbybelle. That is, as long as you wouldn't mind. If so, like I said before, I can make—"

"I don't mind at all." Aunt Gingie grabbed her purse from the pew and placed it on her shoulder. "It sounds like the perfect opportunity for Doris and me to get to know one another."

She clicked her tongue and joined Doris. They eyed each other suspiciously, then pushed through the double doors.

Molly eased her way between Ted and me and chuckled. "Put on your helmet, friends. Things are about to get very interesting."

Everyone laughed, but Molly was right. Aunt Gingie and Doris were a bad combination. Fire and dynamite in one place. And the fact that the whole idea was Doris's suggestion hadn't escaped me. What was she up to?

Chapter Twenty-Four

I opened the refrigerator and stared into it.

Three days had passed since I'd had real contact with Aunt Gingie or Doris.

Whenever I called my aunt, she'd say they were in the middle of something or couldn't talk. Also, I'd yet to have the pleasure of meeting Wolf, Aunt Gingie's husband.

Ted and I knew Doris's husband, Abner, well. I mean, for what there was to know of him. For a man who didn't talk much, he said a lot. We've seen him stop Doris in the middle of her meddling with one look. And if he folded his arms across his chest, Doris would start stuttering, and within minutes, she'd gather their stuff and leave.

I liked Abner.

And he liked cars. Old ones. And apparently, Lonewolf did too because, according to my aunt, that's what he was busy doing every time I'd call to invite them over for dinner.

Either Doris was dead, or the four of them were up to something.

I pulled out a quart of milk, a package of bacon, and a carton of eggs. Molly had grabbed a bagel and yogurt earlier and returned to the guest room. Ted, on the other hand, had to leave for work in half an hour. But because I'd spent most of the morning trying to track down my aunt, his breakfast of crisp bacon, boiled eggs, and buttered toast was seriously late.

I put three eggs inside the egg boiler, then grabbed a skillet and placed it on the stove. I'd just placed a couple of slices of bacon in it when Molly walked into the kitchen.

I reached for the coffee pot. It was time for her refill.

She smiled and placed her mug on the counter. "Am I that predictable?"

I nodded. "When it comes to coffee, you and Ted come in for your refills like clockwork." I poured the steaming brew into her mug and passed the sugar bowl.

She opened the refrigerator for the dairy creamer.

I plugged in the toaster. "Could you please hand me the butter while you're in there?"

"Sure." She handed me the butter, and the doorbell rang. We looked at the stove's digital clock. Bright green numbers glowed 7:02 a.m.

"Were you expecting someone?" she asked.

I shook my head and walked to the door. Then, I peeked through the lacy pattern of the curtained side window next to it.

Molly tiptoed up behind me and whispered, "Who is it?"

I discreetly lifted the curtain to get a better view. The person on the porch was a man, but his back was to the door. He had a head full of silver hair and was dressed in khakis and a dark blue blazer.

"His back is to me, but he doesn't look familiar."

Ted came down the stairs, and we jumped. "Who's at the door?" he asked.

"I don't know." I paused to catch my breath. "I've never seen him before."

Ted's eyes narrowed. "And it's not a package delivery guy?"

I peeked through the curtain again. "There's nothing on the porch or in his hands. As a matter of fact, his hands are in his pockets."

Ted's eyes tightened, and then he ran back up the stairs.

Seconds later, he returned with his pistol tucked into the back of his pants.

Molly sprinted to the kitchen and threw open the cabinet door under the sink. Duct tape ripped from the cabinet surface as she pulled the gun Ted had hidden there free and hid it behind her back. I ran to the sofa and pulled a can of mace and my phone out of the front pocket of my purse. I then dialed Dan's personal cell. He answered on the first ring.

"Jan, what is it?"

"A man we don't recognize is at the door."

I heard the dinging sound of a car door opening. "I'm on my way."

I tapped the phone off.

The bell rang again.

Ted leaned against the door. "Who is it?"

"Bruce Cheatham, former Corinth City Homicide Detective," the voice boomed through the door. "I'd like to speak with January Eller. Is she home?"

"Isn't that the name of the guy who came to town to work with Dan and Gingie?" Molly asked.

I nodded. "But how are we supposed to know what he looks like?" I paused. "Oh, now I remember. Detective Cheatham was the one who arrested Aunt Gingie the night Garringer and his goons kidnapped me from the police station.

I turned to Molly. "He was new to the department back then, I think. He had to be because he was the only one genuinely interested in finding out what really happened to your mom." I shook my head. "That was so long ago. No way will I be able to tell if that's the same guy on the porch."

Ted pulled the gun from his waistband and held it against his leg. He peeled back the curtain covering the side panel with his other hand and called through the window. "Show me an ID."

Something smacked against the windowpane. Ted squinted, then motioned for me to give him my phone.

I tossed it to him.

He dialed quickly. "Dan, the guy at the door says he's Bruce Cheatham. Yeah, he showed a driver's license. Silver hair, light blue eyes? Yeah, that's him. Thanks."

Ted tapped off the phone, slid the pistol back into his waistband, and unlocked the door. He nodded to me and Molly. I held on to the can of mace, but Molly immediately stuck her gun back under the sink and closed the cabinet.

Ted threw open the door and reached for Cheatham's hand. "Sorry that took so long. We usually don't have visitors this early. Please, come in."

Cheatham shook Ted's hand. "No problem. I should've called. Are you Theodore Eller?"

Ted nodded.

The retired detective smiled. "I'd like to talk with your wife if that's okay."

Ted shut the door and turned to me. I nodded and said, "I'm January Eller."

His brows raised. "So, it's true. Sheriff Glass told me it was, but I needed to see you with my own eyes."

"I don't understand."

"Dan called a few weeks ago to ask what I knew about Garringer and his son. I couldn't believe it when he told me what had happened here and mentioned your name and Gingie's. Since the day you disappeared from the police station, my wife and I have prayed for you. And to see you now, all these years later ... " He blew out a long breath. "I'm sorry. I'm going too fast. Do you remember me?"

I couldn't remember exactly what he'd looked like back then, but I did remember the kind blue eyes and the gentle smile. "Yes, I remember."

He lowered his head. "That day, when I let you walk out with Sgt. Mordell, I had no idea he was one of Garringer's men. When Child Services called later that evening and said you'd never arrived, I knew something was off. I called my wife and asked her to pray. After that, I hand-picked a few officers I knew personally and set up a search team, but you were nowhere to be found. Then we heard about the fire at Gingie's. They found Mordell's body but not yours, so we continued the search." He shoved his hands in his pockets. "We continued that search for three years until the department forced me to pull the plug. After that, I personally hired a private eye. He came back with new leads, but none of them panned out. So, to see you here now, alive and safe ..." He swallowed. "It's beyond words."

Every time I started to doubt God, it seemed like He reminded me just how loved and cared for I was. After everything that happened following the incident at the police station, I'd completely forgotten about Detective Cheatham. And to find out now, all these years later, that he'd never forgotten about me and that he'd continued to search and pray for me? I was speechless.

"Thank you," I finally managed to say. "I had no idea."

He looked down, then back at me. "I appreciate the thanks, but it's undeserved. It was my fault things got out of hand."

"What do you mean?" Ted asked.

Cheatham eyed him for a moment, then took a step backward. "Earlier that year, when a few of my colleagues and I were assigned to that department, we were warned that there were dirty cops on the force and were told to keep our eyes open. Mordell was on a short list I'd created to send to the higher-ups so that they could investigate him further." He rubbed the back of his neck. "Corinth was and still is a haven for criminal activity. There were always more cases than detectives to work them. I got caught up in the caseloads and never got around to sending that list. If I had, Mordell wouldn't have been there that day to hear what you said about Ms. Fitzhugh's disappearance." He shuffled slowly toward me. "That's the other reason I wanted to stop by. To let you know, I'm sorry. I dropped the ball. I never should've let you walk out that door with Mordell."

I closed my eyes. Memories of Mordell shoving me into a vehicle flooded my mind, along with images of the three men, the duct tape, their lurid looks, and the dark cabin.

Garringer pulling at my clothes.

My eyes popped open. "I could've been killed." I had no intention of saying those words. Yet, there they were.

Cheatham sucked in a breath. "I know." The words came out soft and heavy. His gaze never drifted from mine.

I stepped toward him. "But I wasn't. And you and your wife's prayers had a lot to do with that. So, once again, thank you."

His head turned to the side as if I'd slapped him. He straightened, then whispered, "You're welcome."

"Is your wife with you?"

He shook his head.

"Please extend my thanks to her. And an invitation to join us for dinner the next time the two of you are in Habakkuk. I can't wait to meet her."

He grinned. "I will do that. Thank you."

I nodded, lifted my hand, the one still holding the mace, and stepped forward to grab my cell phone from Ted. As I did so, the detective ducked and instinctively reached for his weapon, his eyes trained on the mace.

"Oh, my word. I'm so sorry. That's not what I—"

"What are you doing?" Ted yanked the can of mace from my hand and gave it to Molly.

Cheatham stood and spread his arms wide. "You moved so quickly. It surprised me." He turned to Ted. "And thanks for not reaching for your Glock."

Ted slowly moved his hand to his waistband. "You knew I had a weapon?"

Cheatham nodded. "Once a detective, always a detective. And I wouldn't have been much of a detective if I hadn't noticed that, now would I?"

We laughed. After a few moments, Molly extended her hand to Cheatham. "Hi. I'm Molly Fitzhugh. Quiggy—I mean, Terese Katherine Fitzhugh—was my mother."

Cheatham's eyes turned solemn.

"It's okay," she said. "It was horrible what they did to her, but she never gave up my location. She wanted me to live, and that brings me peace. Jan told me you were the only person in the department that night who cared enough to find out what had happened to her. So, on my mother's behalf, thank you."

He swallowed and was about to answer when a car door slammed.

Molly glanced out the window. "It's Dan."

She opened the door for him. "It's about time you got here." She planted a kiss on his cheek. I don't know who looked more surprised, Ted, Cheatham, or Dan.

Dan's face darkened through three different shades of red. He grinned but said nothing.

"Cheatham," Ted motioned toward the living room. "With all the confusion, we never properly asked you to have a seat. Would you like a cup of coffee?"

"I'd love to, but I need to get going. My wife's with our only granddaughter at the hospital. We're expecting our first great-grandchild any minute now."

"That's right!" I pulled my phone from Ted's hand. "That's what I was about to do," I winked at Cheatham. "Before you were about to shoot me, that is."

The grin that had been plastered on Dan's face ever since Molly kissed him disappeared.

"Say what, now?"

"A simple misunderstanding," I said and stood next to Cheatham. I lifted the phone and tapped the camera icon. "Smile!"

He smiled, and I snapped the photo.

Molly dipped her brows at me. "Jan, what are you doing?"

I snapped a few more photos. "This man and his wife prayed for me when I needed it the most. I'd like her to know her prayers didn't go unanswered."

Dan sighed heavily. "Your life's not out of danger yet, Jan."

Ted took the phone from me and asked Molly to stand beside me and Cheatham. "Let Thwart do his worst," he snapped the picture and then looked at Dan. "The three of them standing there together is proof that if God be for us, who can dare be against us?"

~

Ted made one phone call to Abner, and Doris and Aunt Gingie finally called me back.

I got them to agree to a late dinner at our place, though they both said neither had time for it.

I didn't care. I wanted to see my aunt.

Dan and Molly also planned on joining us, so why wasn't I happy?

I leaned against the kitchen counter. Doris was spending more time with my aunt than I was. The muscles in my face tightened. Not only that, she'd also had the chance to meet Wolf, an uncle I had apparently had for three decades. She met him before I did, and I wasn't okay with that.

I slid open the window. Gingie mentioned that Wolf was a meat eater, so Ted went to the market and picked up several steaks. When he came back, he headed straight for the backyard grill. The fresh, crisp November air was no match for the spiced, tangy smell of Ted's homemade sauce and savory grilled meat.

November. Almost two weeks had passed since I found that note in our mailbox. It was now thirty days until Christmas.

"You doing okay?" Molly reached into the drawer beside me for a paring knife.

I turned and finished slicing cucumbers for a salad. "Thanksgiving is in a couple days, and all I can think about is Christmas."

She nodded. "And I bet it has nothing to do with shopping."

"How I wish. You have no idea how much I long for my life to be the way it used to be. Libbybelle, in the kitchen baking her one-hundredth batch of Christmas cookies. Laynee, helping me decorate the tree and wrap gifts. Ted and Adam stringing up enough lights outside to rival the Griswolds."

Molly grabbed an apple from the fruit basket between us. "I know it can't possibly be anywhere near the same—with the threat from Thwart hanging over our heads and another Christmas without Laynee—but you could still enjoy some of those things. I'm sure Adam would love it. I could help you decorate, and I know Dan would help Ted hang the lights."

"I've thought about that, but with Adam staying at Libbybelle's until this is over, it's been hard. Depending on how things go that day, I may not even be able to see him."

I reached into the cabinet and pulled down the salad bowl. "Every year since we've been married, Ted's had my Christmas gift delivered on Christmas morning, and heaven knows I'll miss that, but if it were up to me, none of us would be here on Christmas at all. I suggested we gather everyone and spend the holidays at a nice resort somewhere, but Ted vetoed the idea. He says being around large groups of people won't stop Legion from trying to hurt him. He doesn't want innocent people becoming collateral damage."

Molly nodded. 'He wants to keep it small and contained."

"Which is a good idea, especially since Dan received permission for us to have police protection all day on Christmas. Logically, this is the safest place to be. Adam hopes we'll be able to have Christmas dinner here, like always. But if it were up to me, we'd be long gone."

"I have to admit, if it were me, I'd want to get away,

too." She sliced the Golden Delicious apple, careful that the pieces fell into the bowl in front of her and not on the floor. "I'd go someplace exotic. Like the Fiji Islands."

I laughed. "The South Pacific? That would work for me. That's far enough away to forget things for a while."

The patio door opened. "The steaks are almost done," Ted said. "Also, I just talked with Dan. He should be pulling up any minute. What time did you say the others will be here?"

I glanced at the clock on the wall. "In about fifteen minutes, though, we're running a few minutes behind." Molly and I chuckled. We were more like an hour behind, but Ted didn't need to know that. "I'm finishing the salad now. The potatoes are baked, and the asparagus is ready. But the pie is not."

He shrugged. "All I care about is the meat. And it'll be properly rested before they get here from the sound of it." He gave us a stern look. "Less gabbing and more baking, ladies." He plucked a slice of apple from Molly's bowl. I swatted him away with a dish towel, and he scurried back to the yard.

The doorbell rang.

"Oh, no. It's Dan!" Molly dropped the knife and apple on the counter and rushed to the powder room.

I dried my hands on the towel and hurried to the door. I opened it, and Dan stepped in.

He was dressed in black fitted jeans and a dark brown sweater that made the brown in his eyes pop. He held two bouquets of flowers. One was a colorful array of cut flowers, and the other was a dozen roses.

He extended the beautiful cut flower bouquet to me. "Thanks for inviting me to dinner."

"What?" I stared at the flowers. "You mean the roses aren't for me?" I worked hard to keep a straight face, and he looked as though he wasn't sure how to answer.

Finally, he cleared his throat. "Actually, the roses are

for Molly. I hope you don't mind."

I took the colorful flowers from him and smiled. "Of course, I don't mind. I was just teasing. Ted's out in the yard if you'd like to join him. I'll go light a fire under Molly."

He grinned and glanced down at the roses. "I'd appreciate that. Thanks."

The patio door slid open again. "Hey," Ted waved him over, and they went outside.

I retrieved a vase from underneath the kitchen cabinet, added water and flowers, and placed them in the center of the dining room table. I then headed to the powder room to see what was keeping Molly.

In the few minutes it had taken to open the door for Dan, Molly had transformed the straight ponytail she'd worn when we were in the kitchen into flowing wavy locks. And the make-up she'd applied would make professional make-up artists proud. She was stunning.

I leaned against the door. "The two of you know this is a casual dinner, right?"

She touched up her eyeliner and then looked at me with Hollywood starlet eyes. "Whatever do you mean?"

"Sure. Dan shows up with a dozen roses and dressed better than I've ever seen him …" I straightened and helped her adjust the elegant white blouse she'd bought at the mall the other day. "And you look ready to step out on the red carpet." I giggled and continued, "Are you sure you don't know what I mean?"

"He bought me roses?"

I nodded.

"Good. That means he accepted my apology."

I raised an eyebrow. "When did you apologize?"

"The kiss on his cheek was my way of apologizing."

I blinked. "Oh."

A small, expensive-looking glass bottle sat on the counter. She picked it up, sprayed a little on her fingertips, and dabbed it behind her ears. "Okay, I'm ready."

When we entered the kitchen, we saw that everyone else had arrived.

Dan had come back inside and was talking with Doris and Aunt Gingie, and a quick glance through the patio door showed Abner and another man talking with Ted near the grill.

Doris picked up the knife Molly had abandoned and began slicing the remaining apples into the bowl. Molly walked past her and headed straight for Dan.

"Hi."

He grinned and picked up the rose bouquet from the counter. "For you."

"Good grief," Doris said, smacking the paring knife down on the counter. "If I'd known this was gonna turn into date night, I would've stayed home. Gingie and I got business to tend to."

I turned to my aunt, but her expression said she had no idea what Doris was talking about.

Yeah, right.

Molly touched Dan's arm. "I'll find a vase to put these in, then maybe we can go for a walk?" She spun around. "You wouldn't mind, would you, Jan? Just text me when dinner is ready?"

I nodded. "It's a beautiful evening. You guys go ahead. I need a little time anyway to get this pie in the oven."

"Great. We won't be long."

After they left, Aunt Gingie waved me over. "Come. Wolf's outside with Ted. I know you've been dying to meet him."

I started to follow her out to the yard but realized I'd be leaving Doris to finish the pie by herself. "Wait. Let me help Doris, and I'll be right out."

Doris shot up a hand. "I don't need help. Besides, if you were really interested in this pie, it'd be done already. Who invites people to dinner and don't have a dessert ready?"

"Doris—"

"Don't, Doris, me. Just show me where the cinnamon and nutmeg are, and this thing'll be baked up in a jiffy."

I pointed to the spice shelf in the pantry, then walked out to the yard with Gingie. The chilled air bit through my thin, long-sleeved shirt and quickly reminded me that I'd forgotten to grab a jacket.

Aunt Gingie took my hand and led me toward the tallest man in the bunch. He was extremely handsome and had hair that reminded me of the color of midnight. It was gathered at the nape of his neck by a suede strap, and the rest of the ponytail fell down the back of his jacket and stopped right above his waist.

The jacket was a dark tan and made of soft leather. It sported fringe on the front, shoulders, back, and sleeves and was ornamented with black, red, and turquoise beading. Small eagle medallions crossed over the shoulders. The jacket highlighted the faded blue jeans and black boots he wore.

"Wolf," Aunt Gingie said, then clicked her tongue. "Let me introduce you properly. Lonewolf Rainwater, I'd like you to finally meet my niece, January. June's daughter."

He extended his hand. "Nice to finally meet you, January."

I detected a slight Native American accent. I reached for his hand and shook it. "Please call me Jan. January sounds so . . . cold. But, as I'm sure you're aware, my mother and grandmother thought it would be fun to name their children after their favorite months of the year."

"After all these years, your aunt still refuses to let me call her April. Although she did have it legally changed to Lorraine, her middle name, but she won't let me call her that either."

She gave him a playful punch in the arm.

"So, should I call you Uncle Lonewolf?"

He slipped his hands in his pockets and smiled. "No, Wolf would do just fine."

"These steaks aren't going to taste great forever," Ted wrapped his arm around my waist. "Time to eat."

We stepped inside the kitchen and stopped.

The smell of cinnamon and melted butter filled the air. The pie was in the oven, and the dishes were washed and put away.

In the dining room, everything except the steaks was on the table. The place settings had been set, and the asparagus was on a platter. Baked potatoes and warm bread were lathered in butter, and a cucumber and tomato salad filled the bowls.

I felt like such a slacker.

Doris rubbed her hands together. "Ready?"

As everyone resounded yes and took their seats, Doris stared at me. I couldn't help but wonder if she was asking if we were ready to eat or if we were ready for something else.

Aunt Gingie gave her a scalding look. Doris looked away, but by then, I had my answer.

It was definitely something else.

Chapter Twenty-Five

Dan and Molly returned from their walk just as Ted set the steaks on the table.

Molly knew everyone there except Abner Slater, Doris's husband. After Ted said grace, I introduced them.

Abner smiled, nodded, and adjusted his wire-frame glasses. Dressed in a pair of light brown corduroys and a navy-blue sweater, he looked every bit the stereotypical retired accountant. He was an older gentleman but still had a head full of hair. All of it snow white.

Molly stole curious glances at Doris and Abner as I passed the salad and dinner rolls. The look on her face told me she was thinking about how a nice guy like Abner could be married to someone like Doris.

When everyone was settled, she asked Abner, "How did you and Doris meet?"

"Ah." He set his salad fork on the table and templed his fingers. "The first day I laid eyes on her was at her father's church. I was seven, and she was five. She was throwing a tantrum, and her mother snatched her out of the pew and dragged her up the aisle. Doris screamed the whole time. Her face was red and adorable, and parts of her fancy white dress were balled up in her tiny fists.

"The following Sunday, she introduced herself, and we became friends. Years later, I decided that I wanted her as my wife. My bride teetered at the tender age of twenty when we married. That will be fifty-five years ago this spring."

Molly smiled as Abner talked, but her head jerked at the word *tender*. She had a lot of ways of describing Doris. Tender wasn't one of them.

She was about to prod Abner with more questions when I noticed Doris giving her the evil eye. I decided to change the topic. I knew from personal experience that Doris didn't like people asking questions about her past.

I turned my attention to Lonewolf. "Did you and Aunt Gingie meet in church, too?"

He shook his head. "We met in high school. It was love at first sight." He chuckled. "Well, it was for me anyway. However, she was in love with some cocky, knuckleheaded high-school football star at the time."

Aunt Gingie elbowed him. "It's not like you were sitting back pining for me. If I remember correctly, you also had your fair share of athletic admirers. Like Missy, head of the cheerleading squad?"

Lonewolf picked up his steak knife. "Oh, yeah. Missy. I remember her. We dated for a few weeks, but it wasn't long before I realized it wasn't me she was after. She was just being nice to me to get close to Garringer."

My fork plopped onto my plate. "Garringer went to your high school?"

"Yeah," he took a bite of his steak and chewed. When he noticed everyone at the table staring at him, he turned to Aunt Gingie. "She didn't know you and Garringer went to school together?"

She shook her head.

"Oh," he swallowed the steak and put his knife down. He then looked at Ted. "I'm sorry, I shouldn—"

"Don't worry," Ted put up his hand. "It's okay. The more we know about Garringer's past, the better."

I tried to picture Garringer as a typical high school student. I couldn't. It didn't match with the monster I'd known. But knowing Lonewolf and Aunt Gingie knew him in his younger years intrigued me, yet I couldn't bring myself to ask one single question. Thankfully, I didn't have to. Molly was asking them for me.

"What was he like in high school?" she asked.

Lonewolf looked at Aunt Gingie before he answered. She nodded.

He looked down at the table before looking back up at Molly. "I knew Garringer before high school. We grew up together."

I sat back in my chair.

Molly leaned forward in hers. "You did?"

Lonewolf shifted in his chair several times before answering. "Garringer spent a lot of time with my tribe when we were kids. We no longer lived on a reservation, but my family kept up with many ancient traditions. Garringer loved being involved in those, so we both hung out quite a bit.

"The only thing we knew about him and his family was that his father was killed in a mysterious accident and that his mother was a fortune teller. She had a small shop on the outskirts of town. That was the best place for it because most of the townspeople were terrified of her. But somehow, she made a decent living, and Garringer never lacked anything. He always had the best clothes, cars, women."

Molly sat silent, deep in thought. But there were more questions I needed answered, even though I feared they'd turn my world upside down. Still, I had to know. Ted was right. Information was key. I cleared my throat. "Lonewolf, how long were you and Garringer friends?"

He furrowed his brow. "What year did you arrive at your aunt's?"

"1982."

He rubbed his chin. After a few moments, he said, "Garringer and I probably stopped being friends about two years before that."

This time, it was Molly who sat back in her chair. Words

caught in my throat. That was around the time Garringer had started abusing her.

Lonewolf continued, "Garringer always had a fascination with the dark side. In high school, he just played around with crystals and the weird-looking cards he'd picked up from his mother's shop, but by the time we went to college, he was obsessed. He spent hours sitting in dark rooms, talking with spirits. At least, that's what he told me.

"When we graduated, he returned home and started his own sect. Gingie and I were curious, so we decided to join him." He shook his head. "We had no idea what we were getting ourselves into. I'd heard about God and Satan, but I'd never stepped foot in a church. However, Garringer knew the Bible and used it to trick people. He told us it said things it didn't, and we believed him."

He stopped abruptly and looked at me.

When he said nothing further, I said, "If there's more, please feel free to share."

He looked around the table, and I did the same. Abner was eating, and Molly and Gingie had lowered their heads. Dan had started taking notes, and Doris's gaze was locked on Lonewolf.

"I'm sorry," Lonewolf said. "I didn't mean to make this evening about Garringer."

I chuckled. "Neither did we, but what you're sharing is helpful and important. So, please continue."

He glanced around the table again, then nodded. "Garringer changed after he started the sect. I don't mean gradually. I'm talking overnight. One day, he was the fun-loving guy we all knew and grew up with, and the next, he was cold and heartless. He'd always been able to conjure up supernatural powers to impress new recruits, like levitating furniture, but suddenly, his powers went beyond that. And those who crossed him, or tried to leave, disappeared."

I swallowed.

"The last straw for me," he continued. "Was when he

talked one of our friends into sacrificing herself so that *he* would receive greater powers." He closed his eyes and then looked at me and Ted. "When I found that out, I left the cult and went to the police. I told them everything Garringer had told me. I also gave them the girl's name and where she was from. They swore they'd look into it, but the looks on their faces told me they never would.

"That's when I went home. I packed my bags and Gingie's." He looked over at my aunt, who was still looking down at her lap. "But by that time, she'd been so brainwashed and was so deep into the occultic activity that she refused to leave." He shrugged. "I figured she'd eventually see what I saw happening with Garringer and the cult and later join me. She did, though it took much longer than I thought."

Lonewolf pushed his plate to the side and folded his arms on the table. "About a year after I left, I ran into a pastor friend who used to have a church in Corinth. He told me how much control Garringer had gained over that town. He said members of Garringer's cult were everywhere, including the hospitals, city government, and police department. He also said that they were loyal. Anything that went on in Corinth that Garringer didn't want to get out didn't. Eventually, a lot of churches packed up and left. The constant fires and threats and lack of cooperation from the authorities was too much for them."

"Are you saying the *whole* police department was corrupt?" Dan asked.

"Almost. Those who weren't were too scared to do anything about it. It wasn't until Cheatham and his crew showed up that things changed. After the explosion at Gingie's and Jan's disappearance, Cheatham helped spearhead the IA investigation, and they cleaned house. After he retired, the guy who took his place was young and inexperienced, and Corinth resumed going downhill. But most of the people who were close to Garringer had moved on. Everyone except for Abigail."

I tilted my head. "Abigail?"

"Garringer's wife."

Molly and I sat forward in our chairs at the same time. "Garringer had a wife?"

I wasn't sure if she'd asked the question or if I did because I was more focused on the words that came out of his mouth next.

"Yes," he said. "Thwart's mother."

Chapter Twenty-Six

Everyone started to speak at once.

Doris smacked her hand against the table. "That's why I haven't been able to find that dirty rat rascal. He ran home to his Mommy's house!"

"What do you mean?" I asked, my heart pounding. "I thought you had a tracker ..." I pressed my lips together. I'd said too much.

Ted stood and put his hands in the air. "Everyone calm down."

Dan looked across the table at Doris. "What do you mean you weren't able to find him? Have you been out looking for Thwart? And did Jan say you had a tracker?"

Doris opened her mouth to respond, but Aunt Gingie interrupted her. "Ignore Doris, Dan. You know how she gets when she's riled up."

Molly leaned toward Abner. "Is that what Doris and Gingie have been up to the past couple of days? Looking for Thwart?"

"Doris," Dan threw his napkin on top of his plate. "I swear. If you—"

"Quiet!"

Everyone stared at Ted. He exhaled, and his arms fell to his sides. "Obviously, there are a lot of questions, but none of us will be heard if we continue talking over each other."

He rubbed the back of his neck and focused his gaze on Lonewolf. "You said Garringer was married, and his wife's name is Abigail?"

He nodded.

Ted resumed his seat. "And Thwart is their son. Is it possible he could be hiding out there?"

"No," Dan answered before Lonewolf could. "Cheatham's already checked her out. She hasn't seen or heard from Thwart in months."

Doris let out a loud huff. "She's lying."

Dan ignored her. "Ted, when Cheatham came to town, he brought everything they'd gathered on Legion. Their file is pretty thick, but thankfully, Abigail has been cooperative. We even asked if she'd allow us to tap her phone lines in case Thwart called. She said yes."

Doris shook her head. "Amateurs."

Lonewolf put up his hands. "I don't want you guys getting the wrong impression of Abigail. She is Thwart's mother and Garringer's widow, but she's nothing like them. Never has been."

Dan nodded. "Cheatham agrees. She has no criminal history, but they have a lot of information on her, most of which she provided and it incriminated Garringer.

"There are multiple reports where she talks about the crimes Garringer forced her to watch or participate in. There were also restraining orders, photos, wiretap records, and depositions. She provided enough information for state authorities to nail Garringer to the wall. But they were never able to track him down."

I turned to Lonewolf. "But you said that she was his widow. She did all that but never divorced him?"

"Nope. And she never would have. Just like he was with my family, Garringer was drawn to Abigail. Enamored with her, and they married young. Despite the fact that he was never faithful to her, he told me plenty of times how Abigail was the only woman he ever loved, and he was fiercely protective of her. If you wanted to get on Garringer's bad side, mess with him. But if you wanted to get on his *really* bad side, mess with Abigail."

Molly shook her head. "I don't understand. If she loved him, why was she working with the authorities?"

"I said Garringer was in love with her, not that she was in love with him. Any feelings she had toward him ended when we returned from college. Like I said, he changed overnight. Abigail's a Christian, and she holds strong convictions on marriage. When she'd said the words, 'til death do us part,' she meant it."

An image of Garringer tying me to an altar while flames roared underneath popped into my mind.

"So, no matter what he did," I asked. "Even when he danced with the devil himself, she'd still refuse to divorce him?"

"The only explanation I can give you, Jan, is that it is just how Abigail is. And not only with Garringer, she's like that with her son, Liam. Or, as you guys know him, Thwart. When she finds out he's done something criminal, she reports it to the police. Thwart knows that, so he keeps his distance when he's in trouble. But just like his father, Thwart adores his mother. She loves him, too, but if she says she hasn't seen him, you can take her word for it."

I stood and started clearing the table. The dinner hadn't gone as I'd hoped, and the food had barely been eaten, but I couldn't sit still anymore. I had to move. I had to think.

"I did receive this bit of news," Dan pulled out his phone. "We were able to get a rush job on those items we sent to the state lab. Nothing came back on the note Jan found in the mailbox, and when I say nothing, I mean nothing. The tech said it appeared to not have been touched by human hands. But the photos of the muddy footprints revealed that they were made by boots. A rare type of boot, only made in certain parts of the country. My boys at the station are working on that info now. We should have something by morning."

Doris folded her arms across her chest. "Or we could bring in that lying mother of his and waterboard her."

Dan slid the phone back into his pocket. "There is no *we*, Doris. If you're trying to track this guy down, stop before you get yourself killed. My department can handle this."

"Your department can't handle squat. It's been two weeks since Jan received that letter." She leaned across the table and thrust two wrinkled fingers in Dan's direction. "*Two weeks.* And what do you have to show for it? Nothing, that's what. It was bad enough when you had no distractions, but now," she turned those same two fingers toward Molly. "This one's got your head in the clouds. All those years of being abused by Garringer taught her nothing. If it did, she wouldn't be walking around here dressed like a trollop."

Molly stood so fast that her chair toppled. "You lying red-headed weasel!"

Doris sprang from her seat. "Tramp."

Molly hopped up on the table and lunged toward Doris. Her hands had been inches from Doris's throat. It was only Dan's firm grip on her waist that stopped her from connecting.

Abner gripped Doris's elbow, and she plopped down into her chair.

I set the plates down and looked at her. "Doris, apologize to Molly right now."

"It'll be a cold day—"

Ted put up his hands again, then turned to Lonewolf. "My apologies. This is not the get-to-know-you dinner that Jan and I had planned."

He shook his head. "It's my fault. This wasn't the time or place to bring up my history with Garringer. I should've been more careful with my words."

"It might not have been the best place to do it, but I'm glad you did. The more information we have, the easier it will be for us to stop his son. His mother may be able to help. I don't want anything to happen to her son, and I don't want anything to happen to me or my family, either. I hope to be able to end this peacefully."

Doris let out a loud sigh and threw her back against the chair. "You people just don't get it."

Ted turned to her. "No, Doris, you don't get it. My wife has warned you before about insulting Molly. Apologize now or leave."

Her eyes narrowed. "First, you had me apologize to those dimwitted youth leaders, and now this?" She stood and snatched her purse from the floor. "Everyone here can …"

Aunt Gingie stood quickly and ran to Doris, whispering something in her ear.

Doris straightened and turned to Molly. "I apologize. I'm sorry about the things I said to you."

An apology from Satan himself would've been more convincing.

Molly looked at me, and I nodded. That was as close as she was gonna get to any type of remorse from Doris.

"Jan," Dan said before Molly could reply, "If you don't mind, I think Molls and I will skip dessert. I have tickets to the midnight jazz festival downtown, and we should probably head that way now if we want to make it there on time." He grabbed Molly's hand, and they said their goodbyes to Abner, Lonewolf, and Gingie as they walked to the door.

When they left, Abner stood. The whispering between Aunt Gingie and Doris continued and was so fervent that they didn't even notice when he donned his hat and reached for his jacket.

I leaned in closer to hear what they were saying. Aunt Gingie was chastising Doris. Then she said something about how Doris needed to get her act together or …

The smoke alarm in the kitchen went off.

The apple pie.

I ran into the kitchen. Ted and Lonewolf followed and grabbed dish towels to wave under the alarm.

I turned off the oven and switched on the oven light.

The pie was on fire.

"Don't open it," Ted rushed over and stood in front of the oven door. "As long as it's contained, everything'll be fine. It'll burn itself out."

I glanced at the flames fighting to get through my oven door.

Doris and Aunt Gingie were still in the dining room. I couldn't see them, but I could hear them. Their fevered whispers continued like nothing ever happened, and a flame rose in my gut. Everything in me told me that conversation had to do with Thwart.

And they were keeping me out of the loop.

But unlike the flames in the oven, the flame in my gut wouldn't be contained. I was tired of standing on the sidelines waiting for Thwart or Legion to make a move. It was a deadly game, but for the sake of my family, I had to play it.

I wanted in.

But there was a problem. I'd promised Ted in this very kitchen that if I ever felt the urge to be reckless again, I'd talk to him about it first.

I sighed. No way was he going to let me walk headlong into trouble again. Especially if Aunt Gingie and Doris were involved.

I placed a hand on my belly and moaned. I had to do something and fast.

The flame in my gut was threatening to turn into a five-alarm fire.

Chapter Twenty-Seven

I waited for the fire in the oven to wither out, and Ted asked Lonewolf if the two of them could talk on the patio.

They went outside, but Aunt Gingie insisted she had last-minute business to take care of and that she'd ride back with Doris and Abner.

"That's fine," I said and opened the foyer closet. I grabbed a coat and added, "Molly's with Dan, and Ted's with Lonewolf, so I'll come with you."

Doris frowned and then followed Abner outside to the car.

Aunt Gingie hung my coat back up in the closet. "Jan, you need to stay here." She hugged me, then stepped across the threshold onto the porch. "I have to go. Abner's waiting."

"Is Doris involved in this last-minute *business* you need to take care of?" I asked.

"Jan—"

"Why are you spending so much time with her? What about me? You and I haven't had the chance to talk since you've been back.

"I understand, and please don't think I'm choosing Doris over you. I don't like the woman. The first night I spent at her place almost became a crime scene. Lucky for her, Wolf and Abner were there to break us apart." She sighed. "But … there's a reason she asked me to stay with her. More of a plan than a reason, but it's something I need to do."

"Are you going to tell me about the plan?"

"Why ask me that? You know I'm not. Why would I put you in harm's way?"

"Harm's way? Doris's plan has something to do with Thwart, doesn't it?"

When Aunt Gingie didn't answer, I said, "Whatever it is, I want in. I don't sit back and wait for something to happen."

She placed a hand on my shoulder. "You wouldn't be your mother's daughter if you did. When our parents couldn't take care of us anymore, June did everything in her power to make sure our family stayed together. And that's what you need to do now. Focus on your family. Ted and Adam deserve all of your energy right now. Let me, Dan and Doris, chase after the vermin."

I couldn't help but laugh. "Vermin" was not a word Aunt Gingie would use, so I knew she'd picked it up from Doris's colorful vernacular. I nodded. "You're right."

"Of course, I am. I'm your older and wiser aunt, remember?" She hugged me again. "Listen, I gotta run. Tell Wolf I left the keys to the rental car on the coffee table."

I nodded, closed the door behind her, and retrieved my coat from the closet. I put my right arm through the sleeve and gasped.

Stinging pain traveled down the back of my neck and along my right side. I hitched in a breath and leaned against the closet door. Dizziness came and went in waves.

Ted was right.

My body still hadn't completely healed from Garringer's beating.

When the lightheadedness subsided, I slowly slid the rest of the coat on and joined Ted and Lonewolf on the patio. My body cried out for a hot, relaxing bath and a warm bed, but my mind churned with questions for Lonewolf.

I sat in the patio chair across from him. "Aunt Gingie

left with the Slaters. The keys to the car are on the coffee table."

He nodded.

Ted shifted in his chair to face me. "Honey, are you all right? You look like you're in pain."

"I'll be okay. I'm about to turn in, but I wanted to see what the two of you were up to first."

"I was just telling Lonewolf about some of the things that happened after Garringer and Legion came to town. We just finished talking about Ruin. Miss Flora cast him out of Olivia's house, but Lonewolf thinks he's far from being gone from the town."

I looked at Lonewolf. "Really?"

He nodded. "Ruin follows Legion."

I pulled my coat tight around me. "So, Thwart's going to pick up where his father left off?"

Lonewolf scrubbed a hand over his face. "Hard to say because the Liam I knew wouldn't be capable of any of this. Abigail was pretty good at keeping him on the straight and narrow. But when he got older, he spent a lot of time with his father. It didn't seem to impact him too much at the time, but now?" Lonewolf shrugged his left shoulder. "I'm not so sure."

I nibbled my bottom lip and remembered something Dan had mentioned before. "Sheriff Glass said that Thwart killed the man he suspected of killing his brother, Declan. Was he also Abigail's son?"

"No. Liam is the only child of Garringer and Abigail," he leaned forward. "Like I mentioned earlier, Garringer was never faithful, which was intentional. He was an only child, and he hated every minute of it. When we were kids, he talked constantly about having a large family like mine. Abigail didn't know it, but by the time Liam was born, Garringer already had enough kids to start a small army. He kept up with all of them. He was determined not to let any of his children slip through his fingers. And they didn't. That is until a pregnant Molly disappeared."

Ted nodded. "Leah was the one who got away."

"And according to Abigail, Garringer was obsessed with finding her."

"Which is why he demanded I tell him where Molly was," I shivered as memories of being in the cave with Garringer played like a horror movie before me.

"Yeah. He planned for Molly to suffer a far worse fate than her mother's for disappearing with his child. Gingie helped hide Molly as well, and she was roughed up by his minions for doing that—however, Garringer later killed them that evening for hurting her. They weren't supposed to touch Gingie. She was untouchable."

I cringed. "The look in Garringer's eyes every time he mentioned Molly's name ..." I shook my head and blinked away the images. "Wait. Did you say Gingie was untouchable?"

"Yeah."

"Why?"

"Because of a promise."

"To who?"

He pointed to his chest. "Out of loyalty to our childhood friendship and how my family embraced him as a kid, Garringer promised never to harm Gingie or anyone in my bloodline. That's why Gingie was able to get away with so much more than the other cult members and why I was able to report his activities to the police and walk out of town alive."

Lonewolf looked down at his boots, then back up at me. "That's also why he was hesitant to harm you. After he tried that stint of sacrificing you on the altar, Gingie reminded him that when she took you in, that made you part of our family. That kept him at bay for a while, but when Molly escaped, he was furious. He couldn't touch Gingie, but he would make her pay. He knew the best way to do that was through you. All protection he'd extended to you as a courtesy was revoked."

"Which is why he had Mordell kidnap me from the police station."

Lonewolf nodded. "According to Abigail, he considered what Gingie had done a betrayal, and you were the one who would have to pay the price." He shoved his hands into his jacket pockets. "But the funny thing is that the biggest betrayal would come through Liam—his favorite and only child given to him by his precious Abigail. Liam had been in contact with his sister, Leah, for years. He knew how to contact her. And not once did he mention it to his father."

"Are you sure?"

"I spent hours on the phone the other day with Abigail. She said when Liam first found out about Leah, he called her. When Abigail asked if he would tell his dad, Liam said no and swore he'd take what he knew about Leah to the grave."

I pulled my jacket around me again and wondered why Liam wanted to keep that information to himself.

The frigid night air stirred and swirled around us. Leaves from the yard glided, swept onto the patio, and settled next to our feet.

I picked up one of the leaves. Lonewolf had provided a treasure trove of information about Garringer and his family, but there were so many more unanswered.

The more I learned about Liam/Thwart, the more it sounded like Ted's goal of peacefully ending the standoff with him might work.

Maybe if I met with him, I could stop things from turning bloody.

I remembered my conversation with Gingie and her words about the *business* she and Doris had to take care of.

The leaf crumbled in my hand.

Was it too late?

Had blood already been shed?

Chapter Twenty-Eight

"What can I get you ladies this morning?" Stephanie's smile was as white as the crisp blouse of her uniform.

Molly and I joined Aunt Gingie, Doris, Olivia, Anna, and Miss Flora for breakfast at Barney's, Ted's favorite pancake place and the new employer of Doris's soon-to-be granddaughter-in-law, Stephanie.

Doris glanced at her and frowned. "You know what I like."

"Yes, ma'am," Stephanie's smile brightened as she wrote down Doris's order. "And what about the rest of you ladies? I can start with a cup of coffee for everyone if you'd like more time. Barney's House Blend is half-price today and is very popular with our customers."

Molly, Aunt Gingie, and Olivia agreed to the coffee, and Miss Flora and I asked for hot tea. Anna settled on a glass of orange juice.

"Great. I'll get those to you and then return for your order in a few minutes. Will that be okay?"

Everyone nodded except Doris. Stephanie turned to her, adding, "Barney knows you're here, and he's preparing your order just the way you like it. It'll be out in no time. Can I get you anything else?"

Doris turned and stared out the window. Stephanie slid her order pad and pen into her apron pocket, then pointed to the menus on the table. "If you have any questions about the breakfast entrée, just let me know."

"Thanks, Stephanie," I picked up one of the menus. "We'll be ready to order by the time you get back."

She smiled, and her blonde ponytail bounced endlessly as she spoke to several more customers before returning to the counter.

Miss Flora was seated next to Doris. She leaned toward her and poked her with her elbow. "Why you so mean?"

"Don't start with me, Flora."

Miss Flora pointed one of her bony ebony fingers at Doris. "No, ma'am. Don't you start with me. Everybody knows you don't like the girl bein' engaged to your grandson, but that's no excuse to be rude. And I ain't havin' it. Not in my presence. When you with me, act like you got some sense."

Anna giggled, and Olivia motioned for her to stop. She did, but Anna couldn't hide the huge grin on her face.

Doris murmured something under her breath. I couldn't make it out, but as Doris and Miss Flora sat side by side, I couldn't help but notice the marked difference between the two. Miss Flora's silver hair was cut in a short Afro style that resembled a halo, while Doris's spiked red hair jutted out in all directions and resembled flames.

I laughed loudly.

"Glad to see you ladies enjoying your morning," Stephanie balanced a small circular tray in one hand and, with the other, handed Anna her orange juice and placed five mugs on the table. She poured hot water into two and coffee in the remaining three. Barney, the owner of the pancake house, stood next to her. He set a plate in front of Doris. It was loaded with scrambled eggs and sliced fried potatoes, onions, and red and green peppers. Then he set another plate in front of her that contained two huge pork chops. Next to that, he set a glass mug with a frothy amber liquid inside. Surely that wasn't …

Barney flipped the empty tray under his arm. "Doris, I trust everything is exactly the way you like it?"

She wrapped her fingers around the mug. "Homemade?"

"My own special brew. With a few of the changes you suggested, of course."

She lifted the glass and took a sip. "Mmm." She then picked up her fork and took a bite of the eggs. "Much better than last time. Keep up the good work, kid. You've got potential."

Olivia and I looked at each other. What did she mean by potential? Barney's was the best pancake house within a fifty-mile radius. The tourists knew it, too, and Barney was no kid. He started this place in his early twenties, fifty-plus years ago. And what in the world was Doris drinking with her breakfast?

"Stop judging me, Jan."

I jerked my head back. How on earth did she know what I was thinking?

She picked up her knife and sliced into her pork chop.

When Barney disappeared into the kitchen, Stephanie pulled out her pad and pen. "Ready to order?"

I ordered a stack of their famous blueberry pancakes with apricot syrup and excused myself to the restroom. I had three cups of tea before Molly and I arrived, and my bladder reminded me of it. As usual, Barney's was super busy. I half-ran and half-walked down the hall to the restrooms. Thankfully, there wasn't a line.

I pushed open the door and was surprised to find the bathroom empty. After I was done, I headed to the sink, reached for the foam soap dispenser, and jumped when I looked in the mirror. Standing behind me was the girl who'd befriended Anna and was a part of Legion.

Whisper.

I recognized her from the night she and Thwart stood outside our home and threatened to kill Ted.

I stared at the image in the mirror and met her gaze. "What do you want?"

Her head tilted to the side slowly. It was so slow that, at first, I wasn't sure if it was moving. She kept her eyes locked on mine, and in a voice barely loud enough for me to hear, she said, "Tell Gingie and her red-headed friend that the next time they shoot at me, they'd better not miss."

I swallowed and quickly scanned her reflected image. The night she was with Thwart, she'd worn all black. Today, she wore a short white dress with a thin lace overlay, knee-high dark brown boots, and a tan jean jacket.

Thick, black hair had been loosely gathered on her left side and secured with a white ribbon. Tendrils flowed down the front left side of her jacket.

From what I could tell, she wasn't carrying any weapons.

I shook my head. "I have no idea what you're talking about."

Her head was still tilted. She pressed her lips together, and a smile crept across her face. "Of course not. Everybody wants to protect Jan."

This time, I picked up a slight Spanish accent. I leaned forward against the bathroom sink and gripped it. Everything in me wanted to turn around and face her directly. But something also told me not to take my eyes off her for one second.

I trembled and blew out a breath. "Listen—"

"No, you listen," she stepped closer and straightened her head just as slowly as she'd tilted it. "Pastor Ted can wait for the inevitable or end this tonight. There'll be bloodshed. But he must meet us after dark in Leviathan's Field if the only blood he wants to be shed is his. Our sentinels will let us know when he's arrived."

I tightened my grip on the sink. "Ted'll never turn himself over to you or anyone else. If you want me, my husband, Gingie, Molly, or Leah, you're gonna have to work at it. We outsmarted Garringer over thirty years ago, and I'm sure it'll be twice as easy to outsmart his son."

An invisible shrieking wind blew through the bathroom, and a high-pitched noise pierced my ears.

Lines formed and zigzagged across one of the large bathroom windows, high along the wall. The lines inched along and began to crack. The panes vibrated, and I realized I'd taken my eyes off Whisper.

I glanced back at the mirror. Her eyes had darkened from warm brown to coal black.

And they were just as lifeless.

"I'm not here for Leah. Garringer's gone. I'll be the next princess of darkness, not her."

The crackling sounds in the window grew louder, her voice softer.

"I avenge blood for blood. Pastor Ted *will* die." Her eyes suddenly went warm again, and she smiled. "I'm only here, a part of your world, for as long as you let me be. We disappear once Pastor Ted pays for what he did to our leader."

She backed away from me slowly, and the sound of the window breaking grew louder with each step.

She paused when she reached the bathroom door and walked back toward me. I willed my feet to move and for my body to turn and face her, but fear cemented me to the floor. She leaned in so close that I smelled strawberry shampoo, flowery perfume, and burnt ashes. She whispered, "You left something in the stall."

She jumped back and raised her left arm in the air. I finally spun around and prepared to defend myself.

Her eyes flashed, and her arm sliced through the air like an ax.

The bathroom window popped. I dashed under the bathroom counter as glass shards burst onto the tiled bathroom floor.

I looked to see what Whisper would do next, but she was gone.

I scrambled from under the bathroom counter into the

stall I'd used minutes before. On the ivory-white toilet seat sat a bracelet. A small silver bracelet with bright yellow butterflies in the center of it.

Laynee's bracelet.

Chapter Twenty-Nine

"**What was it** about 'don't go anywhere alone,' didn't you understand?" Dan yelled. "You could've been killed!"

I plopped down on the sofa, Laynee's bracelet still gripped in my hand. The bracelet Ted had given her when she'd turned five. The bracelet that had rested near his grandfather's bible inside his desk at the church. When grief over Laynee overwhelmed him, he'd pull out both and let the Scriptures comfort him.

Somehow, Legion had gotten to it.

"Dan," Molly placed a hand on my shoulder. "It's not her fault. There were six of us still at the table. Any one of us could've gone to the lady's room with her," she wiped at her eyes. "*I* should've gone with her."

"Molly, don't cry." I reached for her hand and placed it in mine. "There's no way you could've known."

Dan scrubbed a hand over his face. "No, ladies. 'Don't go anywhere alone' means Don't. Go. Anywhere. Alone. And if that means you have to sit on top of each other in the bathroom, do it." His face darkened, and the vein in his neck pulsed. "Thank God this didn't end as badly as it could have." He crouched in front of me. "You have to be more careful. Tell me you understand."

I nodded and slowly let it seep in that this wasn't just police business with Dan. It was personal. It was about not losing a friend. And despite everything I'd put him through, the look on his face told me that what Molly said was true. He still considered me a friend.

Ted sat next to me and gently eased the bracelet from my hand. He held the bracelet over his heart for what seemed like an eternity. He sniffed and stood. "I'll be in my office."

When he walked down the hall, I stood to go after him. Dan grabbed my arm. "Jan, please. I need to question you about the incident while it's still fresh in your mind. My guys are scouring the scene at Barney's, but any information you give me now could help speed things up."

I heard a soft click. Ted had closed the door to his office. I turned to Dan. "I want to be with my husband, so make it fast."

He nodded and looked out the window behind me. "Where's Gingie and Doris? I need to question them, too."

Molly shook her head. "All I know is that when Jan ran out of the bathroom crying and told us what happened, they got in Doris's car and sped off."

"Did they say where they were going?"

"No, and they're not answering their phones either." She stood beside him. "But Miss Flora is across the street at Olivia's. I can go get them if you like."

"Thanks, but I already interviewed them." He motioned for me to sit again on the sofa. Molly leaned against the wall near the window.

He reached into his pocket for the all-too-familiar notebook. "You said that on your way to the restroom, you were surprised there was no line and that the bathroom was empty. Did anything else strike you as odd?"

"Not really. The ladies' room at Barney's only has three stalls, so there's always a wait. The place was packed this morning, so I expected more women to be in there. But before I went to the sink and saw Whisper standing behind me, nothing else was out of the ordinary."

"So she was hidden in one of the stalls?"

"No, she wasn't. When I entered the restroom, all three stall doors were open. No one was inside them. Like I told you, the place was empty."

He ran his fingers through his hair. "So she just appeared?"

"It seems that way. The door to that restroom has a loud squeak. I'm sure I would've heard her walk in."

"And the glass windows. They just … shattered on their own?"

I nodded.

He cleared his throat. "You said that she wants Ted to meet her tonight at Leviathan's Field. Did she say what time?"

"No. Why?"

"We have a team ready, but we don't want to tip our hand too soon."

I looked over at Molly. Her furrowed brow and narrowed eyes told me she was just as confused as I was.

The look on his face told me nothing. "Dan, what are you talking about?"

"Ted wants to do the meet."

"*What*?" Molly pushed off the wall and bounded towards Dan. "That's insanity. They'll kill him!"

Dan stood. "We're not going to let that happen."

"Not gonna let that happen?" Molly's voice rose as she leaned forward. "We're talking about Legion here. There's no telling what they'll have waiting for Ted out in that field!"

"Molls," he lowered his voice to counter hers. "We've got this."

She groaned and slapped me hard on the shoulder. "Jan, say something!"

I turned away from her and toward the cobalt blue throw pillows beside me on the sofa. One of them had a loose thread.

Dan sat back down. "Jan, you okay?"

I stared at the pillow.

He gently touched my arm. "Jan?"

My mouth opened, then closed. I didn't know what to tell them. Part of me wanted to jump up and join Molly in her protest. Another part of me wanted to sit still, pray, and lean on God. Then there was another part that wanted to grab every gun Ted had hidden in the house and invade Leviathan's Field like it was Custer's Last Stand.

He squeezed my arm. "It's a lot to take in right now. First the incident with Whisper, then Laynee's bracelet—"

"When did Ted decide to do this?"

"Ted was with me at the station when the call from Barney's came in. When he heard what Whisper wanted, he immediately agreed to it. I tried to talk him out of it, but he said that you and Adam's safety was at stake, and if meeting with Legion would end this madness, he was all in. Then he —"

"Sheriff," Mick Bolt, Dan's lead deputy, barreled through the front door and stopped in front of us. "Shots have been fired at a warehouse near Leviathan's Field."

Dan jumped up. "Mick, get every available squad car out there now." Then he turned back to me and Molly. "Nobody leaves here until they hear back from me. Understand?"

I nodded, but Molly grabbed Dan's elbow. "Please be careful."

They kissed, then he hurried out behind Mick. She locked the door behind them, then stared out the window. Sirens blared in the distance.

I grabbed the pillow with the loose thread and placed it in my lap. I wound the skinny blue strand around my finger and yanked. The sound made her jump.

She turned and walked toward the stairs. "My head is pounding. I'm going to get an aspirin. Do you need one?"

"No, but I could use some water. I'll get us both some."

She nodded and headed up the stairs.

I went to the kitchen and pulled two glasses from the

cabinet. A noise at the back door startled me. I spun around. Doris was standing there.

I let her inside, and she swiped at a streak of blood running down her face. "We need reinforcements."

"You scared the daylights out of me. Where's my aunt?"

"They got her."

"What do you mean, *they got her*?"

She rushed toward me. "Are you gonna stand there and ask questions, or are you gonna help?" She motioned to the kitchen sink. "Grab the gun duct taped under there and meet me in the car." She turned and ran out the door, leaving it open behind her.

My heart raced as every possible worst-case scenario involving Aunt Gingie crossed my mind. I bent and swung open the cabinet. The gun was right where Molly had left it. I reached for it, but my hand, seemingly with a mind of its own, inched away from it.

I slammed the cabinet door, grabbed my keys off the counter, and followed Doris.

Chapter Thirty

I flung open the passenger door to Doris's black Cadillac Escalade. Two amber eyes stared back at me. And they didn't belong to Doris.

She patted the large, well-muscled animal on the rump, and it jumped into the back seat. I'd seen German Shepherd's before, but none had looked so deadly.

Doris revved the engine, then pointed her thumb at the dog. "That's Maestro. He won't attack unless I tell him to. Get in."

I climbed into the SUV and closed the door, fully aware of the panting and growling behind my seat. "Where are we going?"

She shot away from the curb and accelerated until the speedometer reached eighty miles an hour. I went for my seat belt. "Doris, slow down."

The SUV picked up speed. She swerved to the right, and I gripped the door handle. She rounded a corner on what I'm sure were only two wheels.

"Doris!"

She steered the vehicle into the middle of four-lane traffic on the main road. I covered my ears and tried to ignore the blare of horns and shouts.

She pulled sharply to the left at a stop light and cut off a shiny red pickup. The driver slammed on his brakes, but

Doris powered her way through the traffic and onto the entrance ramp of the highway.

I collapsed against the soft leather seat. I had no idea where we were going. My shaking hands told me that it didn't matter. Doris had no intention of getting us there alive.

A sound that resembled a laugh and a roar came from the driver's seat. I turned and stared at her. She narrowed her eyes but never pulled them away from the road. "This will all be over soon."

Cars and other images on the highway went by in a blur, and my heart raced almost as fast as the speedometer. I needed to know about my aunt, and Doris had ignored my questions twice. I straightened in my seat. "Where are we going, and where is my aunt?" The last two words came out in a yell. Maestro barked at me.

"I said we'll be there in no time."

"Doris, tell me where we're going right now, or I'm jumping out of this vehicle."

"And what would that prove?" She turned and gave me one of those 'I-always-knew-you-were-as-dumb-as-I-thought-you-were' looks.

Heat crept from my face to my hands. I wanted them to reach for the door handle, but they ached to be wrapped around Doris's neck.

"Our exit is two miles away."

The SUV slowed barely enough for me to get a good look at the sign. The next exit was Douglas Springs. That's where Doris and Abner lived.

"Why are we going to your place? What's going—"

She slapped her hand over my mouth as Maestro let out a bark so loud it rocked the truck. A quick glance in the review mirror showed bared fangs. I swallowed, then moved as close as I could to the passenger door as he tried to paw his way into the front seat.

Doris said a few words to him in what I assumed was German, then yanked her hand away from my mouth. She glared at me. "You almost said the attack command phrase."

Maestro hadn't budged and was close enough for me to get a good look at his coat. It was spotted with blood. I swallowed again. "What's the command phrase?"

She leaned as far as she could past his massive chest and whispered in my ear, "Just be sure to never ask, *what's going on?*"

I nodded. Maestro's intense stare warned me against making any sudden moves. The blood on his coat was fresh.

I glanced at Doris and saw that a part of her black jeans, near the thigh, was darker than the rest. Slowly, I reached over, touched the spot with my finger, and looked at it. Blood.

"Doris, are you injured?"

She shook her head. "The blood isn't ours."

I turned to look at Maestro again. There were no cuts or marks from which the blood could have come. But if it wasn't theirs, then whose was it?

My phone rang. Doris stretched her arm across Maestro's chest as I reached into my pocket and pulled out my phone. "It's Molly."

"Don't answer it."

My thumb paused over the talk button. "Doris, right before you showed up, Dan and his team left to respond to a shooting. He told us not to leave the house. She's probably worried sick, wondering what happened to me."

The SUV slowed and swerved onto the Douglas Springs exit ramp. At the stop sign, we made a right, and Doris leaned heavily on the accelerator again. "Right now, we have bigger fish to fry."

The town was an old rural one with miles of dusty roads. The road we were on led to her house, and the Escalade was leaving a dust storm in its wake. I placed the phone back in my pocket, and Doris made another sharp right turn onto her gravel driveway.

The rose bushes that lined the driveway and the massive

white oak trees that majestically dotted her landscape didn't take my breath away like they normally had. Neither did the charming wrap-around porch that hugged the lovely country home. They didn't have time too. Doris barreled her SUV into her backyard with the same speed she'd used on the dirt roads. She didn't stop until we got to the wooden doors of her barn.

Maestro barked and paced in the back seat. Doris reached behind her and rubbed him on the neck. "Not this time, boy. I have to tie you up, but I'll come back and get you if we don't get what we want."

She jumped down onto the gravel and then opened the back door. Maestro hopped out and made a mad dash toward the barn. Doris ran after him and grabbed his collar. After she secured her grip, she returned back to the truck. "Abner and Lonewolf have gone to look for Gingie and likely have gotten the police involved by now." She tightened her grip on Maestro as he pulled and barked at the barn. "It'll take them forever to get the information they need to find her. So. I came up with a better plan."

I sat in the SUV and watched Doris walk Maestro to a nearby tree with a heavy dog chain attached. She clipped the chain to Maestro's collar, then disappeared around the side of the barn. She returned seconds later holding a squirrel that looked like it would've still been alive if it hadn't run into Doris five seconds ago. She dropped the squirrel on the ground in front of Maestro and headed to the front of the barn.

I jumped out of the truck and joined her. She gripped the barn door handle and slid it quickly to the right. I gasped at the sight in front of me.

"Doris! What have you done?!"

Chapter Thirty-One

A young man who looked to be in his mid-twenties was suspended from the rafters by a long chain. His face and thin white T-shirt were covered in blood. His wrists were attached to the chain, but the one on the left was clearly broken. The real horror was his left foot. The mangled appendage dripped blood into the dust beneath him.

"Jan," Doris said. "Meet Bane, a member of Legion." She pulled a pole-like tool with four blades on the end of it off the wall. "Bane was there when they took Gingie, but he doesn't want to tell me where they're keeping her." She pressed a button on the tool, and the sharp blades spun at an alarming speed. "Fortunately for Bane, Maestro got to him before I did, but now we're running out of time." Bane moaned, and she pointed the whirring blades at Bane's neck.

"Doris!" I screamed and reached for the tool. She pushed me away and aimed the blades closer to his neck.

Maestro's bark erupted through the air. We spun around. At the entrance to the barn was a young girl dressed only in a black tank top and jeans despite the chilly autumn weather. Her golden blonde mane was parted in the middle and flowed down to the spurs on her boots. In her right hand was a large gun.

"Thirteen," Bane managed to shout out, along with another moan. "Shoot that crazy witch and get me out of here."

Doris lowered the spinning tool and held it like a spear. She then ran toward Thirteen.

Thirteen lifted her arm and pulled the trigger. Doris cried out and fell hard onto the floor.

"Doris!" I ran and knelt beside her.

Thirteen walked slowly toward us. She stopped next to me but pointed the gun at Doris's head.

Doris grabbed a handful of Thirteen's hair and yanked her down to the barn floor next to her. The gun slid and landed next to Doris's pole tool. The steel blades were still whirring.

I scurried across the barn, grabbed the gun, and pointed it at Thirteen, who was on top of Doris, striking her with her fists.

"Get off of her now!"

Thirteen landed another blow to Doris. Maestro's thunderous barks had overpowered my voice. He pulled fiercely against the tree he was tied to. He was a volcano ready to erupt.

I shouted the warning to Thirteen again. This time, she turned and looked at me. She sneered and focused again on Doris, who'd gotten an arm free. Doris dug into the ground beside her and threw dirt in Thirteen's eyes.

She jumped off of Doris and wiped at her face. Doris flipped onto her stomach and crawled toward the whirring tool.

I had a perfect shot at Thirteen, who cursed and rubbed at her eyes. Bane moaned again, and Thirteen ran to him. Doris had made her way to the tool and tried to lift it.

Keeping my eyes on Bane and the gun on Thirteen, I backed out of the barn and made my way to the tree Maestro warred and pulled against. I unclipped the chain, pointed to the barn, and yelled, "What's going on? What's going on?"

He lunged into the barn and headed straight for Thirteen. She turned toward him, and he lunged at her neck.

Doris lifted the tool with one hand and attempted to stand and walk toward Thirteen. Maestro had dug his teeth into her neck, and she writhed in pain on the floor. Doris's gunmetal gray eyes told me that wasn't enough. She wanted to cut up Thirteen and decorate the barn with the pieces.

Maestro growled and gnawed on Bane's foot. The same one he'd apparently started on earlier.

I took the tool from Doris. She was weak and had a bullet in her left arm.

With Thirteen's gun in one hand, I half-dragged, half-carried Doris to the driveway, and laid her next to the Escalade.

I went back inside the barn and pulled Maestro away from Bane. Doris called to him in German, and he ran and stood beside her. I then put him inside the SUV.

A car roared down the gravel driveway and stopped next to the Escalade. Three men dressed in white T-shirts and black pants jumped out and ran toward the screams coming from the barn. Two of them headed for Thirteen and Bane.

The other, toward me.

Chapter Thirty-Two

Sweat poured down my face.

I pressed the accelerator. I'd never driven a vehicle this large before, but desperate times called for desperate measures. And I was desperate.

Desperate enough to shoot a man in the knee.

He'd threatened to kill us for what we'd done to his friends, then tried to wrestle the gun away from me.

He shouldn't have done that.

The last thing I'd wanted to do was shoot him, but it bought me enough time to get Doris inside her SUV and speed off.

I looked in the rearview mirror. So far, they hadn't tried to follow us.

Thirteen had been barely alive when we sped away, and I'd left the guy I shot bleeding in the gravel. Bane would need emergency care and fast.

Would they call for an ambulance? I doubted it.

When I reach Douglas Springs Medical Center, I'll give them Doris's address and tell them to send help.

Maestro was covered in blood and panted heavily beside me in the passenger seat. Thirteen had managed to pull out a knife and stab him, but my guess was that most of the blood on his coat belonged to her and not him. He didn't appear to be seriously injured. He wasn't licking any wounds or wincing in pain. Instead, he sat at the ready, eagerly awaiting another command.

Doris lay quietly in the back seat. When I told her I was heading straight for the E.R., she'd shaken her head no. But it didn't matter. She was going.

I'd already called Abner, who was meeting us at the medical center. He and Lonewolf didn't have any luck finding Aunt Gingie. Still, they were able to round up other members of Legion and hold them at gunpoint until the police arrived.

That was at the warehouse near Leviathan's Field, the last place Doris said she'd seen Gingie. The police report of shots fired there had to have been the shootout between Abner, Lonewolf, and Legion.

I slowed the SUV and took the highway exit for the medical center. Blue informational signs guided me to their Emergency Room.

Abner waited out front, along with two doctors and a stretcher. Abner had his hand on the Escalade's door handle before I completely stopped. When I did, he flung open the back door and helped the physicians ease Doris onto the stretcher. When the doctors rushed her inside, Abner opened the passenger door and motioned for Maestro to hop out. Abner quickly ran his fingers through the dog's fur, then looked at me. "Is he hurt?"

"I don't know. There was a knife lying on the floor next to the girl he attacked, but he hadn't been acting like he was hurt. I think most of that blood belongs to her and the other guy he attacked."

He nodded, then looked behind the SUV towards the street. "Did they follow you?"

"I don't think they were able to. They were seriously injured. You may want to send help."

"Will do." He walked to the driver's side, and I rolled down the window. "Hand me the keys," he said. "I'll park the car. If they did follow you, you'll be safer inside where there's a strong police presence."

I shook my head and started the engine. "Abner, Doris

needs you inside with her. I can't stay here. I have to go find Aunt Gingie."

"Doris would want me to make sure you're safe. Now get out of the car."

"I'm sorry," I shifted the gear from park to drive. "I can't."

He ran around the front of the SUV. "Then I'm going with you."

"I don't want anyone else getting hurt," I yelled at him.

"I'm not letting you drive out there alone," he reached for the passenger door handle.

I sped away before he could grip it.

Chapter Thirty-Three

Leviathan's Field bordered between the cities
of Habakkuk and Corinth.

The Field was rumored to be the place where thousands
of Christians were slaughtered by an unseen enemy hundreds
of years ago. There was no historical data to back that up,
but that was the rumor.

The Field was a mile long across and wide. Next to the
Field was a large, abandoned home that had been turned into
a small warehouse over the years. Both were surrounded by
seven-foot wrought-iron fencing that featured Gothic arches
and intricate scrollwork.

The Field always seemed dark no matter the time of day.
It was creepy, and someone was watching me.

I couldn't see them, but they were there, monitoring
Doris's SUV and every move I made.

I parked the SUV in front of the small makeshift
warehouse and got out. I pushed open the iron gate and
walked along the cracked cobblestone path to the door. Or
what used to be the door. It was made of heavy wood, but
rusted hinges kept it stuck in the open position.

"Hello?" I peeked my head in and called out. "Aunt
Gingie, are you here?"

A bat flew over my head, and a small animal with a
long-pointed nose and burn patches on its fur scurried across
the floor.

"Aunt Gingie?" I called again.

"She's up here."

The voice came from above, and I looked up. Liam leaned heavily against a wooden banister that threatened to collapse and fall.

"I don't want any trouble, Liam. I just want to take my aunt and leave."

"And I just want Pastor Ted," he said calmly.

I sucked in a breath and blew it out. "Where is my aunt? Is she okay?"

"Come see for yourself," he pointed to the old and crumbling concrete steps before me. There were several flights of them, and they looked like they'd barely support the weight of a kitten, let alone my one hundred and thirty pounds.

"What's the matter? Are you scared?" he teased.

Liam was tall, like his father, and was at least eighty pounds heavier than I was. How did he get up there?

The warehouse wasn't as wide as the field next to it and only had four floors. Any walls that used to exist had long ago been knocked down. The space around me was wide and open, yet I couldn't see another way to get to the next floor.

"Behind you," he said.

I turned, and leaning against a far wall was a ladder. It hadn't been there a minute ago. Obviously, we weren't here alone.

"How do I know my aunt is really up there?" I asked.

He didn't respond.

"Aunt Gingie!" I called again.

"She can't respond right now, but she is up here."

"You brute. What did you do to my aunt?"

He yawned.

I ran to the ladder. It was long but it wasn't sturdy, and I sensed someone was waiting above it. If I climbed the ladder, that person could kick it down as soon as I reached the top.

I'd have to take that chance. Aunt Gingie needed me.

I climbed the ladder, paused when it reached the next level and peered over it.

No one was there. I quickly scrambled over the ladder and looked around.

Next to Liam was a cage that resembled a jail cell. Aunt Gingie was inside it, lying on the floor, her back to Liam.

She wasn't moving.

"Aunt Gingie," I ran past him to the cage.

"She wouldn't stop fighting with me," he said, then added, "so I had her tranquilized."

I spun on my heel. "You're a monster."

"If I were a monster, she'd already be dead. She'll be fine once the tranquilizer wears off."

He was calm and relaxed. Evil didn't rage from his pores like it did from his dad's.

I was furious he'd hurt Aunt Gingie, but he seemed willing to work with me.

"Liam, let me take my aunt and leave. Please?"

"I will, as soon as Pastor Ted gets here."

"You're holding my aunt hostage?"

He chuckled. "Would you rather I hold you hostage?"

I tightened my fists. So, he was the type of person who answered a question with a question. I needed to be more direct.

"Why do you want to kill my husband?"

He gritted his teeth, then said, "Because he killed Father."

"Only because Garringer was about to kill our son. Ted was protecting him. It was self-defense."

He ran his hand through damp, dark hair, which brushed the tips of his shoulders. "I know what happened, but he still has to pay."

"Whatever debt you think we owe to Garringer has been paid. He killed our daughter."

Liam shook his head. "He did not. Father could never break through the protection surrounding that little girl."

My heart stopped. "Protection? What are you talking about?"

"The hedge that surrounded her and your home. Father tried plenty of times to break through it but failed. Otherwise, he would've dragged you out and tortured you until he found out where Molly was. But you made it easy in the end by going to him."

I pressed my lips together so my mouth wouldn't hang open. He'd said a lot, but was it to distract me? I didn't know. I'd have to process it later because I had more questions.

"Garringer was spotted at the home where my daughter died."

"He'd heard what happened to her, so he went to check out the scene. Father wasn't sorry she died. He was upset he'd been unable to use her to get to you. He'd never been able to overpower those surrounding her."

"Who inside of Legion has that power?"

"Are you kidding? If Father couldn't do it, there was no chance in hell we would've been able to," he chuckled, then added, "Literally."

I lowered my eyes. Was he telling the truth? Had *everyone* been telling me the truth all along? Had it truly been an accident?

If so, where was her angelic protection when she was drowning?

Heat flamed inside my body, and my mind warred with my heart. I struggled to push away the urge to blame God for, once again, not protecting a loved one.

I reminded myself that He was Sovereign and that He'd blessed me with Laynee. He'd always known how much time we'd have with her from the moment she was born. Should He have told me how many days I'd have with her from the beginning? Would that have helped the heartache? Or added to it? Would I have been able to keep my sanity as the date of her death got nearer?

No, I wouldn't have. And none of that mattered now

because I remembered my promise to Him. I'd promised that if she had been killed, I'd forgive, and if her death was accidental, I'd find peace knowing she rested in His arms.

"Jan," a groggy voice called from behind me.

I turned to the cage. "Aunt Gingie, are you okay?"

She straightened and nodded. "What are you doing here?"

"Looking for you," I said and reached for her hand. She clasped it. I turned again to face Liam. "Please, let her out of here."

His eyes darkened. "Summon Pastor Ted here, and I will."

"I'm not going to do that."

He held out his hand. "Give me your phone. He'll answer when he sees your number. I'll tell him I'm holding you hostage, and he'll come."

"My phone's useless. I tossed my battery on the way here because Ted and Molly wouldn't stop calling."

"Tossed it where?"

I'd only tossed it in the back seat of Doris's car, but he didn't need to know that.

When I didn't answer, he said, "Where's Molly? Didn't she come here with you?"

I shook my head.

"Where's my sister?" He stepped toward me. "Where's Leah?"

"She left Missouri weeks ago," I dropped Gingie's hand. "You never told your father you'd been in contact with Leah. Why?"

He stiffened. "How do you know that?"

"From your mother. I haven't had the pleasure of talking with her, but a friend who knows her well has."

"I didn't tell Father about Leah because she was living a good life, and he would've messed it up." He walked toward the cage. "Gingie, we left your phone in your pocket. Turn it on and hand it to me."

The building shook and shrieked.

"Whisper!" Liam exclaimed.

Gunshots filled the air.

I grabbed Liam's arm. "Where are the keys? I need to get Gingie out of there."

He pulled a leather key ring shaped like a pentagram from his belt loop and tossed it to me. "Hurry. Whisper's dead. You must leave now."

I inserted one of the keys into the lock. "What makes you think she's dead?"

"That was her death shriek that shook the building."

The first key failed, and I inserted another one. It worked. I slid the cage door open, and Gingie grabbed my hand. "Let's go," she said.

When we reached the ladder, I looked for Liam, who had somehow disappeared.

"Hurry," Gingie said, pointing to the ladder. "Dan and Ted may need our help."

Chapter Thirty-Four

Aunt Gingie's legs were wobbly before we descended the ladder. Now, they were basically useless.

Gunshots continued to echo around us. She leaned on my shoulder as we hurried down the broken cobbled path and across the lot to Doris's SUV.

Gingie pressed her back against the passenger door. "They must've given me something," she breathed out heavily. "I can barely feel my legs."

I placed a hand on her shoulder. "Liam said they tranquilized you. Some of that may still be in your system."

"Well," her lips trembled. "We don't have time for it to wear off. We need to follow the sound of those shots."

I nodded and opened the door for her. After I helped her inside, I got in the driver's seat.

There weren't as many shots as before, but they were coming from the northwest end of the field. If Gingie hadn't been tranquilized, we could've easily run across the field.

I started the engine and headed in that direction.

When we got to the field, I drove the SUV across it until an officer jumped out from behind a large rock and pointed a gun at us.

I stopped the vehicle, and we held up our hands.

Dan and Mick Bolt emerged from behind a huge tree. Dan waved a hand at Mick and the officer, and they lowered their weapons.

Dan ran over to us, his hand still on his gun. "Are the two of you alone?"

"Yes," I replied and rolled down all of the windows.

He looked inside and then motioned for us to get out. I nodded and opened the door. "Gingie may need some help."

Dan helped me out. Mick whispered something into the small mic on his shoulder and jogged around the truck to Gingie.

"Is Ted here?" I asked.

"Lonewolf, Ted, and Molly are in a vehicle not too far from here. They're on their way."

I looked around the field. Several black-clad dead bodies were strewn across it. "What happened?"

"I was at the hospital questioning one of the men we'd arrested out here earlier when Abner ran in and told me that you were headed this way to look for Gingie. We jumped in my police car with Maestro and returned this way. Two more police cars followed us.

"So, Ted's not hurt?"

"No. Abner texted him what happened while I drove. When he responded that he, Molly, and Lonewolf were on their way, I told Abner to let him know they'd need to keep their distance until I gave them the all-clear."

I released a breath. It came out shakier and louder than I'd intended it to.

Dan smiled. "I wouldn't relax just yet. Molly's pretty upset with you right now."

"I know," I blinked away tears. "How's Doris?"

"She looks like she's been in a fight, and they had to remove a bullet from her arm, but she's going to be okay."

"And Abner came out here with you? He didn't stay with Doris?"

"He knew she was in good hands. Besides, I'm glad he was with me and had Maestro. That dog saved our lives."

"What? How?"

"The woman that cornered you in the bathroom at Barney's? The one in the white dress?"

"Yeah, Whisper."

"She and her friends attacked my police car when we arrived. Abner and I climbed out and wrestled two of them to the ground. Whisper then whipped out a machine gun and was about to fire at us, but Maestro jumped through one of the broken car windows and lunged at her."

"Oh, my word. Is he hurt?"

"A little, but Abner rushed him to the vet. I think he's going to be okay."

"And Whisper?"

"She's gone. She put up a good fight, but Maestro ripped her … well, let me say it wasn't a pretty scene."

I gasped.

He continued, "There was another gun battle when the other officers showed up, but we've secured the area," he raised his brows. "We haven't seen Thwart. Have you?"

"Yeah, he was the one holding Gingie captive. He let her go and then disappeared."

"Do you know where he's at now?"

I shook my head.

"Excuse me," he turned and talked quietly to Mick.

A brown sedan roared onto the field and stopped inches from the SUV. Ted, Lonewolf, and Molly hopped out of it. Lonewolf ran to Gingie, and Ted embraced me in a hug. Molly leaned into Dan's chest and narrowed her eyes at me.

Ted squeezed me and planted kisses on my face. "Don't worry about Molly," he said between kisses, sensing my mind was elsewhere. "She's only upset because she was frightened to her core. She didn't know what had happened to you."

"I know," I said and responded to his kisses. "I shouldn't have left the house like that. But when Doris said Aunt Gingie was in danger, I—"

"Shhh," he kissed my lips. "It's okay. We'll talk about

that later."

I looked up at him. "No, Ted, it's not okay. I promised you I'd never do anything reckless again, at least not without talking to you about it first. I broke my promise. I shouldn't have let Doris talk me out of letting you and Molly know what was going on. I am so sorry."

He tucked my head under his chin. "Baby steps, sweet one. Baby steps."

Dan patted him on the shoulder. "Gingie's pretty weak, and Lonewolf wants the paramedics to take a look at her. They're on their way. He put Gingie in the sedan, and they'll wait for them in the parking lot."

We nodded.

"We scoured the woods and rock formations around here," Dan continued, motioning toward the warehouse. "My guys and I are headed there to look for Thwart."

"Liam," I corrected, humanizing him. He'd let Gingie and I go when he could've used us as leverage for Ted. The least I could do was call him by the name his mother gave him.

"Liam," Dan corrected.

Molly walked up behind him. He kissed her on the cheek and headed toward the warehouse.

"Molls," I said after Dan and his men sped across the field in their cars. "I should've—"

"You should've answered your blasted phone," she spit out. Tears flooded her eyes. "Do you know how scary it was to go downstairs, and you weren't there? And the patio door had been left open. I thought someone had taken you." She wiped away the tears that had traveled to her cheeks. "I didn't know what to—"

"I hate I did that to you," I embraced her, and she squeezed me tightly. "Will you ever forgive me?"

She gasped and pushed me away. Her eyes were focused on something behind me and Ted.

We turned around.

Liam. Where did he come from? And how did he get that close without us hearing him?

The calm Liam I'd talked to an hour ago was gone. Red rimmed his eyes, and his skin had turned an eerie yellowish color.

In his hand was a black baton. He lifted his arm, and the baton swished through the air as he aimed it at Ted's face. Ted blocked it with his shoulder, and they fell to the ground.

Molly and I screamed. The back of Ted's head had hit a rock protruding from the dirt, but he'd still managed to shake the baton out of Liam's hand, even though Liam was on top of him.

I jumped on Liam's back and clawed at his eyes and face. Molly kicked him in the chin and dragged Ted from underneath him.

Liam stood and shook me off his back. Lonewolf ran across the field and tackled him from behind.

Liam leaped off the ground and pulled a machete from his cloak. It sliced through the air with a sickening sound as it cut its way towards Lonewolf's neck.

"Stand down, Liam!" Dan called as he raced across the field.

Liam roared when Lonewolf used Dan's diversion to roll across the dusty field away from him. Liam then lifted the machete again and charged at Lonewolf.

A bullet whizzed through the air and pierced his chest. He stopped and lifted the machete again, but this time toward Ted and Molly.

Dan shot him again.

And again.

Liam gasped, and his eyes dimmed. I swallowed as I watched his life end before he dropped to the ground.

I stood and ran to Ted. Molly had dragged him behind Dan.

"I'm fine," he said as I wrapped my arms around his neck. "I have a headache, and my shoulder hurts like you wouldn't believe," he kissed my cheek. "But I'm okay."

"Everyone evacuate this place now," Dan said. "Ted, can you make it to the parking lot?"

Ted nodded.

After we were locked inside one of the police vehicles, I separated Ted's hair with my fingers to get a better look at the back of his head.

He winced when I touched the knot, but there was no blood.

I snuggled against him. "You're sure you're okay?"

He shifted in his seat and faced me. "I am because it's all over. No more Garringer or his son." He smiled. "It's over."

I released a sigh and returned the smile. "You're right, babe. It's finally over."

Chapter Thirty-Five

"I had a dream."

I knelt in front of my daughter's gravestone for the first time. "I'm sorry it's taken me so long to get here. It's been quite the journey," I chuckled and laid a bouquet of yellow flowers at the base of the stone. "But I promise to come more often."

I inhaled the cold yet comforting winter air, then blinked back tears as I struggled to wrangle my thoughts. "Oh, my word, Laynee, how could I forget?" I coughed to stop a sob from escaping. "Merry Christmas, my sweet little one. Merry Christmas."

I reached for one of the tissues Ted gave me before I got out of the car and dabbed at the tears. "I'm glad Libbybelle, Dad, and Adam have already talked to you this morning because I feel like I'm going to be here forever. I sniffed and shook my head. "But I won't be able to stay forever, at least not today. Would you like to know why? Today, we're having a large Christmas dinner with all our friends and loved ones. Oh, how I wish you were here to join us." I blew my nose into the tissue. "That reminds me of my dream. I dreamed you were in a bright, colorful place. There were so many colors. Some I recognized, like blue, yellow, gold, and silver—others I didn't. And the music. The music wasn't like any I'd ever heard before. It sounded like thousands of instruments playing simultaneously, and it was the most beautiful music I'd ever heard.

"A chorus of high and low voices sang along perfectly with the music." I cleared my throat. "And you were in the midst of all of those radiant colors and glorious music, smiling and laughing. Joy emanated from you. I can't explain it, but I saw the joy happening with my eyes, and it penetrated my heart as well. But I was so excited to see you that I immediately reached for your hand and begged you to come back to me, but you shook your head and smiled." I wiped away more tears. "The crazy thing is that I wasn't sad when you did that. Somehow, I was able to finally realize you were happy and didn't want to come back.

"I woke up after that and knew I had to come talk to you. Eight short years you were here with us on this earth. Such a short time, yet long enough for you to leave a legacy. So many people have told me about the hearts you touched and the people you led to Christ—including your great aunt Gingie," I chuckled again. "If you'd known her years ago, you'd know what a spectacular feat that was. And you were even able to become friends with Doris. How you managed that, I'll never know. She and I haven't been able to cross that friend bridge yet." The muscles in my cheeks twitched. "You had so little time and yet accomplished so much."

I leaned my head against the gravestone and sobbed. My body shook with the grief I'd held in for so long. "What a blessing it was to know you, Laynee," I choked out. "And what an honor it is to be your mother." I sucked in frosty air and waited until it cooled and soothed my heartache. "I'll always be your mother, Laynee," I released another breath. "Forever and always."

I stood. If I didn't leave now, I wasn't sure I'd be able to. I rubbed my hand gently across the headstone. "Goodbye, for now, my sweet one." I gasped again for air.

"Goodbye. For now."

~

"I can't believe it." I dabbed at my eyes for the thousandth time with tissues that Ted kept handing me. It had been a teary ride home from the cemetery for both of us. Adam and Libbybelle had been in a separate car and left a half hour before us.

"At least they left a place for us to park," Ted laughed and pulled into our driveway.

The road in front of our home and Olivia's was packed with cars. I'd sent an invitation for an impromptu Christmas dinner to everyone we knew. It was extremely short notice, so I didn't ask anyone to RSVP. I just asked if they had time to stop by, that they would.

Libbybelle had been cooking for two days. Doris had even stopped by to help when she was released from the hospital. I thanked God often for her quick recovery and Maestro's.

When we walked through the front door, the savory and delightful scents we'd had to endure the past two days greeted us. Today, though, they were a hundred times more delightful.

My friend Mary, who I'd barely communicated with since Laynee's death, greeted me at the front door and quickly pulled me into a hug. Behind her were Kite Eagle, Priscilla King, Lydia Day, and Eve Stockton.

All of whom were very dear to me, yet I'd ignored them when I struggled with the loss of Laynee and my faith. Now they were here loving on me like none of that ever happened.

"I've missed you ladies," I cried as they formed a circle and embraced me.

"We've missed you, too," Kite wiped away my tears.

"I apologize for my behavior. I can't believe I was so—"

"Human?" Lydia interjected.

"Yeah," I chuckled. "I think that's it."

Eve tilted my chin up. "When you wouldn't answer the door when we stopped by, and you wouldn't respond to our phone calls or texts, it was obvious you needed time and space to grieve the loss alone. There was nothing we could do to ease your pain, but we could pray. We knew you were struggling to do that, so we did it for you. We stood in the gap." She stepped out of the circle and spread her arms wide. "And look at what God has done."

I looked around the home, which, only a few months ago, had been like a prison. It was where I was chained to a grief that almost ended me.

But not today. I choked back tears.

To my right, in my dining room, was Ted, and he was talking and laughing with Bruce Cheatham. Next to Bruce was whom I assumed was his wife, and she was chatting away with Dan and Molly.

Before I'd even met my dear friends, the Cheatham's had already started praying for me. My whole life had been covered in prayer. From my mother's quiet prayers over me before she died to Mr. and Mrs. Gibbons, my childhood church family, the Cheathams, and my best friends who stood behind me now.

God was good. He'd promised never to leave or forsake me, and He hadn't.

Adam and Ted were alive. So were Molly, Dan, Abner, Doris, Lonewolf, and Aunt Gingie. All of whom could've been killed. Instead of celebrating the birth of our Savior on this day, we could've been attending several funerals.

I sighed and took in the sight of all the loved ones surrounding me. I listened intently to their words and laughter and cherished the joy that flowed through all of them.

I was still encircled by friends who looked at me with tender eyes. I didn't want to leave the circle or the love emanating from it, but I needed to mingle.

And I would.

Later.

Right now, I wanted to stay circled in their love, mercy, forgiveness, and grace for a few more minutes while I continued to take in everything around me.

I wanted to do what Eve said.

I wanted to look at all that God had done.

-------THE END -------

Salvation Prayer

Would you like to accept Jesus Christ as your Lord and Savior?

The <u>Billy Graham Evangelistic Association </u>makes it quick and simple using 4 easy steps. You can find out more about these 4 easy steps by clicking <u>here.</u>

Would you like to share your thoughts on this story's characters, storyline, plot, or spiritual elements? Feel free to email me at fictionwithfaith at gmail dot com

I'm looking forward to your feedback!

Are you interested in signing up for Kara's newsletter? Be among the first to hear about giveaways, free books, sales, upcoming releases, and other exciting tidbits. <u>Click here to sign up for the quarterly newsletter.</u>

KARA R. HUNT is the host of the <u>Cheer UP! Podcast</u> and an award-winning author.

Her novels have received the 2023 Golden Scrolls Award for Contemporary Novel of the Year and the coveted 2023 Selah Award for Contemporary Womens Fiction.

Kara is an avid reader and usually can be found reading a novel from one of her favorite authors or listening to one of their audiobooks. Kara and her husband reside in rural Missouri.

Previous books in the Habakkuk Series

Book 1 - <u>Paper Dolls</u>

Book 2 - <u>Paper Dolls: Kite</u>

Book 3 - <u>Paper Dolls: Priscilla</u>

Book 4 – <u>Paper Dolls: Lydia</u>

Book 5 – <u>Paper Dolls: Eve</u>

Book 6 – <u>Paper Dolls: Mary</u>

KARA R. HUNT
BOOK SIX
paper dolls
Mary
THE HABAKKUK SERIES